alive at 5

alive at 5

LINDA
BOND

Entangled Publishing, LLC
2614 South Timberline Road
Suite 105, PMB 159
Fort Collins, CO 80525
rights@entangledpublishing.com

Amara is an imprint of Entangled Publishing, LLC.

Edited by Kate Fall and Nina Bruhns
Cover design by Elizabeth Turner Stokes
Cover photography by smutny pan, alphaspirit, and Checubus/
Shutterstock

Manufactured in the United States of America

First Edition July 2014

Thank you to TK, Randy Swallows Photography, and my friends at Skydive City in Zephyrhills, Florida for all the lessons and all the help. Alive at Five couldn't have dropped without you! And to John Fulton, Eric Moore, Kellie Lightbourn, Matthew Borek, and my other creative, talented friends, you all went above and beyond for me. I hope we can continue to create storylines and videos that move people—forever.

Thank you to all the women writers who have helped and encouraged me, including my critique partners since day one: Vella Day and Houston Havens. To Karen Rose, thanks for your time and good advice. Alive at Five came to life under the guidance of editors Kate Fall and Nina Bruhns. Thank you, Nina, for believing in my voice. And to my husband Jorge, who had faith in me when I didn't have faith in myself, I love you.

Chapter One

Central Florida

Zack Hunter's heart hammered against his ribs in a flurry of painful jabs. Closing his eyes, he forced out his growing anxiety in a wild battle cry and leaped through the plane's open door.

No turning back. The mission begins now.

The usual blast of air slapped his face in rhythmic waves, but the familiarity didn't comfort him.

Plummeting 120 miles an hour toward the Central Florida drop zone, he forced his eyes open. Arms spread wide, belly to the ground, his exposed skin stung as if a thousand tiny millipedes ran up and down his flesh. But it wasn't that sensation making his stomach churn.

Don't think. Just do. He couldn't screw up again.

For one crazy second he thought about not opening his parachute. He would hit the ground so hard, he'd be gone before he felt it. Death might be the only way to extinguish the inferno of guilt slowly burning him alive. His uncaring family wouldn't even miss him.

No, he had to stay alive to right the wrong. He could trust no one else to do it. Three men had died in the last three years on these expensive, high-risk vacations—including his uncle, a man he'd loved like a father. He had to prove their deaths were no accident. He was the only one who still believed justice had to be served.

He deployed his high performance parachute, the nylon filling with air. As the straps jerked against his chest, he grunted, the air whooshing out of his lungs. The burning pain was a well-deserved punishment. Punishment for not being able to save his Florida Department of Law Enforcement partner, who had drowned on a police dive mission. Punishment for being so preoccupied with personal guilt over that failure that he'd let his uncle go on a dangerous adventure vacation without him. If Zack had taken the trip as his uncle had asked, Jackson Hunter would still be alive today.

All Zack had to do now was keep control of the damn parachute—and his fluctuating emotions—and he'd fit right in among the adrenaline junkies kicking off their two-week adventure vacation today. No one would suspect his secret motive for being on this crazy, organized thrill ride: find out what happened to Jackson, the uncle who had saved him from his abusive father.

Against the pull of the atmosphere, Zack glanced down. The altimeter on his wrist read six hundred feet. Pulling on the front risers of the parachute, he dropped into a spiraling dive. His heart beat faster as the shallow pond in the Zephyrhills landing zone rose up and closed in on him.

Another rush of testosterone fueled him. Instinctively, he swooped into an L-shaped turn that took him so close to the pond his toes skimmed the calm surface. As he skidded across the top of the liquid blanket, the water splashed up in fluid bullets. In a strange way, the sting comforted him, made him feel as though he was paying a price for failing both his police partner and his uncle. But he wouldn't fail again. He lifted his gaze from the water. It took half a second to register a woman standing at the end of the pond.

What the—

He only had time to make out long legs, a black skirt, a slender frame, and long, dark brown hair. Was that a *video* camera pointing at him?

Oh, *hell* no.

His heart stomped within his chest. The woman wasn't moving out of his way.

He yanked harder on the canopy brakes, trying to stop his momentum as he skated across the top of the lake. His mouth went dry. *This was going to suck. For both of them.* As his feet hit dirt, he cut diagonally to avoid an accident. *Too late.* Flipping head over heels, he cartwheeled toward the woman.

• • •

Through the viewfinder, Sam Steele saw the blur of a skydiver careening toward her. *Holy shit!* How'd she miss his jump? Sucking in a deep breath, she dove at the ground.

Their bodies collided and pain seared through her. Sam flung her arms forward, the small digital news camera flying out of her hands. She landed face-first in the dirt. The camera whacked the back of her head, and a sharp pain rippled through her skull.

Breathe. Just breathe.

"What the hell?" a deep voice boomed from her right.

She pushed herself up, sucked in a deep breath, and fell back on her butt, blinking to clear her vision. She didn't see any blood, but her head hurt like hell.

The skydiver came into focus. He'd already detached himself from his parachute and was flexing his legs. No obvious injuries on him either. *Thank God.*

The man was tall with short, dark hair, wide shoulders, and a long, lean body. Military? Then wouldn't he know better than to land like that? He could've killed her.

Whipping off his goggles, the skydiver peered around. She intended to give him a good piece of her mind, but stalled when his heated gaze zeroed in on her.

He stormed her way with fisted hands, closing the distance between them in a few powerful strides. He dropped to a knee, his chest rising and falling. "Are you okay?"

"Well, you scared me to death, but I don't think you broke any of my bones." She flexed her arms. One ached like it had been bruised.

"Good to hear." A vein pulsed at his temple. "Now, let me ask you this. What in the *hell* were you thinking?" His chest continued to rise and fall as if adrenaline still fueled his muscles. "This is a landing zone. You were standing right in the middle of it."

Oh, so this was *her* fault? Taken aback, Sam barely managed to suck in enough air to speak. "My job. That's what I was doing." She cringed as a sharp pain pinched under her rib cage. She wanted to reach up and touch her chin, make sure it wasn't bleeding, but she didn't want to show any sign of weakness. Not in front of this guy. "If you knew what you were doing, you wouldn't have slammed into me."

"Is that so?" He rocked back on his heels. His jaw flexed.

Not good.

Finally, he jumped up and stuck out his right hand. "Let me help you."

She hesitated before accepting his offer. With a firm grip, he pulled her to her feet.

Big mistake. Instantly, a wave of nausea rolled through

She shifted on the bench, and focused on her hands. "Not me." Her dad had been an affluent boy from New England who had romanced her mom and said all the right things one spring break at Clearwater Beach. He'd disappeared when her mother needed him the most. Sam thought about explaining, but then thought better of it. As if Zack Hunter, thrill-seeker, would care.

She needed to get back to work. Maxwell must be landing soon. She had a deadline to meet, and a job to keep.

He cleared his throat. "Well, now that I know you're okay, I'll let you get back to your reporting." As he stood, he glanced skyward and shielded his eyes. "Yep, there they go. See those black dots in the sky? Your friend is about to open his parachute. Keep your eyes to the sky." He peered down at her, and his face relaxed into a lopsided grin. "And keep your cute little ass out of the landing zone."

As she attempted to formulate a witty response, a thunderous noise boomed overhead, making her jump. She peered up, half expecting to see lightning coming from a dark rain cloud, but there wasn't a single cloud in the crisp, blue sky.

Scrambling up, Zack cupped his hands around his mouth and yelled back toward the office, "Hard opening!"

"What does that mean?" She feared the answer.

"Someone's in trouble."

She grabbed the video camera, turned it on, and hit the zoom button. Frantic, she searched the sky for Maxwell's signature red jumpsuit.

There!

She zeroed in on him. He hung limp as a rag doll in his harness, his parachute open and spinning out of control. Her heart galloped. "That's Maxwell! What's wrong with him? He's going to overshoot the landing zone!"

"He's got bigger problems than that."

A man in a Skydive Drop Zone uniform ran out of the main office. Zack grabbed him by the arm. "Call 911. Get the paramedics here quickly. Maxwell Wentworth may be unconscious. He's coming in for a rough landing."

Sam's knees buckled and sweat beaded on her forehead. She slammed the camera onto the table and grabbed the edge in an attempt to stop herself from collapsing.

Zack steadied her with a firm hand. "Sit down, Samantha," he ordered, but not without sympathy. "Let us help your friend."

The skydive employee pulled out his cell phone and made a call.

Once she'd dropped onto the bench, Zack took off running.

What was she doing? That was *Maxwell* out there. "Wait! I'm coming with you." Kicking off her high heels, she ran after him. Grass slick with humidity slid between her toes. She slipped, but righted herself and kept going.

Zack spun around to face her and she plowed into him. He grabbed her by the shoulders, fingers pinching her flesh. "You have to go back. You don't want to see this." His black eyes glowed with intensity.

She lifted her chin. "He's like a father to me." Warm tears slid down her cheeks. She slapped them away, needing to get to Maxwell.

Zack released a male sound of disapproval. "Then prepare yourself for the worst. I've seen hard landings before. If your friend isn't already dead, trust me, this landing will kill him."

Chapter Two

Sam's lungs burned from running full speed toward the landing zone. A powerful breeze kicked up, pushing Maxwell hard into the ground. He hit feet first, and his legs collapsed beneath him, slamming him into the grassy field with such force his body bounced and flipped over.

"No!" Her heart banged in her chest. She pushed herself to run faster, but her side cramped, making it impossible to keep up with Zack. Maxwell's parachute floated down over him in slow motion, covering him in a colorful nylon shroud.

Zack and a couple of skydivers reached Maxwell and gathered up the parachute, jerking it away from his body.

Out of breath, she reached them and collapsed to her knees beside her friend. "Maxwell!" Grabbing his limp and clammy hand, she stared at his chest, desperate for any movement. Just a half inch, anything to show he was still breathing. "Maxwell, please," she choked out.

A fist of fear lodged in the back of her throat. She needed to look into his eyes and find life there. She started to remove his goggles.

"Don't move him."

The urgency in Zack's tone stalled her. "I need to make sure he's not dead."

"You could make his injuries worse," he said.

He was right. Instead, she placed two fingers on Maxwell's carotid artery.

Nothing.

She pressed her ear gingerly against his chest.

No movement. No sound.

"Oh, my God, he's not breathing. I have to do something!"

"Sam, wait for the—"

Ignoring Zack's warning, she gently pulled the goggles from Maxwell's face. His eyes stared straight ahead. Glassy. Empty. Dead. "We've got to revive him."

Her hands shook as she carefully tilted his head back. She placed her mouth over his and breathed for him. His cool lips convinced her he was probably already gone, but she couldn't give up. Sitting up, she fumbled with the hook on the harness across the center of his chest. Damn it, she couldn't undo the clasp. "Come on, come on."

This couldn't be happening! This was supposed to be such an easy assignment. A feature on her friend. He'd jumped hundreds of times before.

A siren wailed in the distance. Help on the way. She could do CPR until they arrived.

No way could she lose her father figure, mentor, and her job all on the same day.

• • •

Zack reached over and undid the latch without saying a word. A sickening feeling of déjà vu washed over him.

He watched as Samantha felt for the lower tip of Maxwell's breastbone and pressed down with both hands. Did she even have the strength to do this the right way? He should jump in, but knew she wouldn't let him. This was personal for her. The minutes passed as she performed CPR, and her tears falling onto her friend's body brought the memories tumbling out from deep inside of him.

My God. This could not be happening again. He remembered all too well the panic he'd felt after bringing his police partner up after his diving accident. Zack had tried CPR, too.

"Samantha."

"What?"

She'd blame herself for failing to bring him back. "It's too late." If only he could spare her that burning hell of guilt.

"I'm not going to let him go." She pushed harder against her friend's chest.

A paramedic in a light-colored polo shirt and black pants squatted next to him. Zack had been so transfixed on both the present and the past, he hadn't heard the EMTs rush onto the scene. "How long has the victim been down?"

"About fifteen minutes. When he hit the ground he was probably already unconscious." *Or dead.* "I haven't seen any obvious bleeding. We couldn't find a pulse, either. His friend has been administering CPR for maybe ten minutes."

"Miss…?"

Samantha ignored the paramedic, pressing even harder against Wentworth's chest. Her windblown hair, red cheeks, and wild eyes made her look like a woman possessed.

"Let the paramedics do their job." Zack tried to keep his voice low and nonthreatening.

"I know how to do this."

"No one's questioning that." He stood and stepped around Wentworth's body, peeling her away from her lifeless friend. "Please, just let the experts help him." She was going to freak when they pronounced him dead. He wouldn't wish that moment on his worst enemy.

"Leave me alone." She tried to throw him off, but her effort was weak.

"Not a chance. Not right now." He pulled her up against his chest. The dam holding back a tsunami of emotions finally broke—her knees gave out and she fell into his arms, surrendering to her tears.

He was unsure of what to do next. It had been a while since he'd allowed himself to get this close to any woman. Under any condition. Wrapping her in a stronger embrace, he stiffened as she buried her face against his chest, wetting his jumpsuit with her hot, messy, tears.

"I'm sorry." The energy around them shifted after the paramedic's words registered.

Here it comes.

She started to tremble, her sobs growing louder. He wrapped his arms around her tighter. This grief, this hurting, was exactly why he'd never work with a partner again. Ever.

But the warmth of her body against his, the way she'd collapsed into him, trusting him so completely in this moment of grief, was awakening an emotion in him he'd buried deep long ago.

Oh, hell no. He'd sworn off emotional attachments for good reasons. He'd failed the people who cared about him. *They'd died.* He'd never get deeply connected again. That way, no one got hurt.

• • •

The sudden vibration of Sam's cell phone made her jump out of the protective embrace she'd melted into. Instinctively, she glanced down to check the number and her heart sank. *Not now. Please.* Reluctantly, she backed away from Zack. Her heavy limbs were hard to lift, but she pulled the phone up to her ear and answered. As if she had a choice.

"This is Sam."

"What the hell is going on up there?" Her boss' sharp tone immobilized her. "I hear scanner traffic up at the assignment desk. Why are police and paramedics rushing to Skydive Drop Zone?"

"He's dead." Was that her voice cracking?

"What? Who's dead?"

"Maxwell Wentworth." She couldn't even look at his body.

"Shit." Her boss covered the receiver and shouted, "Get the satellite truck to Skydive Drop Zone, ASAP." Then he made a disapproving click with his tongue. "Why am I just hearing about this now?"

Gripping the phone with the limited strength she had left, Sam fought the urge to launch her cell skyward. "I guess I could have called you sooner, but I've been a little busy pushing air into the lungs of a dying man." God, she felt like throwing up.

Zack placed a hand on her back. He was so close now he could certainly hear her boss' loud, demanding voice. "You're killing me, Steele."

Zack grabbed the phone from her. "Nice choice of words, asshole."

Mortified, she struggled to get the phone back. She'd never heard anyone talk to her boss that way. Clawing her fingers into Zack's palm, she ripped the cell from his hands. She couldn't lose her job. She alone supported her mother and sister, and her contract with the TV station was almost up. Not to mention the probation she was under.

Despite the anxiety tearing up her belly, she had to keep it together. Reluctantly, she put the phone back to her ear and walked away so Zack could no longer hear the conversation. "Sorry about that. I—"

"The satellite truck is on the way." Her boss still seemed hot, but at least he wasn't yelling anymore. "I expect you live at five."

Live at five? She chewed her bottom lip. "Maxwell's death was an accident."

"So? He's a well-known member of this community."

"He died skydiving. It's not like he was shot or stabbed. It was an accident." She could barely breathe, and the familiar fingers of anxiety began to get a grip on her lungs. This was how her panic attacks always started, with a tightening in her stomach and then her chest. Next, she'd get light-headed, and her heart would race so fast it physically hurt. "You really want me to do a live shot at five?"

"Ya think?" Her boss sighed. "His death is news. Well-known members of our community don't die skydiving everyday."

She wondered if her boss could hear the pounding of her heart through the phone. She couldn't do it. She could barely even talk right now. Her throat was closing up. How was she supposed to—

"Reporting the news is still your job. Don't let me down again, Steele."

She closed her eyes, the not-so-veiled threat forcing her blood pressure up another notch.

"If you can't put your personal feelings aside, I'll send another reporter. But I can't get them to Skydive Drop Zone by five p.m. It's too far away. We'll miss our chance at an exclusive."

An exclusive. Her mentor and friend had become a news exclusive. Just like that.

"Feed the video in early. I want to approve any pictures before they air." Her boss paused. "And Sam?" His voice took on a gentler tone. "I'm sorry."

Right. "Live at five. Just like you said." She disconnected the call and dropped to her knees. She desperately needed George. Her photographer had been so excited to fly and shoot video of Maxwell as he jumped. The Otter should have landed by now, but she still didn't see George in the gathering crowd. Her photographer would help her. He had a way of making her laugh or distracting her so the panic would subside.

A dozen skydivers remained at the scene, talking in clusters. The noise level had dropped from frantic to subdued. Another paramedic arrived, talking to someone on a cell phone. Suddenly, she felt so small, so alone, completely lost in the buzz of activity. She took a series of deep breaths, trying to slow her pulse and ward off the panic attack.

Looking up, she caught Zack circling Maxwell's body, a pensive look on his movie-star face.

He stopped every few seconds to pick up a part of the parachute and examine it. At one point, he held a piece of the nylon in his hands, rubbing it, and staring at it almost reverently. Then he closed his eyes, balled the material in his fist, and appeared to be saying a prayer, or maybe reciting a curse. Why did Zack Hunter care so much about Maxwell's death?

He shook his head and knelt to examine more of the equipment attached to the body. She glanced around. The police hadn't arrived yet.

Reluctantly, she hauled herself off the ground and approached Zack, trying to avoid her late friend's vacant stare. "What are you looking for?" At least she was breathing somewhat regularly again.

He glanced at her. "Any sign that this wasn't an accident."

She jerked back, bringing her hand to her chest. "Why on earth would you even think that?"

He continued examining the parachute parts. "Because I've been skydiving a long time. Hard openings are rare."

"What does that mean?"

"It means his chute opened too quickly in the air. When that happens, a skydiver can pass out or suffer internal injuries—maybe even die instantly. During my career with the rangers, I never saw that happen. Not once. And we did some crazy, risky shit."

Dread raced up her spine, growing in intensity, along with the police siren wailing in the distance.

Zack swiveled in the direction of the sound, his eyebrows pinched together. He continued to feel around the parachute and pack, quickly now, his eyes firing up with determination "Wentworth was a skilled skydiver, which makes me wonder…"

"What?"

"If someone tampered with his chute before he jumped."

She tried to swallow, but guilt hardened into a huge lump. "He…um, let a young rigger pack his bag this morning."

"What? He didn't pack his own?"

"He usually does. Today, I asked him to do a quick interview with me before he jumped." Tears welled up, and the burning made her blink. "So he passed his gear off to a teenager who said he'd do it for ten bucks. You know, those young skydivers trying to make a buck." She wiped her cheeks with the back of both hands.

He stood. "It's not your fault."

She nodded, but tasted the gritty truth in her mouth. She surveyed the area. "We have to talk to the guy who packed his parachute."

"Yeah. My gut tells me this wasn't an accident."

Her jaw dropped as his meaning sank in. "Then, what? Murder? You've got to be kidding?"

And why would Zack, ex-military man, care if it were?

What she really wanted to do was go home, take a sleeping aid, and crash for twelve days. But she couldn't.

She had a job to keep. And if she wanted to help Maxwell now, the best thing would be to figure out what had really happened to him.

She forced herself to look down at her mentor. Maxwell's glassy eyes stared right through her. Her stomach heaved. She gagged as the acid taste of her breakfast rose up in her throat. She *would* find out what happened to her mentor, and she wouldn't let anyone stop her. She had to do this.

For you, Maxwell, she silently swore. *And for me, too.*

Chapter Three

A fading five o'clock sun continued to pulsate heat over the Skydive Drop Zone. Sweat rolled down the curve in Sam's spine as she stood in front of the Eyewitness News TV camera, her chest burning with a rising rush of panic. *Great. Just freaking great. Here it comes again.*

How could she do this? Maxwell was barely dead. She rubbed her arms, feeling dirty. Mud stains were embedded in her new dress. She'd barely had time to run a brush through her hair and redo her smudged mascara.

She prayed her photographer's frantic movements behind his TV camera meant technical difficulties would prevent her from having to go through with this live shot. These freaking panic attacks were the ultimate irony for a live news reporter to be suddenly afflicted with. The debilitating problem had started six months ago, right after her mother's accident. After she had to take on the financial and emotional responsibility of providing for a parent who needed extensive medical care. She'd been seeing a therapist for a few months, but none of his suggestions calmed her once the camera started rolling. Sam desperately wanted the attacks to just go away so she'd stop screwing up live shots at work. If she didn't... She couldn't even think about losing her job.

"I still don't hear any audio, George," she said hopefully.

"I'm working on it." Sweat fell from the forehead of her tall, skinny colleague. He struggled with the cords leading into his camera, pulling one out and replacing it with another.

They were supposed to shoot a live news headline straight up at five. She glanced down at her smartphone. *4:58.* Her chest tightened even more. Two minutes until the start of the five o'clock news, and she still couldn't hear anything in her earpiece. *There was a God.* The device connected her to the producer in the TV studio forty-five miles away, but so far she hadn't heard the producer's voice or the commercials leading up to the news. She whispered a silent thank you for the divine intervention, while rubbing away the tension spreading between her breasts.

George's camera jostled precariously on the tripod, his movements rapid but controlled. After a day in the hot sun, his pale Irish skin raged as red as his hair. The stress of the situation didn't help. She knew better than to say another word. Instead, she gave thumbs down to the camera, hoping her producer could see her, and stepped out of range of the camera's lens. A sigh of relief escaped. Whenever she felt a panic attack coming on, she knew she had to ruthlessly control her breathing. Just inhale and count to five before exhaling.

"Sam, can you hear me?" The female voice blasting through her earpiece gave her a jolt. She froze. What should she do now? Ignore her producer's question? Pretend the audio problem hadn't been fixed? Her heartbeat picked up speed and her mouth went dry. She heard the commercials leading up to the news open. She balled her fists, forcing her French-tipped nails into her palms, looking for a little pain to stop the flow of adrenaline coursing through her veins in a headlong rush. *Seconds away from the live newscast.* Her throat tightened.

"Damn cable." George stood behind the camera, ready for action, but his eye wasn't on the eyepiece. "Steele, did you hear the producer?" He stared at her, eyebrows up.

She shuffled back into place, head down. "I hear you." She could barely even hear herself over the blood pounding in her ears.

"You're at the top of the show." The producer had the high-squeaky enthusiasm of a kid just out of college. "Your headline is forty-five seconds away." The young woman probably didn't even know Sam had just watched her friend die. Her demanding and often insensitive news director wouldn't have bothered to mention that. "I also need a roll cue to your package. That hits two minutes into the show."

Roll cue. Right. She'd been doing her job for so many years, her brain kicked into autopilot, despite the simmering panic. "Here's a look at the shocking accident." The words flew out of her mouth as crazy thoughts banged around inside her head like out-of-control bumper cars.

"Twenty to the top of the show."

Her brain registered the producer's voice, but she couldn't respond.

Breathe in. Breathe out. Just breathe.

Finding a quiet place in her mind had enabled her to survive the painful journey of her life—her father's abandonment, their lack of money, her mother's failed searches for a well-to-do knight in shining armor, and most recently her mother's near-fatal accident. Why was her skill at meditation failing her these days? Anxiety had her in its wicked claws, and was squeezing her breathless.

"Sam, go. You're live." Her producer shouted into her earpiece.

Sam opened her eyes, and looked directly into the TV camera.

And froze.

...

Ice Queen.

That was what Zack thought as he watched Samantha Steele perform her job as a TV reporter. How could anyone look so hot and be so frigid? When they'd talked earlier, when he'd seen her emotional reaction to Wentworth's death, he'd thought she was different from others in her trade.

Apparently not.

She'd just watched a man she cared about die, cried in his arms, and an hour later, she was cool as a cucumber on TV, her face looking animated as she spoke to the camera in front of her. *Vulture.*

He wasn't close enough to hear her words, but what could she possibly be saying to make what had happened here today all right? His stomach churned in distaste. She'd sold out her friend's privacy for a few minutes on the evening news. No telling what she'd do to him if she knew who he really was, and why he was here.

He was tempted to walk away, but knew he couldn't. He had a mission to accomplish. The clueless reporter would pack up and leave after the five o'clock news. The local cops would finish their questioning, and then he could get back to his own private investigation.

Gaze drawn back to her, he watched Samantha jerk something out of her ear. Both hands covered her face, and her shoulders shook as if she was crying. At least she appeared to feel a little guilt over turning her friend's death into a news story.

Suddenly, she swayed and bent over, her hands resting

on her knees for support. She seemed woozy. He took a step forward, but knew he couldn't reach her fast enough to break a fall. Thankfully, she steadied herself, then stood and looked his way.

He tried to deflect his gaze, but too late. Their eyes met and held as if glued together. He shifted his weight and finally felt compelled to look down.

Men probably stared at her all the time. He had to admit she was great looking, and he had enjoyed flirting with her earlier, sympathized with her after Maxwell's death. Even thought about looking her up and asking her out after he got back to his normal life. But when the satellite news truck pulled up, and he realized she was about to throw a huge spotlight on the company he was investigating, he'd gone stone cold. It had to be all business between them now. He couldn't risk anything else.

Reluctantly, he looked up again. She held his gaze for a moment, then abruptly turned away.

He pulled his Ray Ban's back into place so Samantha couldn't read the intent in his gaze and strode toward her. He had to convince her to leave immediately, before she stuck her reporter nose in where it didn't belong, asking questions and stirring up even more interest in the adventure vacation company.

She remained near the camera, but luckily her photographer was walking back to their truck in the parking lot. The last thing he needed was the cameraman running around taking more pictures that might later air on TV. The publicity generated today would make his job much more difficult. He didn't want either of them hanging around asking more invasive questions, scaring witnesses—and possibly the killer—and blasting crucial evidence across the evening news. Not to mention what she might dig up on him personally.

Be nice, he told himself as he approached.

That was his goal, but when he reached her, and she cocked her head as if in challenge, his true feelings stormed out. "How can you do that?"

"Do what?" Her face was still red and puffy under a new layer of makeup that didn't quite hide her distress.

"Turn your emotions on and off like that. One minute you're crying hysterically on my shoulder, the next you're this indifferent journalist reporting a death as if the man was a stranger to you. Don't you feel bad about that?"

Her eyes looked as if they would pop out of her head. "It's my job. It's what I have to do, like it or not. Some of us have to *work* to survive."

"What you did was cold." He knew he was pushing her buttons, but couldn't help it. His past experiences with reporters had left a bitter taste in his mouth.

Samantha cast an icy stare his way. "Then I'm sure you'll be glad to know I froze on live TV. Couldn't speak a word. No one knows what happened to Maxwell because I couldn't even breathe long enough to get the story out." With each word, her voice rose in pitch and volume. She swiped the back of her palm against her cheek, smudging a black streak of mascara across it. "Now, I'm probably going to be fired."

Taken aback, a flash of regret slugged him. And shame. When he was a kid, his dad's condescending words had cut through him on a regular basis, making him feel small and worthless. Stupid and unworthy. How could he be so quick to make another person feel the same way, deserved or not? And apparently he'd been wrong about her.

"I'm sorry. I didn't—" He shook his head. He really was sorry. But he also wondered how much information had made the broadcast despite her freeze-up.

A man behind them cleared his throat.

Zack whipped around.

One of the cops who'd arrived earlier in a marked

cruiser sauntered up to Samantha. He was dressed in khakis and a dark green polo shirt with a Pasco County Sheriff's Department emblem on one side. *Casual for a detective.* Zack could spot a Homicide dick a mile away.

"Am I interrupting anything?" the detective asked Samantha. The dude was tall, with a body-builder's physique, and he moved toward her in a familiar way.

"Not at all, Stuart." She shot Zack a guilty look. "I mean, Detective Johnson. I wish you'd arrived a few minutes earlier. Maybe you could have saved me from a total meltdown on TV. Again."

"Meltdown?" The cop seemed puzzled by her response.

Samantha's phone rang. She glanced down at the number, sighed, and looked back at the detective.

"You going to get that?" Johnson watched her, his brow wrinkling.

"Nope. If my boss wants to fire me, I'm going to make him do it in person." She pressed a button on her phone. The ringtone ended. "Can this day get any worse?"

"Talk to me, Sam." The big man moved closer as if to offer comfort, but he stopped short of touching her. Unexpectedly, he turned to Zack. "And you are?"

"This is Zack Hunter," Samantha jumped in. "Ex-Army Ranger, current adventure seeker."

He shook the detective's hand. The cop's grip was firm, strong, and serious. Zack casually checked the ID clipped to the man's belt and confirmed his name.

Johnson turned back to Samantha. "So, what happened out here today?"

Zack bristled at the subtle blow off, even though he should have been glad the cop hadn't recognized him. The law enforcement world was a small one. He didn't want his cover blown in front of this reporter.

"Isn't it your job to tell me?" She placed both hands on

her hips.

The detective smiled, as though they'd faced off in this contest before. "I need to see the video you shot before, during, and after the accident. Including the footage you didn't have time to air."

"And I need to see a subpoena," she stated, but her words lacked bite.

"Come on now, we're old friends." A compassionate smile spread across the detective's face as he put an arm around her and gave her a friendly squeeze. "And I can tell you've been crying. Let's work together on this, okay? Let's just forget the normal red tape bullshit."

"Stuart." She glanced Zack's way. "I mean, Detective." She cleared her throat and pulled slightly away from him. "I can't give you the raw video. Station policy. You know that. I can't afford to piss off my boss any more than I already have, so you're going to have to go through the red tape." She shrugged and made a sympathetic face. "And besides, no one shot video of Maxwell's landing. I put the camera down before I ran over to him. George was still up in the plane."

"How well do you know the deceased?"

Her gaze dropped, and her chest rose and fell. "Maxwell Wentworth and I were good friends. He dated my mother for a while before he got married again, kind of took me under his wing."

"I'm sorry." The detective gave her another squeeze. "Hell, no wonder you froze. Your boss is an asshole for making you do it."

Zack's respect for the man went up a notch.

Johnson's gaze moved to the dead man still on the landing field. Then he took his arm from around Samantha's shoulder and pulled out a small notepad. "Okay. Let's go over it. You were here covering a story, right? On Wentworth?"

She nodded. Her phone made a humming noise. She

glanced down at it, but didn't pick it up.

Zack wondered how long she would continue to ignore her boss, kind of admiring her for being that bold.

"Notice anything suspicious? Did Wentworth do anything out of the ordinary before this jump?"

She shot the detective a resigned look and told him about the kid packing Wentworth's chute.

The cop nodded. "Forensics will check out the parachute and every piece of gear the deceased—Mr. Wentworth—had on him. We'll process it all. You know the name of this kid?"

She shook her head. "I don't even know if I'd recognize him. I wasn't really paying attention."

Zack watched her energy sink even further and felt a little sorry for her. "Only a handful of teenagers hang around here trying to make a buck or two packing gear," he offered. "I'm sure we can find him."

Now why had he said that? He wanted her out of here. Like, right now.

Johnson scribbled a note. "Did Mr. Wentworth jump a lot?"

"Every other weekend. He practically lived up here."

"You think this was an accident?" The detective directed his comment to Samantha, but watched Zack.

"I don't think Wentworth's death was an accident and neither do you, Detective. Am I right?" Zack said. "Are you investigating Skydive Drop Zone or the X-Force Adventure Vacation Company?"

The big man puffed up and stepped closer to him. Zack could smell the sharp tang of a hot day hanging off him.

"He's okay, Stuart." Samantha tried to step between the two, but Zack put an arm out to stop her.

He didn't need her protection. Or her help. He stared down the detective. "I think someone tampered with Wentworth's parachute before he jumped. They did something to force that parachute to spring open too quickly. That sudden impact could kill a man instantly." He watched the detective carefully.

"You seem very interested in Wentworth's death. Why is that?"

"I'm on this vacation, too, and I don't want to be the next one to have…an accident."

The detective's gaze ran up and down the length of him, his jaw set, but Zack didn't even begin to flinch. He'd held up to much worse in the military. *Bring it on.*

"You vouch for this guy, Sam?"

"I—I don't really know him."

Zack's stomach tightened as he broke eye contact and glanced at her. Her face was a hot mess, makeup gummy and mascara running down her cheek.

"Okay, here's the deal." Johnson flipped his notebook closed. "Off the record, of course."

Samantha nodded.

Zack nodded, as well. Why the hell not? So far, they were both making this easy.

Wiping drops off his brow, the detective pursed his lips. "Maxwell Wentworth wasn't the first person to die during one of these fancy-ass adventure vacations. About eighteen months ago, a man named Scott Fitzpatrick died during an underwater cave dive at Peacock Springs State Park up in the Panhandle. He went down in the Orange Grove sink with a couple of other men, got separated, and never resurfaced."

Samantha gasped. "Another accident?"

Zack managed to cover his reaction, but his body went on full alert. So, this guy knew about the other incidents. Was he putting two and two together? So far, no one else had been able to.

Johnson shrugged. "Maybe. Took a couple of days to find this Fitzpatrick guy's body. When the local police hauled him up, they didn't find any trace of foul play. A friend of mine is with the local force up there and said Fitzpatrick had run out of air in his tank. Probably got lost and died trying to find his way out of those underground caves. It's happened before. An employee with the adventure vacation company and a family member ID'd the body. Case closed."

"Then...how does that relate to Maxwell?" Samantha worried her lip.

"Six months later, *another* guy died cave diving at Peacock Springs."

Zack's mind filled with white noise and his shoulder blades pressed together until the pain in his body kept the pain in his heart at bay. He knew this story all too well. The face of the dead man—his uncle—regularly haunted his dreams...and nightmares. His heart thumped, but he fought to keep his expression stoic. They couldn't know about his personal connection. Not yet. He could learn so much more if he remained undercover.

"Some uptown corporate guy from New York came down looking for a thrill," he heard Johnson tell Samantha. "He died alone, lost in the caves. The medical examiner ruled his death an accidental drowning."

Accidental, my ass. Zack chewed the inside of his mouth to keep the words from seeing the light of day. He had gone on many dives with his uncle and Jackson's son. On vacation away from his abusive father, Zack had found these underwater caverns to be a place of peace. And his deaf cousin reveled in a world where sound wasn't as important as the varying visual feast. Jackson Hunter had been too skilled to *accidentally* get lost and die. Zack's fisted hands drummed the side of his thighs.

"And the X-Force Adventure Vacation Company? He was on one of their vacations, too?" She leaned forward.

"Righto."

Samantha nodded slowly, lost in thought.

Great. The detective had dangled the information like a carrot in front of a desperate reporter about to lose her job. No doubt she'd take a big, fat bite. Did she even have a choice? The woman had something to prove, and a lot to lose.

"I definitely see a pattern here." Her hand moved up to massage her temple.

He wondered what she was thinking. Was she excited about this new information because it meant she was onto a good story that would save her ass? Or was she feeling sick at the implication someone could have murdered her friend?

"But both deaths were ruled accidental, right?" she said.

The detective sighed. "Only because the Florida Department of Law Enforcement couldn't find evidence of anything otherwise. And each accident happened in different counties and under different jurisdictions, so maybe notes aren't being shared. But now this little mystery has landed in *my* county, and in *my* lap, and I think something stinks like a pig's ass."

Samantha cracked a sad smile at his language. "Why are you telling me—" She paused and surveyed Zack. "I mean, why are you telling *us* this information?"

Zack held his breath. Why was she including him? He certainly didn't intend to do the same. He worked alone. Solo. No partner. Ever again.

"You have access to the X-Force Adventure Vacation Company in ways I don't," Johnson said matter-of-factly.

She drew back. "But…you're a cop."

"And you're an attractive woman who can get closer to these filthy rich bastards than I can." He crossed his arms. "Look, I'm going to be honest with you, Sam. I've dealt with men like this before. Most are arrogant egomaniacs who love nothing more than bragging about themselves and their accomplishments." His gaze lasered directly on Zack.

If this investigation wasn't so damn important to him, he'd have shown the cop exactly how accomplished he was. He ground his teeth instead.

The detective turned his attention to Samantha. "They don't like cops, but I bet they'd love to spill some secrets to impress a beautiful woman like you."

Zack opened his mouth to protest, but then thought better of it. The detective was whetting the reporter's appetite, giving her a chance to redeem herself while also seeking justice for her friend. If he tried to interfere now, convince her to leave, it would look suspicious. He'd just end up making things worse. He swallowed his anger and remained quiet.

"Are you tipping me off to investigate the X-Force Adventure Vacation Company?" she asked Johnson.

"You know I can't do that."

"You just did."

The detective grinned. "Did I? Nah."

You sure as hell did. Zack groaned inwardly, but kept his face passive. He wanted to kick a deep hole in the dirt—or better yet, in the man's cop radar for picking up on all this too soon...or too late—but refrained.

"Why can't you get a court order and investigate it yourself?" she asked.

"I intend to devour this scene like my mother's Thanksgiving meal, but the medical examiner said the previous deaths were accidental. If someone is making these murders look like accidents, they're covering their tracks pretty damn well."

"You think that's what's happening?" Samantha's eyebrows furrowed together.

The detective nodded, then gestured his way. "So does your friend, here."

Zack narrowed his eyes. The detective was baiting him, but Zack knew all of these cop tricks. Had used them himself.

Samantha turned to him.

He shrugged and said, "I believe I've already stated my opinion."

Finally, she directed her attention back to the detective. "I'll think about expanding the story. But no promises, because I don't even know if my boss will trust me enough to pursue this kind of investigative story now..."

The detective threw in another plea. "If you liked this Wentworth guy, don't let his death be for nothing."

Zack watched those words resonate with Samantha, and his stomach sank when he saw the instant she made up her mind. Her chin jutted out, and she opened her mouth to say something—just as her skinny photographer charged up to them.

"Hey, you gonna answer your damn phone, or what?" the kid groused. "'Cause I'm sick of Stan calling my ass and telling me he's going to fire you if you don't pick up."

Samantha whipped around and threw both hands up. "Tell Stan I'm working the damn story. Okay?"

"I think maybe you should have been working that damn live shot earlier." He made a face. "Shit, I'll call him but—"

"Tell him I just found out Maxwell may have been murdered, and I have exclusive inside information I'm working. I'll call him back when I can."

The cameraman gawked at her as if she'd gone crazy, his eyes as wild as his messy red hair. "What the hell are you talking about?" He glanced over at the detective, at Zack, then back at Samantha. "You serious? That's some shit, if you are."

"We're still going on this adventure vacation, George, but it's no longer just a fluff feature. Tell the boss we're bringing him back an investigative piece. If he still gives us the two weeks, he won't be sorry."

The camera guy's shoulder's dropped, but he nodded.

"He's still going to wanna talk to you. He's fucking pissed."

She put her hand together as if in prayer. "Put him off. Just for now. Please." She pulled off a smile. George shrugged and stomped off.

Fabulous.

Zack could not believe his bad luck. Now, not only would he have to deal with keeping his cover intact with the adventure company and evading a killer's notice, he'd also have to keep a nosy reporter and her too-observant cameraman from asking dangerous questions, stirring up suspicion, and broadcasting rumors and allegations on the evening news. He must have made a sound of disgust because both Samantha and the detective were now staring at him.

After an uncomfortable moment of silence Johnson pocketed his notebook. "You've got my number, Sam. Keep in close touch with me on this." The confident smile on his face irritated Zack, but he took the business card the detective also handed to him. "Both of you, call me with any new information you come up with. Anytime, day or night."

But Johnson's narrowed look told him he still distrusted Zack.

Samantha nodded, but pressed a hand against her stomach as the homicide investigator sauntered back to the viewing deck.

Instantly, a wave of guilt slammed into Zack.

Suddenly, she whipped around to face him, suspicion coloring her expression. Her unexpected move, and the heat of her gaze, was enough to make him take a step back.

"I know you're not a local cop because if you were, Stuart would have recognized you."

Startled by the accusatory tone of her voice, he stuttered, "I— N-no, I'm not. Why on earth would you think that?"

"I guess you could be just another guy with too much time and money who can afford this kind of crazy vacation. But I think there's more to your story. You think there's something funny going on, and you're here to investigate. Aren't you?" It wasn't really a question, more like an accusation.

She was trying to bait him, too. She couldn't possibly know his reason for being here. He bit his lip to keep from delivering a smart-ass reply. It didn't work. "And you think I'm willing to pay twenty-five grand to investigate some random hunch? You're nuts." Or too smart for her own good…

She tipped her head considering. "Maybe not so random."

He curled his lip. "And your reporter's instinct is always right, is it?"

Her steely brown eyes shot ice bullets at him. "I want to look into Maxwell's death as well, and I'd like you to work with me."

She had to be kidding. "No. No way." He worked alone.

"Here's my plan." She widened her stance, completely ignoring his rejection. "I was supposed to follow Maxwell on his two-week adventure vacation. I'll just tell the manager of the adventure vacation company that I'll be following you, instead."

He couldn't hold back a laugh. "Not a chance in hell. I'm here to have fun and unwind. I don't want to have a TV camera up my butt all day."

Her face remained a blank shield.

His blood pressure hitched up. "What makes you think the company will want more attention from the media?"

She rolled her eyes. "Now that a number of people have ended up *dead* on one of their vacations," she explained, "who in their right mind would book a trip with them? We'll convince the management they need the positive publicity to survive."

"*We*?" He was running out of arguments.

"Yes, *we*. That will give me the access I need to poke around and investigate."

He tried another tactic. "I could have sworn you said you don't even fly. Sure you're up for F-16s, cave diving, and swimming with sharks?" She seemed way too skittish and high-strung to handle this kind of jacked-up adventure.

She paled for a second, but that chin went up again. "I'm hoping George can do all that stuff. He loves diving and flying. Lives for this kind of life-risking craziness. And it'll give me more time for investigating."

He pushed out a long breath. "What part of *hell no* don't you get?" But he knew a losing battle when he was in the middle of one.

"I don't really expect you to help me, just give me a cover."

He groaned in a blast of disbelief. The irony of this situation was not lost on him. If he wanted to remain undercover for real, he had to provide *her* with a pretend cover. The woman did have balls, he had to admit. He forced a smile. "And if I don't go along with your plan?"

"I walk right over to my detective friend and tell him my suspicions." She stared boldly his way, hands on hips, legs slightly apart. "I'll tell him that Maxwell was killed and you know all about it. That you're here investigating the other suspicious deaths. I don't know what agency you're working for, but Stuart could find out in less than ten minutes, and I imagine you don't want to blow your cover just yet. Am I right?"

His jaw dropped. "Blackmail? Really? Do you know the penalty for that if I really *am* a cop?"

She snorted. "Extortion, actually. Well?"

He snapped his jaw shut. He knew very well what would happen if the adventure vacation company knew his real identity, and what his bosses would do if they found out he was still investigating this case after they'd specifically pulled him off it.

Wow. She had him. He was impressed, and a little turned

on.

He ground his teeth. He would agree to her plan, only because he had no choice. He was determined to find and nail the son of a bitch who had killed his uncle.

"All right, fine," he reluctantly said.

She might lose her job if she didn't come back with her investigative story. But he would definitely lose his job if she exposed his undercover activities and his family's private life on the news. So he would have to keep the nosy reporter under his thumb and under his control.

One way or another.

Chapter Four

Sam and George caught up with the X-Force Adventure Vacation Company in Peacock Springs State Park—250 acres of wilderness in Florida's Panhandle. Two of the "accidents" had occurred in this very park.

After driving all night, they'd made camp shortly after sunrise. Now, in mid-afternoon, the sun's heat poured through the openings in the treetops' canopy. The air hung heavy, like the leaves on the live oak and silver maples surrounding them.

Sam sat next to Zack on a wooden bench just a few feet from the entrance to the Orange Grove Sink, a mocha-colored pool that struck her as too murky to dive in.

She'd done her research last night while George drove. She knew what a sinkhole was. They opened up all the time in Florida. But Peacock Springs was different. Rainwater and the flow of groundwater had dissolved the limestone in the area over time to form the largest underwater cave system in Florida. Five-and-a-half miles of passages had been surveyed by cave divers. That meant plenty of places for lone divers to get lost and in trouble.

The Orange Grove Sink was one doorway to that underground world of wonder. More like a deathtrap. Just the thought of diving in those passages made beads of anxiety bubble up on her forehead.

Patting the sweat away with a tissue, she cut a glance at George, who stood behind his camera. "Are we ready?" Her fingertips were starting to prickle, another sign a full-fledged panic attack had started. She didn't have to dive today, so what was her freakin' problem?

"Yep, ready." The red light on George's camera flickered on, indicating he was recording.

Zack leaned back against the bench in a tight, Batman-looking scuba suit, one arm casually thrown over the benchtop, but his eyes remained alive and focused, alerting her to the fact he wasn't as relaxed as he wanted her to think.

"Cave diving is inherently risky. So, why take the chance?" she asked, playing her role as reporter for the crowd gathering around the sink.

"Why *not* take the chance?" He rolled out the same charismatic smile she'd seen right before Maxwell's landing, when he was flirting with her, before the closed off and difficult side of his personality had surfaced. Which Zack would she be dealing with today?

"That's not an answer."

"Don't judge my answers, or I'll stop listening to your questions." His gaze challenged her.

Ever since she and George had arrived, Zack had been playing this frustrating game with her. He'd been flirty, but uncooperative. If she talked to a group of people, he'd join them and listen. When she was alone, he'd avoid her. She still had no idea if Zack Hunter was an arrogant player or an accomplished investigator. Probably both.

She bit the inside of her mouth. No use. It didn't stop

angry words from storming out. “You’re not cooperating.”

“I’m sitting here, aren’t I?”

“You’re not answering my questions.”

“This isn’t a real interview.”

“Sure it is. We may use some of the footage.” She wanted to stomp her foot or do something childish that would make her feel better, but the camera was rolling. “And even if we don’t, they don’t know it.” She gestured toward the other vacationers nearby, using her eyes to make sure he understood the importance of convincing the X-Force Adventure group they were for real. Some were shuffling around the Orange Grove Sink. Others were testing out their dive gear. A few were joking around near a food cart. A couple of the vacationers had stopped to watch the interview.

Zack followed her gaze. “They aren’t close enough to hear what we’re saying.”

“How would you know that?”

He slid off his sunglasses. “Okay, boss.” His dark eyes danced with questionable intent. “Ask me again.”

George interrupted, “Hold up.” Shaking his head, he fiddled with a button on the side of his camera. “Dead battery. I’ve gotta run to the truck for another one.” He unlatched the old camera battery. “We weren’t getting any good shit anyway.” He jerked the battery off the camera and stalked toward the parking lot, mumbling under his breath.

As soon as she thought he was out of hearing range, Sam lit into her stubborn new partner. “You have no idea what I had to do to convince my boss to give me another chance and let me go on this investigation. I have to come back with a story. And you’re looking for answers too, right? So, what’s your problem?”

Zack’s posture stiffened. “This isn’t a game. You shouldn’t be here. No job is worth your life.”

“Well, I am here, so let’s at least try to act like teammates.”

She checked out the area again. Monica, a tall, blond field manager for X-Force Adventure Vacations, stood about ten feet away with a group of three other employees. Her attention appeared to be firmly anchored on Zack.

Leaning into him, Sam pretended to adjust the small microphone attached to his wet suit. "Have you found anything?"

"Like what?"

"I don't know. Information on Maxwell's death?" He smelled so earthy, so masculine in the wet suit, and his hair glistened with moisture as if he'd just taken a shower. What the hell? She didn't even *like* this man, and she certainly didn't like how she noticed all these details about him and reacted physically to them.

"Haven't found a thing." He inhaled slowly. "And you?"

"I just got here. So far the only person I've interviewed is *you*." She made the mistake of glancing up. His pupils expanded. The flutter of butterfly wings teased her belly. She straightened, wondering again why he affected her like this. She'd interviewed the president, for Christ's sake. Of the United States. She slid down the bench away from him. "What's our next move?"

"We don't have a next move. I'm cave diving in about fifteen minutes."

"George is going with you."

"No, he's not." Zack's eyes flashed as he spoke, and he crossed his arms over his chest in a manner that left nothing open for interpretation. "I don't dive with amateurs."

"He's not an amateur." *Swallow. Take a breath.* "Will you stop challenging me and play along?" She fumbled for a place to hide her agitated fingers.

His big hands covered hers. His fingers were warm and his grip firm. "Play along with *your* rules, right?"

Damn it. The butterflies were dancing in her stomach

again. What was she, fifteen? She freed herself from the heated cocoon of his hold. "Don't take this so personally. We're partners on a mission." This time she forced herself to stare him down.

The air between them popped with electricity.

"When you look at me like that, it makes this personal." He inhaled again, this time so slowly she knew it was for effect. "Lavender. I like it. Very sexy."

Her shoulders dropped. Of course he'd come back with an inappropriate comment like that. Yet, she *had* splashed on lavender body spray earlier that morning, knowing she would see him. "Don't flirt with me. We've got a serious job to do here. To find a murderer."

"Okay, problem solved."

Sam jumped. She hadn't heard George return. Behind his camera now, her photographer reattached the battery.

Silence hovered over the three of them, like a blanket of suffocating humidity. She shifted on the bench, rubbing her forearms, hoping heat and friction would force the baby fine hair on her skin to settle back down.

The red light on the front of the camera blinked. "Let's take it from the top," George placed his right eye behind the viewfinder.

"Mind if I listen?"

Sam turned toward the approaching voice. Monica had strolled over and now towered over her. *Great.* "Of course not." Sam gritted her teeth while plastering on a smile. "But you'll have to stand behind George."

"Excuse me?" Monica drew back.

"So you won't be in the camera shot." She pointed to where she wanted the vacation manager to stand. As Monica walked by, a wave of jasmine assaulted Sam. Apparently, she hadn't been the only one who'd splashed on body spray this morning. She made a disgusted sound under her breath.

"Let's do it." Now they *had* to make this look real. Turning to face Zack, Sam suddenly realized the chemistry of the moment had stopped her anxiety from building. She was nervous, but it felt different today. "So, cave diving is inherently dangerous. Why do it?"

He cocked his head and grinned like Tom Cruise in *Top Gun*. "I'm an adventurer."

Those simple words ignited heat in her belly. Or maybe it was that confident smile. She licked her lips.

"I want to explore the unknown," he continued, looking right into her eyes. "To seek out what I've never explored before. I want to run my fingers down a virgin passage, squeeze through a small opening. I may get stuck a few times, move back and forth, and work my way through, you know, into this mysterious place where I've never been. It's magical."

Oh. My. God. She took a deep breath, her heart drumming like tiny, nervous fingertips. He was just playing with her. She had to remember that.

"There's no audience, no crowd." He motioned to the sinkhole. "It's your own personal achievement. The ultimate pleasure."

She started to ask a question. "But—"

He cut her off. "I'm a man who loves beauty."

His gaze bathed her again, warming her with its intensity.

"Very few people can say they've seen the light as it breaks through crevices in the rock, painting an underwater cave in a rainbow of colors." He closed his eyes, the vision in his mind obviously blissful enough to raise his lips into a smile. "There are no computers, no phones, no interruptions." He opened his eyes and stared deep into hers. "Do you know what I do when I'm in an unexplored cavern?"

Her heart pounded loud enough in the silent pause she was sure her microphone would pick up the beat. "What?" She held her breath.

"I leave my fingerprints all over the new territory, marking it as mine forever."

She exhaled. *Jesus, he's good.* She glanced over at Monica, who had a dreamy look on her face. An idea struck her. If Zack Hunter could make her own guarded heart race, then he could probably seduce Monica with little effort. Maybe he could get the vacation manager to tell him everything she knew about the X-Force Adventure Vacation Company. Including the dirt.

"No more questions?" Amusement filled Zack's voice. His gaze bounced back and forth between her and Monica.

Sam rolled her eyes. "Just one. Does that crap always work for you?"

He blinked. Then he barked out a laugh. "Yeah. Usually."

"Amazing." She stood. She wasn't going to end up like Monica, quick to fall under his spell. She had his number. He was definitely a player. "No more questions right now. But I reserve the right to ask more after your dive with George." She emphasized the last two words.

Zack lifted his chin, but he said nothing.

George switched off the video cam. "Whoa, that shit was much better."

Why the hell was George grinning at her? A quick, bright flash startled her and made her stumble and drop back onto the bench, her body inadvertently colliding with Zack's. Her muscles tensed.

"Perfect. I want to get a photograph of you two together," a new voice interrupted, this one male.

Sam looked up. The X-Force Vacation Company photographer stood a few feet away, snapping shots of her and Zack.

"Sorry, because you're back lit I have to use the flash."

He was a short, balding guy, and easy to miss if not for the company T-shirt, the camera, and the annoying flash that followed him everywhere.

"Can you two move closer together? And smile, please. It's for the X-Force website."

Zack's arm snaked around her waist. In one strong, fluid movement, he slid her body tight to his.

She willed herself not to react, even though the heat of him seemed to melt her skin.

His breath warmed her ear. "Follow my lead, so no one gets hurt," he whispered. "We may be in the company of a killer, remember?"

She forced herself to smile and nod.

He moved one hand down to a sensitive area at her waist. She suddenly couldn't breathe. His fingers grazed her skin and she flinched as he gently tickled her. What the heck!

The flash went off again.

"That's it. Thanks." The photographer stepped away, his attention on his camera.

Zack's hot gaze burned through her.

Sam shot to her feet and walked a few steps away, trying to regain her composure. She couldn't look at him because she couldn't believe the effect he was having on her.

"Let me pack up real quick, and I'll be ready to change into my dive gear," George's voice boomed, eagerness lighting up his expression.

He flipped his camera off the tripod and sprinted to their TV truck in the parking lot, his gawky gait impaired by the camera swinging at his side.

She peeked at Zack to see if he was going to protest again, but Monica had walked up to him, and they were engaged in conversation. Sam took a step closer so she could listen.

"What a great interview. I've never heard anyone describe cave diving with more color or passion." Monica placed a hand on his arm. "Your interview will be great advertising for our company. I'll put it up on our website."

Of course she would.

But only if Sam gave her permission to use the footage. She smiled to herself.

Zack whispered something to Monica and the young woman grinned and nodded, glancing at Sam.

Embarrassed at being caught watching them, she turned away and helped gather the rest of George's equipment. She fought the urge to glance at Zack again. But the need to know tugged at her, and she lost the battle within seconds. When she looked up, Monica was walking away and Zack was two steps from Sam's side. She stood taller. "What did Monica say to you?"

He shook his head. "You're always asking questions."

"And you're always avoiding answers."

"I told her I'd take her diving tomorrow."

"Really?" For some inexplicable reason, Sam's chest burned at the thought. "You said earlier you don't dive with amateurs."

"She's not an amateur."

Oh. Right. "To question her more about the deaths?" she asked to cover her embarrassment.

"You can't actually talk underwater." He grinned.

Clenching her jaw, she said, "Funny."

He chuckled softly. "Yes, of course to dig for information. That's why we're both here, right?"

So he'd finally admitted it. Enough of his playing around. "Who do you work for?"

"I'm a rich, arrogant egomaniac, remember?" he drawled. "I couldn't possibly work for a living."

She leaned into his space. "Don't you think I have the right to know?" She couldn't stop her fingers from fidgeting. He was getting to her. "You know who I work for."

"Maybe I work for myself."

"And maybe you don't."

"Why does it matter?"

"I need to know I can trust you."

"One has nothing to do with the other. You can trust me."

She wanted to scream. His words tangled her up with frustration. Getting anything out of him was harder than figuring out a damn Rubik's cube. "I've been a reporter for a long time. I usually read people quickly, but you're a real mystery."

"Don't try to solve the mystery of me." He patted her on the back like a little sister, which only made her blood pressure rise. "Stick to your original game plan. Find clues that someone killed Maxwell Wentworth. That's a goal we both share."

His eyes always had such intensity behind them. What was behind all that passion? She had to know. *All in good time.* Taking a deep breath, she made an earnest appeal. "Please watch out for George."

"I'm not diving with George." Zack balled both fists. "I told you that. I work alone. Always." He gave her a quick salute and headed toward the ridge above the Orange Grove Sink.

She didn't even realize she was holding her breath until a tap on her shoulder startled her, and an exhale *whoosh*ed out.

"Do you want to see the pictures?"

She spun around. "Oh, hi." Her hand clutched reflexively at her chest as she willed her heart to slow down again. It was just the X-Force photographer. "Sure. Are they good?"

The bald man smiled at her like a shy schoolboy. "You take a great picture." He held out the digital camera in front of her.

Zack's smile took up most of the shot, but hey, it was a nice smile. She relaxed her shoulders.

"Do you think his dive will bring up bad memories?"

"I'm sorry?"

The small man was standing a bit too close now. "Zack's dive." Wide-eyed, he shuffled even closer to her. "Don't you think it's odd he wants to do this?"

"Why?" She took a step away from him. "Isn't this what he's *paying* for?"

The little creep followed her, moving into her personal space. "You know Zack's uncle died last year on a dive in this same cave, right?"

His revelation sucked the air right out of her. It was like a vacuum had been attached to her mouth, and he had flipped on the switch. She started to flush, despite having felt a chill just a moment ago. "No. I didn't know."

"I'm surprised he didn't tell you."

So am I. Her shock at hearing the news must be splashed all over her face. She struggled to school her features. "Um. Why would he? I doubt he wants to talk about it on camera."

She searched out Zack, but he was concentrating on his preparations for the underwater cave dive, and didn't notice her. Well, this explained his interest in Maxwell's accident scene, and his reason for investigating the so-called accidents happening on the adventure trips in the first place.

"Yeah, I was shooting pictures last year when his uncle dove the sink with three other vacationers. He never surfaced."

"That's terrible." She would have to call Stuart to confirm this information and find out what he knew about Zack's dead uncle. That had to be the wealthy guy from New York that Stuart had referred to.

The X-Force vacation photographer shook his head. "They found his body trapped in one of the underwater tunnels. Such a shame. The man was still in his prime. Fifty-five, I think."

She put a hand to his shoulder and firmly backed him

away from her, sending what she hoped was a definitive message.

"Do you know his name?" she asked. Why wouldn't Zack have told her this very important detail? They'd had plenty of time alone to share information. And why was this creep dishing out Zack's family dirt to her?

He shook his head thoughtfully. "Can't remember, but I can look it up for you."

"Thanks. That would be great."

"You really didn't know?" The photographer placed his hand on her arm, as if to comfort her.

"No, but hey, he's not my friend or anything." Her stomach rolled. "I'm just a reporter here to do a story on him."

The photographer watched her with a question in his gaze. "Yeah, I guess. But, if I were a reporter, I'd wonder what else he hadn't told me. And why."

No kidding.

And as soon as she could get rid of the little weirdo, she intended to ask Zack exactly that.

Chapter Five

Staring at the cement staircase leading down into the murky Orange Grove Sink, a sense of dread clawed at Zack's gut. After more than a year of not diving, the uncomfortable cramping proved he was still nervous about going under.

The last time he'd taken a dive, he'd been working, looking for a missing kid who'd gone under jet skiing off Florida's west coast.

He and his police partner had been searching in the Gulf, off St. Petersburg, when his coworker's gear had malfunctioned and he'd drowned. A sour taste lingered in the back of Zack's throat. He hadn't been paying attention when his buddy had failed to keep up with him. He couldn't stop blaming himself for not backing up his partner.

On the heels of that unfortunate accident, his uncle had died diving in this very sink.

Right now, as he stared down at the rippling surface below the rocky edge, the muddiness of the water mirrored his thoughts, and he wondered if it would be safer for everyone if he stayed topside.

No. He had to see this through. For his uncle. And for his own peace of mind.

He adjusted his regulator, and descended into the Orange Grove Sink in his scuba gear, moving slowly and deliberately until the chilly water covered his head and he could swim freely. The rhythmic sound of his breathing and the chill of the water began to lull him into a numb state.

Which was exactly what he needed right now.

Drifting down through the water, his thoughts traveled back to days when he'd gone diving with his uncle. His heart began to beat faster as the sunlight from above dimmed and the water around him grew darker, matching his memories. The light strapped around his head and a handheld flashlight guided him.

His uncle used to sneak him away from his father in order to give him a break from the constant verbal and physical abuse. Jackson knew this incredibly different world would give him hope. His eyes watered behind his mask, but he fought back the raw grief still living deep inside him.

His gaze darted around the cavern, drinking in the rich environment he used to crave seeing. The pyrotechnic display of daylight refracted into beautiful curtains of color that stained the limestone walls. The murky brown of the water dissolved into a mesmerizing blue-green, and he allowed himself to be swept away by the awesome power of the experience.

But only for a few too-short moments.

He had a responsibility, a mission to fulfill down here today. He needed to use all his skill to try and find some clue that might explain how—and why—his uncle had died.

A team of medically certified cave divers had recovered Jackson's body and the medical examiner had ruled his uncle's death an accidental drowning. Just like that Pasco County detective had told Samantha. No more details had followed, even when Zack had used his pull as a law officer to dig.

He was near the bottom of the Orange Sink now and he saw there were a few smaller, tunnel-like caves that branched out from the main cavern. He stopped in front of the one bearing a warning sign with a large picture of a dark, scowling Grim Reaper.

He'd bet anything that sign had enticed his thrill-seeking uncle.

For a moment, he treaded water in indecision. But his instincts told him he was on the right track and he made up his mind. Before he entered the smaller cave, he secured his guideline on a rock near the entrance and snapped on an arrow pointing to the surface, in case he became disoriented. Then he reeled out more line.

Out of habit, he glanced back. He gasped, almost losing his regulator.

The fucking TV cameraman was swimming right behind him, underwater camera in hand, probably shooting video of him. *Damn it.*

His body temperature rose, despite the cool water. Motioning for the kid not to follow, he pointed repeatedly to the warning sign of the Grim Reaper.

How the fuck had he not noticed a partner *again*? *Because he'd been too preoccupied, inside his own damn head.* But he wasn't down here today with an experienced police diver. He was dealing with a TV cameraman who was probably an amateur diver—and a stubbornly persistent reporter waiting at the top of the sink ready to spew questions his way when they surfaced. *Fuck.*

His frustration exited in a stream of bubbles. He could either swim with the kid back to the surface, making the required stops for decompression, which would eat precious minutes from his total allowed dive time, or he could go just a little further now...and keep a careful eye on the kid.

He was so close to possible answers.

He motioned for the cameraman to follow.

George nodded. The tunnel narrowed precipitously, so Zack had to swim slowly to avoid stirring up silt from the cave floor.

A ripple of water hit his back. The hair on his neck floated on end as the energy behind him shifted. Years in the special forces had fine-tuned each of his senses so acutely that his body alerted him to a crisis almost before it appeared.

He stilled instantly.

The water continued to move.

Careful not to further stir up silt, he looked back at George.

His bright light hit George's mask, making the kid's eyes pop wide open like some horror movie victim. George's hand rose to shield his face. He twisted away from the light. His sudden, erratic movements kicked up a cloud of silt from the cave floor, encircling them in a thick, sandy cloak.

Shit! Had his light frightened George? Or was the photographer reacting to something else? The kid was big and tall, flailing around in the tight tunnel. Zack reached for the side of the cave, bracing himself for the impact of the resulting sandstorm. His fingers found a crevice in which he could anchor another guideline.

Just in time.

A wave of brown obscured his vision to zero despite the headlight. He took slow, steady breaths, fighting not to feel claustrophobic in his sudden blindness. He swept his flashlight beam around.

A flash of black swirled past. George's wet suit? With one hand tight on the reel that held his guideline, he quickly attached the flashlight to his dive belt and reached out with his free hand. He swiped at the cloud of sand, hoping to find an arm or a leg. His fingers grazed George's wrist. Zack latched on. His heart rapped against his chest so fiercely he had trouble breathing.

George struggled with something Zack couldn't see. The cameraman wrenched to one side, then the other, pulling against his hold.

Zack held tight, his body absorbing the jerky motions. Apprehension tightened his throat. Was he in trouble? Even in a narrow tunnel, a diver could drift and get lost in a matter of minutes. Or lose his regulator and his air.

His fingers slipped off the slick neoprene of George's dive suit. *Shit!* His pulse lurched as he lost contact. He sliced his hand around in the liquid murkiness, trying to find him again.

But it was no use. He sensed the water go still and empty around him.

The kid had disappeared.

Chapter Six

Sam sat on the edge of her hotel room bed. Her fingers drummed against the beige and brown bedspread, her right foot tapped the floor as if she was keeping time to some high-intensity rock song.

But silence filled the room.

Maybe she should have stayed at the Orange Grove Sink and waited for Zack and George to surface, but George had told her they'd be down for a while and frankly, she'd been itching to do a little investigating and some online research on Jackson Hunter and Scott Fitzpatrick. She wasn't able to get a wireless connection in the woods near the sink, but she'd connected at a diner near the Holiday Inn in Live Oak. She'd been reading up on Zack's dead uncle and the first man who died so she could grill Stuart Johnson about what else local law enforcement knew, when her waitress, a cute redhead named Rita, had asked her about the headlines she was reading online.

It turned out that Rita had hooked up with a former vacationer last year. After much subtle manipulation on

Sam's part, Rita finally spilled some interesting information about her "boyfriend" and how he'd been diving one day when another vacationer from New York had died in the caves. Bingo! The waitress had been busy juggling about seven tables but had promised to swing by the motel after she got off work and bring Sam a dive DVD that she hoped would be their first real clue. She had been so excited to share this info with Zack, she'd barely been able to eat.

Now, three hours later, the detective hadn't called her back, the waitress still hadn't gotten in touch with her, and neither George nor Zack were answering their cell phones.

A knock came at the door. She sprang off the bed and yanked the door open.

"George!"

He leaned up against the doorframe, his head down and his shoulders slumped.

Slightly annoyed, the words blew out of her. "Where have you been? I've been trying to call you."

When he slowly brought his head up, Sam took a step back, stunned by the haunted look in his eyes and the tangled mess of his red hair. His skin, normally white with freckles and a hint of sunburn, looked ashen and downright alarming. She blinked to make sure she was seeing correctly. "My God, are you okay? You look like death."

He groped toward her. "I need to sit down."

She reached out and took his camera bag, ushering him inside. Quickly, she stepped outside the hotel room and checked the hallway, then the parking lot. "Where's Zack?"

George didn't respond.

When she turned back around, he was lowering himself onto the king-sized bed, carefully, as if injured. He eased his head onto a pillow and gingerly threw an arm over his forehead. "I almost died today."

"What?" She sprinted back into the room, but left the

door open in case Zack was parking the car or something. George looked like a man who'd just thrown up his dinner. "What the hell happened?"

"It all went down so fast. Shit."

Her heart fluttered. Where was Zack? She hurried over to the bed, sat at George's side, and grasped his arm. His skin felt cold and clammy. "You need to tell me what's going on."

George rubbed his head agitatedly. "The dive started out great. The first rush of cold water freaked me out, but as soon as my body adjusted, I fell right into the groove. I followed Zack after he went in, just like you suggested." He sat up and filled her in on the scary details of his dive gone wrong. "He led but, you know, I don't think he knew I was with him at first." He lifted a shoulder. "The dude was, like, in his own zone or something." His eyebrows bunched toward the center of his forehead. "Eventually we got to an entrance where the cave narrowed into a small tunnel. There was this big sign with the Grim Reaper on it."

She was getting a bad feeling about this. "Let me guess. Zack ignored it."

"Yeah."

Her pulse kicked up. She was actually a bit envious of Zack's obvious lust for excitement and total lack of fear. "And you followed him in there?"

"You told me not to let him out of my sight. And shit, I didn't want to be down there alone. Jesus. That guy has got balls the size of—"

She put her hand up. "Yeah, I get it. What happened next?"

"The ceiling was so low in some places it was impossible for me to lift my head without bumping into rock. Pretty freaky."

Her stomach clenched. She hated confined spaces. She grew increasingly nauseous as George described how he'd freaked out when something brushed up against his fins, setting off a sand storm underground.

She closed her eyes and envisioned that moment deep in the underwater cave. On second thought, she could do without those images in her head. When she opened her eyes, he had started shaking. That was a first. Damn, he was really traumatized.

Or maybe he was suffering from hypothermia? She got up and searched the closet for a blanket.

"Oh man, did I fuck up. I kicked up all that shit on the cave floor, and in, like, five seconds I couldn't see a damn thing. The lights didn't help. The water had turned brown—like a whiteout on the ski slopes." He clutched at his chest. "I didn't have any guideline attached to me. Both my hands were gripping the underwater camera casing, and"—he took a deep breath—"I didn't know what the hell to do. I was thinking, do I drop the camera and swim for the wall? Or do I keep the equipment and lose my sense of direction? I just panicked. I mean, fuck."

She walked back to the bed, the blanket under her arm. His muscles were actually twitching. Adrenaline, no doubt. She wrapped the thin, white blanket around his shoulders. He shivered so hard his teeth rattled.

"How did you get out?" Her mouth had gone bone dry. She reached across for a bottle of water on the other nightstand, took a sip, then handed it to him.

"I swam straight with the current, with my arms outstretched, and damn if I didn't run right into Zack. He grabbed my wrist, but then I lost my bearings again and my wrist slipped from his grip." His shoulders rounded over, and he took a deep breath. "I thought I was a goner for sure."

"Jesus, then what happened?" Why was her stomach cramping? George had survived.

"Zack reached out for me again. He grabbed my wrist

and—he saved my ass. That's what he did. He got my hand and led me to the guideline. Let me tell you, I did not let go of that line until I saw sky—and I don't mean through the water."

She watched her friend as he rubbed his temples.

"Maybe you should see a doctor."

"I did. One of the guys on the trip is an ER doc. He checked my vitals and said I was fine." He let out a long breath and nudged her in the arm. "Where the hell were you when I came up?"

"I came back here to look something up online. Did you know—"

"Here's the best part." His red-rimmed eyes regained some life. "Not once did I let go of that camera. I rolled the whole time." He let out a strained laugh. "Fuck, I just forgot to shut the damn thing off. Should make for a great video, though. The kind of shit that gets all kinds of hits on YouTube. Stan will piss his pants over it."

"Great. Maybe your brush with death will buy me another week on the payroll," she drawled, relieved that he could make light of his potentially deadly adventure. She pulled him into a hug. "I'm so glad you're okay." She held him until he stopped shaking, and his heart slowed its pace. Finally, she asked, "And Zack?"

"He took off right after he made sure I was okay. Said he had to meet someone."

Breaking the hug, she pushed back. "He abandoned you? To meet someone?"

"Doc said I was fine."

"Who is he meeting in the backwoods of the Florida Panhandle?"

"He didn't say."

"Did you ask?"

"No, that's your job."

She pierced him with an irritated look. “So helpful.”

“Hey. Guys don’t pry into each other’s personal business. We leave that to you women.”

“Neanderthal,” she scolded. “Listen, I found out something today that you need to know.” She held his shoulders so he’d pay close attention. “Zack’s uncle died in that same sink last year. He went cave diving, and never surfaced.”

“His *uncle*? No shit.” His eyes widened in surprise. “Zack told you that?”

“No, he did *not* tell me that, and that’s the point I’m trying to make.”

“Can’t be true, then.”

“It is true. I looked it up online.”

George straightened his back and pressed his lips firmly together. “What are you getting at?”

“I don’t trust him. First, this news about his uncle, and then he leaves you right after you almost die. Something’s going on, and I don’t like being left out.”

“He saved my life. Don’t make this into something sinister.”

She stood up and started pacing. As if she could sit still. “Obviously he doesn’t trust us enough to tell us his real motivation for being here, and he has no problem endangering our lives while we help him investigate. Aren’t you curious who he’s working for? Maybe he’s a private investigator. Maybe he had a meeting with his boss.”

“Maybe he just wants to find out what happened to his uncle, but he isn’t a sharing kind of guy. A lot of us aren’t.” He gave her a pointed look.

“Yeah, I get we’re different, but this is serious. I don’t trust him.”

“You don’t trust any man.”

Her jaw dropped. “I trust you.”

A ringtone cut off his response. He reached for his cell. "Yeah?" He sent her a smug glance. "I'm cool, man. A little wiped out, but fine."

She mouthed, "Zack?"

George nodded.

She scooted closer and reached for his phone.

He gently pushed her hand away. "Yeah, she's right here. I think she'd like to talk to you, too."

She grabbed the phone. "Zack? I've been calling you. I have a couple of questions I need you to answer."

"I'm sure you do."

She took a deep breath. "I want to know—"

"No, I didn't get hurt during that diving accident. I'm fine. Thank you for asking."

"George already told me," she said, ignoring the sarcasm in his voice, swept away by an overwhelming feeling of déjà vu. *Skydiving accident. Cave diving accident.* "Why didn't you tell me about—?"

"I think I know what you're about to ask me," he interrupted. His voice had that gravely edge to it that came with exhaustion. "I'll answer your questions, but not over the phone. Meet me at Skipper's. It's a bar and grill on Spencer Avenue. I'll be there at eight."

"I don't—" She quivered with uncertainty.

"And Samantha, I want you to come alone."

Chapter Seven

Zack swirled Grey Goose Vodka around his mouth. Leaning back in an ancient wooden chair, he wrapped one of his boots around the leg and focused on the front door of Skipper's Bar and Grill.

Even chilled, it burned his throat as he swallowed, but the liquid fire did nothing to extinguish the guilt assaulting him like a bad migraine. He'd almost lost another partner.

He closed his eyes, hoping the alcohol entering his bloodstream would dissolve the stress embedded in his muscles. As he shook his glass, the ice cubes rattled in the emptiness.

He hadn't found any clues in the sink today. He was getting nowhere fast. Why not give the reporter a real chance to use her investigative skills? The whole idea made him groan. What he needed first was another Grey Goose, but before he could signal the waitress, he spotted Samantha Steele in the doorway.

Her dark hair was slicked back in a tight, business-like bun. Of course. She was always inappropriately dressed for the occasion. What would she do if he walked right over there, pulled out the bobby pins, and messed up that perfect hair?

Embarrassed by the direction of his thoughts, he dropped his gaze lower and instantly regretted it. Her form-fitting white shirt clung to her breasts, and was open just enough to let ample cleavage peak through, inciting a rise in his… blood pressure. She wore her trademark black stiletto heels, probably the same damn ones she'd had on today at the Orange Grove Sink.

What was this woman thinking?

Hell, what was *he* thinking?

That I can't take my eyes off her.

He had deliberately picked the working class honky-tonk to make sure he had the advantage, knowing Ms. Steele would feel completely out of her element here. He needed to be in control, because he was about to do something he rarely did. Ask for help.

Just the thought made his throat tighten. He'd never trusted a reporter before. Never thought he'd see the day.

With her mouth set in a determined line, Samantha's fiery gaze scoured the bar.

"Can I get you another Grey Goose, honey?"

He tore his gaze away from the stunning control freak standing in the doorway. His waitress, a thin woman in tight blue jeans and a stained T-shirt, gave him a flirty smile.

He made the peace sign. "Make that two, please."

She smiled and sashayed away.

His gaze drifted back to Samantha. When she finally spotted him, she moved toward his table with long, purpose-filled strides. Her eyes, even in dim lighting, flamed with determination.

With his heartbeat picking up, he wondered what it would take to break through that chilly exterior and warm her up to the idea of starting their partnership all over again—this time as a real team.

When she reached his table, he stood up to pull out her chair.

She beat him to it, then sat down with a definite *don't touch me* attitude, taking in the empty shot glass.

"Hello, Zack. Glad to see you survived this afternoon's adventure."

He couldn't blame her if she felt angry or hurt. He'd run out after the diving accident, freaked out by the close call and his own inner demons. This wasn't going to be easy.

She placed both elbows on the table and rested her chin in her hands, staring right at him. "Want to know what I was doing while you and George almost got yourselves killed this afternoon?"

"I have no idea." But he did. Why was he still not coming clean with her?

Because old habits die hard.

"Working. That's what I was doing. Want to know what I discovered?"

The waitress arrived and gave Samantha a slow once over before placing a tumbler in front of each of them.

"Oh, no, thank you. I'm on the job." Samantha pushed the drink back toward the waitress.

He placed his hand over the glass. "Keep it. You need to relax, so we can talk."

Samantha eyed him warily.

The waitress raised an eyebrow, and then smiled at them before leaving.

Slowly, he slid the drink in front of Samantha, hoping his smile would disarm her enough that she would at least take a good chug.

She ignored both the smile and the drink.

Her defiance only raised his body temperature another

degree. Damn, he wanted to reach out and touch her, just to see if her skin was as cool as her stare. Instead, he picked up his newly delivered drink and took a slow sip.

She cocked her head. "While you were cave diving, I was online looking up Jackson Hunter."

He held his features in check, sipping his drink. So, she'd found out. What had he expected? The first thing any good reporter would do was dig for information on the people who had died on these vacations.

"I found out your uncle died while on an X-Force Adventure Vacation one year ago this week. Imagine my surprise when I learned you were taking my cameraman on the same dangerous dive your uncle took. And then you abandoned George after the accident."

She had a thing about abandonment. He'd have to be more sensitive. "I specifically forbade him from diving with me, remember? More than once. And I only left after I made sure he was fine."

She sat back in her chair and peered at him with hurt in her eyes.

He swallowed. "Fine. No excuses. He followed me and I didn't make him go back. I'm sorry. I really am. And I should have driven him back to the motel." Okay, the apology was out. "But I did make him see the doctor on the trip."

"You made sure he did that?" She looked vaguely surprised by that. And somewhat mollified.

"I did."

Silence settled between them for a moment before she broke it. "Your father hated your uncle," she said.

His turn to be surprised. Now, how would she know *that*?

"Jackson Hunter orchestrated a hostile takeover of his brother's company. Your father's company."

He swallowed, his spine straightening against the back of his chair. "You learned all that this afternoon?"

"From the *New York Post*'s website. I didn't have to search far into their archives."

He bit back an angry remark. The hostile takeover had been in the news for months in New York. It wasn't exactly a secret. But this wasn't the way he'd wanted the night to proceed. He should have told her about his uncle right from the get go. Doing that wouldn't have jeopardized his investigation. But, he wasn't used to sharing.

"Sounds like your father may have had motive for revenge."

She only knew the half of it.

Suddenly, she reached across the table and wrapped her hands around one of his. Her skin was warm and a little moist—the opposite of what he'd expected from an ice queen. Her gesture of compassion flustered his already churning stomach. The only calories he'd ingested since the dive were from the vodka.

"I could have helped you," she said. "If you had been honest with me from the start, we could have been working together to figure out what happened to both Maxwell and your uncle." Her tone softened and the frost in her look appeared to melt. "We were supposed to be partners."

The unbidden sense of longing that swept through him caught him off guard. It was swift and all consuming, a rush of sensations he hadn't felt since childhood. He shifted in his seat. "I can explain."

"Good, because I'm only going to give you one more chance to tell me the truth about what you're doing here," Samantha said. "What we're going to be doing together."

He couldn't help it. He smiled. Thinking about what he'd *like* them to be doing together. It must've been the Grey Goose scrambling his brains. Or his hormones.

Something of his thoughts must have shown on his face. She blushed and quickly glanced away.

A break in her icy armor at last. A plan to continue breaking through formulated in his slightly…relaxed mind. "All right. I'll make you a deal. I'll tell you what you want to know. I'll tell you the truth, and answer any of your questions about my uncle—if you give me one hour."

Her lips parted. "One hour for what?"

"One hour when you're not in control. Not asking any questions. I want you just to relax and let go, for once."

She made a sound of disgust. "Right. No way."

Originally, when he'd invited her here, he had simply planned to come clean, apologize, and get her to forgive him and start over. But now he realized he was going to have to regain her trust if they were going to work together. So far, neither an apology nor the alcohol had worked on her. He had to try something else.

"Is this about sex?" she demanded uncomfortably.

Leave it to a female to cut right to the subtext. "Samantha, *trust me.*" He smiled at his own poor choice of words. "There are at least three women in this bar right now who would go home with me if I asked." *Probably true.* "This isn't about sex." *Not quite true.* "It's about trust." *Very true.* "And until I have yours, we won't be able to work together successfully."

"But—"

He held up a hand. "You know I've had reservations about this arrangement from day one. It's dangerous. Nothing proves that more than today. You have to trust me to call the shots—and actually *listen* to me—to keep us all safe. You have to admit you like to be in control."

She regarded him evenly. "Stop playing games with me."

"Give me an hour." He waved off her instant objection. "No games. An exercise in trust."

They'd done similar drills in the military, without the sexually charged atmosphere, of course. It was all about learning to trust one's partner, come what may.

"I think you're the one with the trust issues, Zack."

Touché. "If you show me you can trust me by doing this, it will help me trust you."

She placed one hand on her chest, covering her heart... and drawing his attention to bits of anatomy he'd just sworn he wasn't thinking about. Damn. A drop of perspiration trickled down his back.

"Okay." She sat straight up, as if she'd made a business decision and not a personal one, which, naturally, disappointed him.

"If we make it through this hour," she said crisply, "and we still want to be partners, I'll trust you with what else I learned today." Her eyes shone now as if she held some secret information that gave her the upper hand.

"Which is?"

"I got the medical examiner's report for Maxwell Wentworth." She switched her legs, crossing them at the knee. Her black high heels swung back and forth slowly, hypnotizing him. "I'll let you read it."

Zack was impressed. How the hell had she managed to get that kind of information so quickly? The detective from Pasco County emailed it to her, of course.

"And, I may have just found our first real clue."

"What kind of clue?

Her eyes sparkled. "I'll tell you in an hour."

He couldn't help but grin. *Feisty tonight.* He had information Samantha wanted to know about his uncle's death, but now she also had information he needed. And she had him curious about this clue. The balance of power had shifted.

For once, he really didn't care.

That Grey Goose must've been *really* getting to him.

She fiddled with the strap on her black high heels and slowly stroked her hand up her calf and over her knee.

He couldn't take his eyes off it. Was she teasing him on purpose?

She stopped mid-thigh to smooth the hem of her skirt, raising it just enough to increase his heart rate.

Oh, yeah. She was definitely playing dirty.

The question was, did she mean it?

He picked up his fresh drink, and met her half-lidded gaze. She seemed to be feeling this strange chemistry, too.

It had been a while since he'd felt this kind of attraction for any woman, and never quite like this. But Samantha Steele was the last person he should be getting romantically involved with. She was investigating his uncle's death. She could blast his family's private details over the public airways, even if that wasn't her intended goal. He wanted to do the right thing by them both tonight. Build trust. Share information. Ignore the chemistry.

But as the ice-cold vodka slid down his throat, and he watched her hand slide another few inches up her thigh, so went the last of those good intentions.

Chapter Eight

Sam pressed her legs together, hoping to extinguish the unexpected heat building between them, but that action only made the ache worse. She'd promised herself before she walked through the front door that she would maintain a professional distance, no matter what tactic Zack used. Or no matter what her traitorous body enticed her to do. She'd give him an ultimatum—either share the whole truth with her or their deal was off.

But when she finally saw him, in the corner of the bar, in the tightest of blue jeans and a fitted T-shirt, with a sexy five o'clock shadow and half-drunk, hooded eyes, he'd taken her breath away. Quite literally. She had to admit a growing desire to get to know him better, to find a way under that shield he always had up. And maybe to touch him. Find out if those muscles of his were really as big and as hard as they looked.

God help her.

And imagine her surprise when he'd actually willingly offered to share what he knew.

Her willpower was wavering.

He was staring at her again now, with those dark eyes blazing, but his other features unreadable. God, he must have spent years perfecting the art of hiding his real feelings. He was so damn good at it.

All at once, he stood up, the chair legs rattling against the floor. "I'll be right back." He leaned over the table, both hands braced on the tabletop. "Don't run out on me. Please."

She swallowed. The way he leaned forward made those muscles in his upper arms bulge. "An exercise in trust. That's all, right?"

"Yes, and in letting go."

"What exactly do you mean by letting go?"

He reached out and gently touched a strand of hair that had fallen out of her bun. "Nothing bad is going to happen to you if you let your hair down a little."

She grasped the wayward strand and tucked it back into the band holding her hair in place. She'd worn it this way to give her confidence, and to show Zack she meant business, but right now, a part of her ached to shake it all out. And exhale.

"I'll be right back." He strode off toward the bar.

Her gaze landed on the Grey Goose. She picked up the tumbler of alcohol and took a nice, hearty sip. The liquid was cold, yet it burned her throat. To her surprise, she enjoyed the contradictory sensations.

She was going to do this. Let go. Slowly, she finished sipping the liquid courage.

A few moments later, the skin on the back of her neck tingled but not from the rush of alcohol. She couldn't see Zack, but he had to be standing behind her. She could smell his cologne over the musty odors of the bar. His masculine scent was as bold as he was.

"Close your eyes again." His breath caressed her right

ear.

A shiver of anticipation shimmied down her back. What was he up to? Despite knowing she was supposed to play along to move their mission forward, she couldn't stop herself from turning in her chair and looking at him.

He shook his head and smiled. "All I'm asking for is one hour." He held up one finger.

Before she could decide what to do next, he moved her shoulders so her back was to him again. Then he slid a cool piece of cloth across her face, covering her eyes and part of her nose. The material smelled like him.

A blindfold? Seriously? She'd watched this in a movie, secretly dreamed of having this done to her—but not in a public place and certainly not by a man she didn't trust.

Or did she?

Her heart bumped against her chest, but it wasn't fear making her pulse race. It was the pleasure of anticipation. God, she was actually *enjoying* this. Still, there were people watching.

Reaching up, she tugged the cloth down. "There are people here." She didn't want to attract any more attention than they probably already had.

"Forget about them and focus on me." He pulled the cloth up and tied the ends into a tighter knot. "In order to trust completely, you have to give up control, and that means blocking out anything and everything around you." His breath warmed her ear again.

"I don't understand." Yes, she actually did. She just didn't want to do it. The thought terrified her.

"You can't always trust what you *see*." His lips brushed the skin near her cheek. "A reporter should know that. You have to dig deeper."

She turned her face toward his and in doing so his lips barely brushed hers before he pulled away. But that slight action shot a burst of electricity into her core. "And how is a blindfold going to help me dig deeper?"

"By forcing you to use and trust your other senses."

A new feeling churned in her center. She was so used to being in control. It was expected of her. She expected it of herself. But her stomach fluttered at the idea of giving into these new sensations he was stirring up in her. "Fine. I'm trusting you not to embarrass me."

He chuckled softly. "That's a good start."

The energy shifted, and a draft of cooler air swept over her, giving her goosies. He'd moved away. Where was he? Had he left her? She reached up to tug at the blindfold, then stopped. She dropped her hands and laced them in her lap. She wouldn't think about all the people who could be staring at her. She *wanted* to be able to let go.

"What do you hear?"

He hadn't left. From the direction of his voice, he must have taken the seat across from her. "People talking."

She could sense his letdown in the click of his tongue and the shuffle of his shoes on the floor.

"You're not really listening."

She tried again. To her left, she heard a pool game underway. "I hear the click of a cue ball. Someone just broke to start a new game." Then she caught a sound behind her. "And a door slamming." A man burst out in a boisterous laugh, followed by a woman's high-pitched giggle. "That woman would laugh at anything the man said. She's flirting. I can tell by the tone of her voice."

"Good. Now you're getting it."

She blushed at his compliment. "Right now, that woman is hanging all over that man. I bet those two leave soon."

"Very good." Zack's voice sounded satisfied.

She grinned again and concentrated, hoping to pick up on something else. The click of ice cubes shaking in a tumbler—

that sound came from directly in front of her. Zack must have bought her another drink. She reached out in the direction of the sound.

As her fingers found the glass, her first reaction was to pull back. The coldness almost burned against her heated skin. She reached out with her other hand to steady the glass and slowly brought the drink to her lips. The liquid had a sharp after-bite. She licked her lips, wiping a drop of Grey Goose off the skin right below her bottom lip.

Zack exhaled slowly.

"I heard *that*." A shot of adrenaline rushed through her. Having the power swing back and forth between them was as delicious as the Grey Goose. Every nerve ending in her ears fired, and she even heard the sound of a plate being placed gently on their table.

"Anything else?" An unfamiliar voice.

Zack must have shaken his head because she heard footsteps heading away from their table.

"Open your mouth."

She hesitated, and he repeated the order. The feeling of control that had surged through her seconds ago vanished with his gentle but firm command. She felt for the tabletop and set down her drink. She parted her lips slightly, hoping she could close her mouth quickly if the exercise got out of hand.

Something rough touched her lips and then the tip of her tongue. She pulled back but the food followed. Fried something on a stick? The greasy smell smothered any other clue as to what he was feeding her.

"What do you taste?"

She took a small bite and chewed slowly. Once she broke through the fried exterior, she could tell the texture was rubbery, hard to chew. The word "exotic" flashed into her mind. "It tastes like really rich chicken, maybe a little tougher like steak. And it's salty."

"It's alligator."

She gagged and spit the meat into her hand.

His deep laugh made her stomach flip.

He removed the chewed gator from her hand with a napkin. "Okay, you don't have a taste for reptiles. I'll skip the snake, which was next."

She shuddered, but couldn't help but be a little curious. "You'd really eat snake?"

"Snake blood is considered an aphrodisiac in Asia. They serve it in a shot glass."

He'd been to Asia? An erotic image of Zack as a Samurai formed in her mind. "Does it work?"

"We were about to find out."

She laughed, assuming he was joking. He'd promised he wouldn't take advantage of her. Would they even have exotic Asian snake blood at a North Florida honky-tonk? Highly doubtful. Zack Hunter, ex-soldier, was turning out to be quite an interesting character.

She decided to switch up her strategy a bit. "Now how about something sweet?"

"Another question. You couldn't even make it fifteen minutes without asking one."

She could picture his grin as he said it. "Not a question. A request."

A woman giggled as though she'd had one too many beers, and someone broke another game of pool.

"Zack?" Where was he now?

Sweet juice dripped onto her lips, startling her. He must be standing next to her. She opened her mouth slightly to keep the juice flowing onto her tongue. The rich nectar rolled over her taste buds in ripples of peach, pineapple, and mango, a rainbow of flavors that brought a moan to her lips. "*Ooh*, now, this I love."

"I'm not surprised you'd love this delicacy."

"What is it?" She opened her mouth for more.

"Mangosteen, an exotic fruit from southeast Asia. It's expensive and almost impossible to import into the United States."

"Then how did you get your hands on it?"

He tapped her gently on the nose. "That's another question."

She licked her lips, getting lost in the pleasure of the moment. When was the last time she'd allowed herself to do that? "*Mmm.* It smells like candied pineapple."

He rubbed the fleshy meat across her bottom lip. A thin trickle of juice dribbled down her chin. Just as she was about to feel around for a napkin, his warm tongue licked up the juice.

Oh, my God.

She pressed her legs together and held her breath as his tongue traveled slowly up to her lips. Her chin wasn't the only part of her that was wet now.

Holy crap.

He stopped just short of kissing her.

"More please," she murmured on a sigh.

"Let's test another one of your senses first. Stand up."

"What? You're kidding me, right? I can't even see where the table is." Not to mention he had knocked her totally off balance. And she was finally enjoying herself.

She reached out, trying to find the edge of the table, but he dragged her chair, with her in it, away from the table and lifted her into a standing position.

"Dance with me."

His hands were around her waist already. "What does dancing have to do with trust?"

A Rascal Flats country ballad was playing in the background. The twangy song had a slow, steady beat. She swayed back on her heels, a bit dizzy.

One of his hands moved around her back, and he gently pulled her against his body.

Her arms instinctively looped around his neck, and her cheek found his. The roughness of his five o'clock shadow scraped her cheek. She licked her lips, pressing into him just a little more. This *exercise in trust* was getting way out of control, but she couldn't bring herself to pull away. She couldn't remember the last time a man had held her this way. She couldn't remember the last time she'd wanted a man to do more. She couldn't remember the last time she'd let herself go like this.

"Now tell me what you hear." His voice had a rougher edge to it.

The out of control beating of my heart. "Rascal Flats, and your voice."

He continued whispering in her ear. "Tell me what you smell."

The alcohol on your breath, and the musky smell of your skin. "Stale beer on the floor."

"And what do you feel?"

Ohmigod, I feel your big hands sliding down my back. "You touching me."

"And how does that make you feel inside?"

Dizzy, wet, hungry for you to stop whispering in my ear and use those lips to kiss me instead.

She couldn't believe the desire controlling her body. Maybe this was why her mother had made so many bad mistakes with smooth-talking men. But her instincts told her Zack was so much more than his silver tongue.

Though, she'd definitely take it…

His hands found the curve of her lower back. With a subtle pressure, he moved her hips into his. He didn't need any words to show her how he was feeling at this moment. His erection was undeniable. His lips nuzzled her neck, and he pressed her against it. “What do you taste?” he murmured.

She inhaled and pulled back just a little bit. “I still taste the mangosteen.”

“I want to taste it, too.”

He moved his lips up her neck, taking his time, pressing his mouth against her throbbing artery. She let the raw emotion of desire sweep over her. Her hand moved up through his hair, hungry for the feel of him. His lips brushed hers, making her knees actually go weak, but abruptly he pulled away. “Damn. I promised I wouldn’t do this.”

“What? Are you kidding me?” No more teasing. No more games. No more exercises. She’d had enough. “You aren’t taking advantage of me.” Oblivious to where she was and who might be watching, she pulled him to her, anxious to crush his lips with hers in a way she’d never tried before.

So, this was what it felt like to let yourself go. *Passion.* It was turning her core into a roaring fire. She’d always kept this feeling bottled up. Why? It felt so damn good.

After a brief hesitation, his lips pressed down on hers—firm and demanding. She opened her mouth to let his tongue mix with hers, and moaned as his grinding erection pushed against her.

Holy cow, she’d never been kissed like this before. She could taste his need, and feel his desire for her, and the rawness of both made her long for even more. She deepened the kiss, pulling him closer still, amazed at herself for being the aggressor, enjoying every damn moment of it. She wanted this kiss to last forever.

“Hey, kids.”

Fingers tapped her shoulder. She jumped.

“Don’t mean to break up the dance floor grind, but I’ve got someone here with something she says you wanted to see.”

George? She pulled back and whipped off the blindfold. What the hell was her cameraman doing here? And with Rita by his side? *Holy shit.* Her heart sped up even more.

"Can't it wait?" Zack had both fists on his hips.

"For your sake, dude, I wish it could." George grinned at them both, but his smile seemed tight. "Sam, Rita here came knocking on your motel room door and then mine saying you wanted her to bring you this DVD as soon as she got off work."

"I did." Sam pulled away, knowing she should be embarrassed to be caught in Zack's arms, but more interested and concerned about what they were about to find on Rita's DVD. "Rita, this is Zack Hunter. His uncle died on one of these adventure vacations."

"Oh, I'm sorry." Rita pulled a DVD out of her purse. "Then you're the one who needs to see this."

Zack's jaw clenched and his shoulders hitched up. "What the hell is going on here?" He stepped away from Sam and gave Rita the once over. "Who are you?"

"She's a waitress I talked to at a diner near our motel while I was doing some work. I actually talked to a number of people, trying to find someone who had come in contact with previous vacation groups, but Rita was the only one who had useful information."

Zack's eyes narrowed and his voice lowered. "What kind of information?"

"You'll be proud of me, partner." She reached out for Rita's DVD. "While you and George we're in those caves searching for evidence, I may have found a clue as to how your uncle died."

Chapter Nine

Sam glanced around the sparse living room of the mobile home they'd driven to. The rickety, two-bedroom doublewide was hidden off a one-lane dirt road with no streetlights, way outside of town. This was where Rita lived? She pursed her lips. Too bad they didn't have DVD players back at their motel.

She moved a wadded up T-shirt and a pair of faded black jeans from the couch to the floor and sat down. A weirdly upbeat George sat on her right, and a silent, brooding Zack sat on her left. The conflicting vibes had her stomach in knots.

Rita was fiddling around in her tiny, box-like kitchen.

Sam wrinkled her nose at what smelled like leftover meatloaf sprinkled with a hint of not-so-fresh kitty litter, and stole a quick glance at Zack. After the intimate moment they'd shared at the honky-tonk, she didn't understand why he'd insisted on driving here alone. Especially when she told him about the DVD. The cool energy he was putting off right now was in sharp contrast to the heated lines his fingers had drawn on her flesh less than an hour ago. She shivered. What was with the guy?

She wanted to touch him and make that connection again, but Zack cleared his throat and yelled toward the kitchen, "Can we get on with this?" He sat forward on the couch, his hands clasped tightly in his lap, looking like a man ready to spring up and run out at a moment's notice. He still wasn't making eye contact with her.

"Sorry, Zack, I know you want to see that DVD." So did she. Rita had told her about it at the diner, but had stopped short with details after her boss had yelled at her about delivering hot food to one of her other tables. "When Rita saw me reading articles on X-Force Adventure Vacations, she stopped to warn me to be careful. At first she wouldn't say why, but when I told her about Maxwell and Jackson, she told me about hooking up a year ago with one of the X-Force vacationers passing through town, a guy named Michael Flint."

Zack whipped around to face her, interest firing in his eyes.

Looked like Zack knew Michael Flint. Or had at least heard of him.

"Apparently, this Flint guy had some suspicions about what was going on at the adventure vacation company. Rita told me he wrote down notes in a journal. She also said he'd been diving with a guy from up north who never made it back to the surface."

Zack's body tensed. "The timing is right." His gaze sought the silent, black TV screen.

"I've got Bud or Mic Light." Rita walked into the living room with a beer in each hand.

"Bud. Thanks." George took the beer, allowing his fingers to linger on her skin.

Rita smiled, her heated gaze traveling to George's hands.

What was up with that? George was hitting it off with the

waitress? She certainly gave off a friendly air, and up close, she was quite pretty, despite the hole in her apron and the grease stains on her skirt. Her living space gave away her financial situation—desperate.

An avalanche of bad memories along with a pang of sympathy rushed through Sam. How many times had the popular boys called *her* trailer trash while growing up? And look how far she'd come. With any luck they were all watching her on the evening news from the beat-up sofas in *their* doublewides.

Not that she was bitter or anything.

"How about you, honey?" Rita's gaze landed on Sam.

She smiled, but the remnants of Grey Goose and Zack's bizarre behavior had her stomach in a tizzy, so she declined.

Rita turned to Zack, who was still staring at the TV. "What about you, good-looking? What do you want?"

For a second, Sam thought Zack was so deep in thought that he didn't hear Rita. Slowly, he acknowledged her. "I want the truth."

Surprise washed over Rita's face.

Sam had never heard that tone of voice from him before. "Zack," she cautioned. If he was rude, Rita could ask them to leave.

"That's what we're here for, right?" Gone was the flirtatious playboy. "I'm not here to party. I want to know what Michael Flint knew about my uncle's death."

The waitress put the second beer down on the table next to Zack and sat in a chair across from him. "Oh, lordy, I'm sorry." She kept blinking as she spoke. "I don't know what Michael knew about your uncle's death. I just know he thought something bad was going on with the adventure vacation company. He was always asking people to call him if they saw anything they thought might be shady. He never did go into detail."

When no one spoke, Sam prompted her, "Go on."

Rita continued. "One night Michael and I were watching a movie here, and he gets this call on his cell phone. He took it in the bedroom, but I wanted to hear, you know, so I put my ear to the door." She shot a nervous glance at both Sam and George. "I thought maybe it was a wife or girlfriend. Like, I don't do that shit, y'all. Anyway. I only heard bits and pieces. I think he said he couldn't pull out now. He didn't have the proof."

"Proof of what?" Sam frowned. Now they were getting to the details Rita didn't have time to tell earlier. "Was he an undercover cop?"

"I don't know." Rita shrugged. "Could have been. Had that air about him. Michael came rushing out of the bedroom that night and said he had to go. Then he hauled ass. Never saw him again."

Sam had spent years learning how to assess people's credibility in mere minutes. The way Rita leaned forward, the way she used her hands and made eye contact, convinced her Rita was telling them the truth. At least the truth as she knew it.

"Two days after Michael left, I'm cleaning up around here, and I find his backpack on a chair under some of my clothes." She blushed as she peeked over at George again. "I tried to return it, but when I went to the hotel, the kid at the front desk told me Michael had checked out the day before and left town with the adventure vacation company. I thought it was weird, but I thought maybe he'd left it as an excuse to come back and visit me, you know. But then I thought, hell no. He never needed an excuse. He didn't want no one to find that backpack. That's what I think. I was going to track the company down, but the next day I heard on the news that a man named Michael Flint had died during a shark dive off the Bahamas."

"What?" Sam straightened. Rita hadn't told her they

guy she'd been hooking up with had died! It made sense now why she'd warned her. Sam checked out Zack's reaction and froze. The guarded expression on his face told her he wasn't surprised at all. "You knew about Michael Flint dying?" Words flew out of her mouth, prickly balls of anger. "Why didn't you fill me in that? Don't you think it's relevant?"

"Samantha, can we talk about this later?"

She stood and fisted her hands on her hips. A bonfire of bad feelings ignited in her belly. "And I was so excited to share this clue with you."

Zack sighed. "How did you find this DVD, Rita?"

Rita hesitated, picking at her clothes. "I opened up his backpack and checked out what was inside, of course."

"And?" Zack scooted to the edge of the couch. Both hands gripped the cushion's edge.

"I found the journal and the DVD."

Indignation still burned in Sam's belly, but curiosity extinguished some of the heat. She took a long, deep breath and sat back down. "You've watched the whole DVD, right?" Her mouth had gone dry. She picked up George's beer and took a swig.

"I'd like to see it. Now." Zack motioned toward the TV.

Rita looked from person to person. "Do you think we should all watch it together?" Her gaze landed on Zack. "Or do you want to watch it alone?"

Zack's shoulders sank. "No need. I already know how it ends."

Rita took the cue and stood.

As she walked over to her small, lopsided kitchen table, the reporter in Sam took over. She fired off questions she hadn't had a chance to ask earlier. "You kept the DVD all this time? For at least a year? Why didn't you turn the DVD over to the X-Force Adventure Vacation Company?"

Rita picked up a simple camouflage backpack sitting on

one of the kitchen chairs. “Michael obviously didn’t trust the folks working at X-Force Adventure Vacations, so why the hell should I? Plus, Michael ended up dead, and I don’t know if it was an accident or if someone at the company killed him because he’d been asking too many questions.” Rita headed back toward them with the backpack slung over her shoulder. “Where I come from, you keep your mouth shut and your nose out of other people’s business. That’s how you stay alive.”

Silently, Sam applauded her statement. Rita Wright was a smart cookie, with good survival instincts.

The waitress placed the backpack on the coffee table in front of the three of them. Sam stared at it, her suspicion growing by the minute. A Semper Fi patch was sewn onto the right side of the backpack. Michael Flint was a Marine? Military, just like Zack?

She waited, giving him a chance to say something about the patch. He didn’t even acknowledge it. He was too busy opening the backpack and pulling out a black, leather-bound journal. He flipped open the pages and started reading. To himself, of course.

She shot George a look, raising her eyebrows in a silent question. Shrugging, he remained silent.

“Rita.” She pressed on despite the urgent desire to wring Zack’s neck—right after she pulled him out of the trance-like state he’d fallen into. But maybe he would have told her about Michael Flint. George had interrupted them before the promised hour had passed. “Why didn’t you call the police if this DVD showed something incriminating?”

Rita picked up the DVD, and then stopped. “I don’t know that it does. You watch it, and you tell me. Besides, I’m on probation—doesn’t matter why. But if you even think about calling the police, we’re done here.” She shook the DVD at them.

"Play the DVD." Zack's eyes had gone dark.

A wave of empathy moved through Sam, washing away most of her anger. Zack was about to watch a beloved uncle die. He deserved a little compassion. Nothing hurt more than losing a loved one, as she knew first hand. Although her mother was technically still alive, in a coma she was more like the living dead. Every time Sam visited her, that harsh reality killed her a little, too.

She reached over and placed her hand on his, curling her fingers over his clenched fist. She gave him a gentle squeeze.

Zack didn't return the gesture of affection, but he did turn to look at her. She pulled back a bit, startled by the haunted look in his eyes.

No one in the room said a thing as the DVD cycled and began to play.

Chapter Ten

Samantha's soft touch surprised him.

Zack hadn't told her about the death of Michael Flint. When Detective Johnson hadn't mentioned Flint after Wentworth died, Zack had felt no obligation to fill them in.

Would he have mentioned it when he made his full confession after the hour she'd promised him at the bar? Maybe. Probably. Who knew? He'd never gotten a chance to find out just how serious he'd been about trusting her. And judging by the look on her face two minutes ago, he would have bet last year's salary he'd never get another chance.

Now, he wasn't so sure.

The gentle squeeze of her hand made him want to curl up in her arms to watch the video, the possible clue she'd found for him. Embarrassed, he pulled away from her.

She didn't reach for him again. Which made him feel even shittier.

The sound of someone breathing through a regulator drew his attention to the TV screen. A diver descended through the waters of the Orange Grove Sink. The date on the screen indicated the dive had taken place on the day his uncle died. Zack tried to swallow, but the invisible obstruction lodged there would not go down.

The water and landscape looked much the same as it had on his dive earlier. Bubbles rose up from below through an increasingly darkening pool of water. The diver shooting the video wasn't alone. Another diver was swimming below him, letting out air bubbles as he breathed. Michael Flint?

The video had obviously been shot with a helmet cam worn by the first diver. If that man was indeed his uncle, they were now seeing through his Uncle Jackson's eyes.

He shuddered, suddenly chilled despite the lack of air-conditioning in the mobile home.

A second diver moved in front of the main diver's helmet camera. His pulse picked up speed. "Can you pause the DVD?"

When Rita did so, he squinted, trying to find something about the new diver that would identify him. The full wet suit, bug eye goggles, and large regulator, along with the murkiness of the deep water, made it impossible to pick out details of a face. He knew what Michael Flint looked like. Flint had been a New York undercover cop, and he'd been investigating Scott Fitzpatrick's death. It had been such a hush-hush investigation that even the local police didn't know about it.

But Zack did. At the time, the Florida Department of Law Enforcement had been actively investigating Jackson's death at Zack's request. When the FDLE shifted their attention toward Flint's death, Zack had been taken off the X-Force investigation all together. Too personally involved, they had told him. Well, tough shit. Here he was anyway. And Fitzgerald's, Jackson's, and Flint's cases were still open, unproven, and unresolved.

The person captured on the video could have been Flint,

but he could also have been any one of the vacationers diving that day.

He blew out air he'd been holding in. "Go ahead and push play."

Proof. He needed proof. Or at least a good clue.

The diver and his dive buddy came upon the familiar sign with the Grim Reaper. The first diver with the camera surged ahead. That was exactly what Jackson would have done. He'd always wanted to be in the lead. At least his uncle, if it was him, was following a guideline that had already been laid down. By now, visibility under the water was severely limited, so all they could see on the screen was what the diver's headlight revealed.

Further down the narrow tunnel, the main diver checked his wrist depth monitor. He held out the box-shaped device on his right wrist as if he *wanted* the camera to pick it up. Zack lurched forward. He drew in a sharp breath. "Pause."

"What? What do you see?" Samantha's voice cracked as Rita froze the picture.

"Look right above the computer console on the diver's wrist. See the initials J.H.? Jackson's initials are on the depth gage. I know that's his. I was with him the day he bought it. The diver *is* my uncle." Fingers of both relief and fear entwined deep in his gut.

"So, this is a clue." Samantha's eyes lit up.

"Where did his dive buddy go?" George scooted closer, too. "Your uncle is a hundred feet deep. Why doesn't he look backward to check for his backup?"

Zack had no answer.

"Maybe he didn't want to go past that awful sign," Samantha suggested with a grimace.

Rita handed Zack the remote control. He pressed forward. A couple of times it looked as though his uncle did turn to check out what was behind him, but by now there was no sign of the other diver. He pressed play again. The readout on his uncle's wrist now said a hundred-thirty feet deep.

"Shouldn't he be switching to his primary tank now?" George asked.

"Is that important?" Samantha asked.

"Divers must breathe different mixtures of gas at different depths," Zack explained. "You start breathing mostly oxygen, but at this depth you have to switch to a tank that contains a blend of oxygen, nitrogen, and helium. The combination allows you to breathe under the pressure of the water." He didn't really think she wanted such a detailed explanation, but frankly, he wanted to hear his own voice right now rather than the sound of his uncle's laboring regulator. A slow horror was creeping up inside him, as if he were down in that cave, struggling to breathe right beside his uncle.

As if on cue, his uncle reached behind his head and maneuvered the switch that changed the mixture. He continued to swim inside the dark tunnel. Occasionally, he'd glance back. Zack rubbed his eyes, but knew nothing would change the outcome ahead.

Jackson had almost reached the area where George had freaked out.

The mechanical air sounds were getting more intense. Why was his uncle breathing so hard? Jackson had been in good shape for his age, and he didn't look like he was overexerting himself. He'd just switched to his other tank. His heavy breathing didn't make sense.

A sudden dread sank deep into Zack's bones. "Something's wrong with the other tank. He isn't getting enough oxygen."

"How can you tell?" Samantha's voice sounded far away, even though she was still sitting right next to him.

"Listen to the way he's struggling to breathe."

The eerie sound of air bubbles being released into the

water filled the room, followed by an electronic noise that sounded like it came from a robot, not a man.

"Elp."

Zack turned his ear toward the TV. Had he heard right?

"It sounded like he said help!" George exclaimed.

"Maybe the sound came from his equipment?" Samantha said cautiously.

"Elp!"

Zack dropped his head into his hands, his elbows resting against his knees. The weight of that one simple word pulled down his shoulders. His heart felt like it was tearing in two. "Jackson obviously knew something was wrong."

He probably also knew help wasn't coming.

"What could it be?" Samantha whispered.

Zack could feel her leaning closer to him.

"The mixture of air in his tanks," George said. "If Zack's uncle wasn't getting enough oxygen, he would pass out or have a seizure. Why didn't he turn around and head back up? Where the hell did his dive partner go?"

All good questions. Ones Zack would never be able to answer. A lack of oxygen to the brain did cause divers to do crazy things deep underwater. He forced himself to keep his focus on the TV.

"But... If your uncle was able to make a sound like help, he couldn't be suffocating, right?" Just as Samantha finished making that logical statement, little gasps rippled through the speakers.

Zack's stomach plummeted. He couldn't watch this. But he had to. He forced himself to keep his eyes open, though he wanted to shut them tight.

His uncle had stopped moving. He rested on the cave floor, his breathing shallow. With the limited light from his uncle's gear, Zack found it difficult to see what Jackson was doing. But...he appeared to be moving his hands, struggling with something at his side.

Jackson turned his head and gazed down. That directed the headlamp toward a guideline hooked into a rock.

Zack shot to his feet.

"What? What?" Samantha asked.

He opened his mouth, but the response balled up in his throat.

"Jackson is tangled in a guideline." George frowned. "Many times there's more than one. When you can't see very well, your gear can get hooked or tangled on someone else's line."

Jackson's body twisted and turned in a frantic dance of desperation. The light on his helmet cam moved across the gray rocks like an out of control strobe in some liquid '80s disco.

"He's panicking," Samantha whispered.

Zack desperately needed to hold her hand again. Instead of reaching for it, he collapsed onto the couch and watched the man he had loved like a father thrash around in the near darkness. His heart ached in a way it never had before. The pain choked him. Jackson tugged at the lines for dear life. The exertion no doubt made him suck in even more of the faulty mixture from the tank. Maybe his death really had been an accident.

Come on, Jackson, give me something. Anything. He prayed for his uncle to show him something that could lead to an answer, like what had happened to his tank.

As silt danced around the dying man, a sandy veil cloaked him, but Jackson's hands came up before the camera, and he gestured in a flurry of finger and hand movements. Sign language! Then the cloud of debris erased his hands from the camera's view.

"That's it!" He couldn't stop the rush of excited adrenaline dumping into his system. He started to shake.

"That's what?" Samantha asked.

"The end?" Rita whispered.

"The clue." His mind anguished over the way Jackson had fought his death, but a new sense of purpose washed over him. The rush of excitement made him a bit nauseous and dizzy. He ran up to the TV and popped out the DVD. "I know what happened."

Chapter Eleven

Zack ran to the front door of the mobile home, ripped it open, and flew out without so much as a good-bye.

"He's leaving?" Hot rage burned through Sam. *Oh, hell, no.* He wasn't going to abandon them again. She jumped off the couch and raced to the door as it swung shut. She managed to stop it seconds before it crushed her fingers. "What did you find out? Where are you going?"

"Meet me back at the motel." He yelled as he ran toward his car. "I've got to do something."

She stumbled down the steps after him, catching her stiletto in a crack in one of the wooden stairs. "I'm coming with—" She fell forward, using her arms to steady herself.

The car engine fired up.

"Tell me what you saw in the DVD. Zack!" His car peeled out of the dirt driveway, kicking up dust in her face. Furious, she stomped her foot and her expensive heel sunk into the damp earth. She almost toppled over. *Damn it!*

George loped down the steps behind her. "Well, I guess you're riding back to the motel with me." He threw an arm around her shoulders.

She glared at him.

He was grinning. Of course. Just like him to think this was funny.

Just as she was conjuring up a good smart-ass reply, her cell phone buzzed. She ripped the phone from her purse. "This is Sam." She knew her voice sounded testy. If it was Zack, she wanted him to know she was pissed off.

"Sis?"

Oh no. Instantly, she shifted gears. Panic assaulted her.

Her sister never, ever called unless something was wrong. Or she needed money.

"Sam? Are you there?"

"Yes." She could barely breathe, her chest heaving from alarm, and the effort of running after Zack.

"I have bad news and I have bad news. Which do you want first?"

• • •

Sam sprawled in a lounge chair by the motel pool, watching the amber fingers of dawn reach out across the horizon through slitted eyes.

She sucked down her second Diet Coke and prayed the caffeine would make her mild headache melt away. Unfortunately, the stimulant also sped up her heart.

God, what was she going to do?

She still couldn't believe the nursing home intended to kick her mom out. Her invalid, comatose, fragile, incapacitated mother was going to be dumped on the sidewalk in days if Sam didn't find a way to pay the overdue bill. Her stomach clenched. Money. It came down to that. It always did.

She'd been paying a discounted rate, thanks to Maxwell who failed to make provisions for this in the event of his death. Great men think they'll never die. Of course, the home wanted her mother's bed for someone who could pay the full amount. Now.

The metallic fizz of the soda surged up into her throat. She spit on the ground, and fell back again onto the lounge chair while squeezing her eyes shut. She'd been waiting for Zack to "meet her at the motel" for hours.

She fingered the stack of papers on her lap. Thanks to Stuart, her detective friend, the Pasco County Medical Examiner's office had emailed the report on Maxwell Wentworth's cause of death to her late yesterday. At least one mystery had been solved. She could go back to Tampa now that the ME had ruled Maxwell's death accidental.

"My father used to beat me."

At the sound of Zack's voice, she twisted in her lounge chair. Even in the dark of early morning, she recognized the silhouette of those long, lean legs and well-built shoulders. "Where the hell have you been? I've been waiting for hours."

"Did you hear what I said?" He ran a hand over his short hair.

She struggled to control her chaotic emotions. "I–" Something about his father? "I'm tired and hurting, Zack. I barely slept."

The red and orange rays of sunrise gave her enough light to see that his clothes were wrinkled, his face drawn, and his posture slumped as if he'd spent the night wrestling with demons, too. What a pair they made.

"I said my father used to beat me."

She heard him this time. Her heart skipped a beat. "Oh." *Crap.* "I'm sorry. That–"

"I've never told anyone other than my uncle."

She stared at him, speechless, jumbled thoughts speed-racing through her mind.

He finally broke the silence. "I promised you if you gave

me an hour, I would tell you everything. Including about my uncle. To understand how much I loved Jackson Hunter, you have to first understand how much I *hated* my father." His voice cracked.

She couldn't even speak. The headache and the lack of sleep had exhausted her, and the emotional impact of Zack's words left her depleted. This was not what she'd expected. She needed to leave and head for home, but she couldn't force a single muscle in her body to move.

He walked over to the closest lounge chair and dragged it next to hers. The iron legs scraped the pool deck, but she didn't flinch. He sat down and stretched his long legs until his feet rested under her chair.

She couldn't stop staring at him. He smelled musky, like he hadn't showered. His troubled, bloodshot eyes bore into hers, and she couldn't look away.

"I remember the sound of my father's footsteps at night, coming down the hallway to my room. His expensive dress shoes would make a brittle sound against our hardwood floors. I could tell by the dragging sound of his shoes when he'd been drinking." Zack snorted. "He drank almost every night."

"Oh, Zack."

"I always wondered how a man could be so smart and successful by day but so fucked up at night." His gaze dropped to his hands. They clenched and unclenched repeatedly. "My father would walk into my room, stop at the doorway, and stare. I used to hold my breath, pretending to be asleep, praying he'd just leave. Even without looking, I could feel his energy. I knew when the alcohol had made him angry and when it had made him sad. On the good nights, he'd stay awhile and then go to bed without touching me. On the bad nights—" His whole body stiffened.

His hurt washed over her like an incoming tide, leaving

her mind spinning.

His head fell into his hands and a wounded sound erupted from him.

She got up, dropped the ME's report on a table, and sat next to him, rubbing his back, tentatively at first.

He didn't acknowledge her. Nor did he push her away.

What had happened after he ran out of Rita's mobile home last night that brought him back to her this morning pouring emotion like water from a broken levee? Whatever it was, she wouldn't ask, because she was finally getting to know the *real* Zack Hunter, and she didn't want prying questions to shut him down again.

His head still in his hands, his voice sounded muffled. "My uncle found the bruises I tried to cover up."

She leaned closer. "From your father's beatings?"

He nodded, his head bobbing in his hands. "Jackson rescued me from that hell. He used every excuse in the book to pry me away from my parents. Eventually I went to live with him. I was ten at the time." His back was military rigid.

She moved back. "Didn't your mother help?"

He ran a hand slowly over his chin. "Let's just say, neither my father or my mother missed me very much."

She swallowed, understanding all too well how a parent's rejection wounded you. Her father had never even made the effort to meet her. Not one phone call, not one card, not one single inquiry her entire life. She totally connected to Zack's desire to veil the pain. Sometimes hiding the hurt was the only way to bury the shame and make it through another day.

"I'm so sorry," she whispered.

He waved his hand as if dismissing the horror of his last statement. "Jackson took me into his home and taught me about living. He taught me and my cousin Josh, to scuba dive, to skydive, to golf. He made it okay to laugh and have fun. He taught me to let go and live. He rewarded my good grades, and paid attention to me when I offered an opinion. He *rescued* me."

And yesterday, he'd watched that beloved uncle die.

"I lived with him, my aunt, and Josh, on and off for about five years." His features hardened. He stared off at some distance place. "I finally returned home a man. My father couldn't hit me anymore, so he started in with the verbal abuse. He was relentless, which was probably how he built such a thriving business empire. He never cared who he hurt."

She reached out to hold his hand, but she couldn't pry his clenched fist apart.

He pulled away. "No, let me finish. I need to get this all out." He shook his head. "Despite hating me, I guess my father always expected me to take over the family business someday. To spite him, I joined the Army the day after I graduated from that fancy, expensive private school he made me attend. I became a grunt. A *nobody*. My father never told his friends. The thought of an enlisted man in the family embarrassed the hell out of him." He stretched his arms above his head, a satisfied smile moving across his face. "I loved every minute of it. I thrived in boot camp, probably because I was so used to being beaten down. I excelled in training."

"If you enlisted, how did you become an Army Ranger?"

"My uncle rescued me once again, this time using his influence to get me into Special Forces training at Fort Bragg. I took college courses online."

A perfect fit, she thought. A young man with his issues could jump out of airplanes, run survival drills, and learn how to murder the enemy, working the anger and hatred out of his system in a productive way.

His face clouded over. "While I was fulfilling my obligations to the military and transitioning into law enforcement, the family feud had become legendary in New York. Finally, Jackson orchestrated a hostile takeover of my father's company. You know the rest—you looked it up."

"Sounds like your father and uncle literally wanted to kill each other."

Their eyes locked. After a heartbeat, Zack dropped his gaze.

She swallowed. "You don't think your *father* would really have paid someone to kill your uncle, do you?" Who was she kidding? Domestic situations ended in murder all the time, in trailer parks and in mansions. She reported the awful truth every night on the news.

He ignored her question, but this time it didn't appear to be intentional. He was staring at the pool as if mesmerized. "Jackson was always an adventurer at heart. He decided to take a break from the chaos and go on an X-Force Adventure Vacation. He asked me to go with him. I said no. I had just lost a partner on a dive at work and I was right in the middle of dealing with that accident, both personally and professionally." He shook his head. "Truth be told, I just didn't want to get in the middle of another family battle."

"So, Jackson went alone."

"Yes."

This time, when she reached for his hand, he didn't pull away. His fingers found hers and they entwined, his grip fierce. "And you think if you had gone with your uncle, you could have prevented his death?"

"I wouldn't have let Jackson go off alone on that dive."

"Zack. Stop."

He looked up, and his need to be rid of his guilt poured over her.

A strong wave of yearning swept through her. She longed to be the one to make him whole again. "You have to forgive yourself." She lifted a hand to his cheek. "Your uncle would have never wanted you to blame yourself for his death."

In slow motion, he reached out and returned the gesture,

touching her face and brushing a strand of hair away from her eyes. A twist of emotion went through her, the feeling so intense it held her breath hostage in her lungs. But honestly, part of her was still afraid to get too close, still sure that he'd hurt her. Even though she now understood what was driving him, he was still a runner. And she couldn't handle someone else abandoning her because she wasn't good enough.

He moved his hand to the back of her neck, his fingers caressing her hairline. "I give in."

"What?" Her nerves felt on fire.

"I want you to help me."

"Of course I will."

She could feel his warm breath on her lips.

"I don't want to do this alone." As his mouth found hers, she closed her eyes. His lips pressed down on hers with fierce longing. His kiss was not gentle. He opened her lips with his tongue, and she tasted him.

She hesitated, a thought pulsating in the back of her mind. *Oh, hell.*

He forced her mouth to move under his. His other hand pressed her backside forward, urging her to move closer. He ran his hands under her shirt, his fingers leaving a burning trail up her side.

She wanted to touch him, feel the hardness under his shirt, ease the ache building in her center, but she held back.

He must have sensed her hesitation. His lips stilled and he pulled away just enough to look into her eyes. "Samantha?"

"I'm sorry." And truth be told, she was. Sorry for so much. Sorry she'd even attempted to do a live shot after Maxwell's death. Sorry she'd lied to get permission to be on this adventure vacation. Sorry she'd ever doubted Zack. Sorry she'd chosen work over her mother. Sorry for so damn much. "I—I can't. I have to go home." She choked on the last words. "Today."

• • •

"What?" Zack pulled back, holding her by both shoulders. He couldn't have heard her right. She was leaving? *What the hell?*

"I'm sorry," she repeated, looking devastated.

He couldn't stop himself from digging his fingers into her flesh. He didn't know which was worse, the ringing in his ears or the throbbing in his groin. *Jesus. Please don't do this.* "What's wrong?"

He knew it. He should never have opened up to her.

She seemed to recoil from him. "I shouldn't have promised to help. I really have to leave. This morning." She dropped her gaze.

Was she repulsed that he wasn't perfect, but damaged, forever fucked-up goods?

He sat back, surprised at himself. He should be happy about this. A few days ago, he had wanted her out of his way so he could do his job.

A lot had changed in forty-eight hours.

"Is this because I left last night?" He hoped that was it. He couldn't blame her for losing faith in him after that. But something inside him had cracked. Watching his uncle die and decoding the message his uncle had recorded as he slowly ran out of air had broken him.

He still needed justice for his uncle, but he no longer wanted to do this alone. Besides, Samantha and her photographer were very good at their jobs. Samantha had uncovered the most crucial piece of evidence yet. Together, they could actually succeed.

Then there was the physical attraction—the raw chemistry that heated up whenever he got near her. That kiss they'd shared… Her lips were so soft. It had been a long time since anything in his life had been as pleasurable as that kiss.

She moved out of his reach. "No. I was upset, but hell, nothing compared to what you must have been feeling." She shook her head. "It's… I have to go home and take care of my family."

He frowned. "Is everyone okay?"

"After you left last night, I got a call from my sister."

The look on her face told him it wasn't a good call. "And?"

"The nursing home is kicking my mom out on Friday if I don't pay the three thousand dollars for next month up front." Her shoulders fell.

He blinked. "That's criminal. Surely, they can't just kick her out."

"Surely they can. It's a private facility. And I don't have three thousand dollars sitting in the bank." Her cheeks turned a pale shade of pink. "What am I going to do with my mother if I have to take her home? She's in a coma. She needs nursing care 24-7. I can't work and take care of her, too. Her insurance won't cover the cost of daily care at this facility." Samantha's gaze darted from her hands, to him, back to her hands.

"Take a deep breath," he said. "Why are they doing this now?"

Samantha bit her lip. "Maxwell's foundation paid part of her bill every month. He dated my mother for a couple of years, between marriages. They didn't work out, but he was always fond of us, and helped us out whenever there was a crisis." Her heart lurched thinking about her mother. "Now that he's dead, those contributions have stopped. There's apparently some kind of estate glitch, or he didn't remember my mom in his will. I'm waiting for it all to be settled."

"I see."

He scrubbed a hand over his face. He knew he should let her go. She had a family emergency. Besides, she'd be a lot safer at home. God knew he'd almost led her cameraman into a death trap yesterday. Wanting to keep her around was just plain selfish. But she'd gotten under his skin.

She stared into the pool despondently.

He'd learned his lesson, too. Working together *was* better than going it alone. Without her and George's help, he'd still be searching for the truth. Now he had proof someone had tampered with his uncle's tanks, and it changed everything.

If he told her what he'd learned on the DVD, what his uncle had signed to the camera, she'd stay. He knew she would. But could he ask it of her?

"I can help you with the money. So you can stay and continue investigating." The words tumbled out of his mouth before he could stop them.

She shook her head sadly. "Thanks, but I need to figure out how to make this work on my own." Both hands lifted, as if in surrender. "You can't lend me money every month." Her lips thinned. "And I can't keep chasing a story that isn't really there."

His throat tightened up. "Let me at least make one phone call on your behalf."

"That's just one of my problems." Her hand shook as she wiped her forehead. "Try fixing this one. My eighteen-year-old sister just told me she's pregnant by her twenty-one-year-old, spoon-fed, so-called boyfriend. She's in total denial, but he's never going to marry her. She doesn't have the right pedigree."

Zack's gut clenched on her behalf. "Shit."

Her shoulders dropped. "Yeah. Shit."

Her despair hit him like an unexpected blow. "How can I help?" He needed to help her. Somehow. "Tell me."

"Oh, God." She reached out to him, wrapping her small hands around his. "I'm sorry. I didn't mean to take my frustration out on you."

"We have unfinished business here." He was referring to their investigation, but what he really wanted to do was kiss her again. Hold her in his arms and take away all the pain he saw in her eyes. Let her take away the pain in his heart…

She smiled, but slowly shook her head. "There's really nothing left for me to investigate."

He stared at her incredulously. "What about Wentworth's death?"

She pulled her hands away and reached for a stack of papers on the table next to her lounge chair. She handed them to him. "This is the autopsy report. Maxwell died from the impact of a hard opening. The jolt ripped his aorta away from his heart and severed his spine." She shivered at the thought. "His death was ruled accidental. The ME found no signs of foul play."

He wanted to reach out and pull her into his embrace. But something in the rigid set of her body stopped him.

"Jesus, I don't know why you crazy men think jumping out of planes is fun."

He glanced down at the report cover. Very official. "This ruling doesn't mean a thing. Someone set him up for the fall. The medical examiner wouldn't know if his parachute had been tampered with."

"The police haven't found any evidence of that," she told him.

He ground his teeth to keep from saying the FAA would determine that, not the local police. He didn't want to upset her.

"And your uncle… It looked like he got tangled on a guideline and just couldn't get back to the surface. An accident, too."

She pitied him with those big, dark, troubled eyes. But she had no idea what he'd seen. There was no way she could know.

"God rest his soul." She sighed again, and stood. "Unless you saw something in that DVD that I didn't?"

He hesitated.

She froze and stared at him. "Zack. *Did* you see something?"

He should tell her. It would make her stay. All he had to do was tell her how Jackson had used sign language to tell him who prepared his tanks before his dive. He had spelled the name Robert. If they found this Robert, whoever he was, they'd find the man who not only tampered with Jackson's tank, but probably also Maxwell's chute.

"Oh my God." Her hand flew to her mouth. "You did."

He stared at her, really seeing her for the first time this morning. Her hair, which had been so tightly secured earlier, now fell around her shoulders in a tumbled, unbrushed mess. Her skin, which had glowed when he'd seen her in the bar, now appeared ashen, with smudged flakes of black mascara on her cheeks. And she'd thrown on jeans and a shirt two sizes too big. Stress had beaten her down in a way she now wore all over her body.

Hell. He had to let her go. Even though his heart twisted at the thought of it. At the thought of never seeing her again. Of losing her forever.

He smiled. "Nothing really. Just a hunch."

Her lips rolled inward, and for a moment he thought she was going to burst into tears. But she didn't. "Well, then..." she murmured hoarsely.

"Yeah."

"It's just, that I, well, I've always done whatever it took to get the story. But now I need to—I *have to*—put my family before work." She stuttered out a breath. "Even if it gets me fired."

What he would have given for a mother or a sister who wanted to put him first, who would have loved him enough to face her worst fears in order to stand by him.

"I'll call you if I find out anything," he promised. But he knew he wouldn't call. Letting her go meant just that. The Lone Ranger would ride solo again.

Whether he wanted to or not.

Chapter Twelve

Sam's heart beat quickly as she walked across the steamy, black tarmac at Tampa's MacDill Air Force Base. The X-Force Adventure Vacation Company had moved onto Tampa's Central Command for the next leg of the thrill ride. The vacationers were flying in F-16s, courtesy of the United States Air Force Thunderbirds, who were using MacDill as their home base today in preparation for the base's annual air show. The next adventure was about to begin, and she and George had somehow managed to make it in time.

She hadn't called Zack to give him the heads up that she'd be here today. She wanted to surprise him and thank him in person for making that one phone call on her behalf as he'd suggested the other night. That was all it had taken to get her mother's facility to extend her contract and care for three more months. Zack had bought her time to figure that problem out. She'd be forever grateful.

She didn't call Monica either. Her reporter's intuition told her to sneak up on the rest of the X-Force Adventure Vacation crew. The element of surprise always worked in a journalist's favor.

Heat blasted her in waves, rolling over her like invisible fingers leaving a moist track in their wake.

She strode across the asphalt, her silver sling backs sinking a bit in the softening tar. She knew they were totally inappropriate shoes for an air show. She didn't care. She wet her lips. Today, she wanted to look sexy.

"Holy shit! Get a load of that." George's voice skyrocketed. Her cameraman moved past her, power walking across the airfield. She laughed aloud, knowing what had him smiling. George loved machines, and sitting outside a hangar near the longest runway at MacDill, the fleet of Air Force Thunderbirds gleamed in the high noon sun.

She wasn't a jet freak like George, but she had to admit there was a majestic and powerful aura around the line of white jets, with their cool blue stripes and red noses.

"I feel the need for speed!" George yelled as he glanced back at her, pumping his fist in the air.

"Top Gun!" she yelled back. His euphoria was contagious.

"Top Gun's the navy, but whatever. I dig 'em all!"

As she caught up to George, he leaned over and planted a big, wet kiss on her cheek. "I love you for bringing us back. This shit rocks. Beats the hell out of covering court or traffic accidents."

George may have agreed to come back for the jets, but she was coming back to show Zack a picture she'd found researching online while waiting at her mother's nursing home. As a cop, he should know already about Scott Fitzpatrick's fifty-eight counts of alleged fraud. News clips galore popped up online, but Zack might not have dug deep enough into Google Images to find the one picture that had fired off a connection in Sam's brain.

Where was Zack? She couldn't wait to show him. Her gaze landed on two jets set apart from the formation. The

Air Force had two F-16 twin-seat trainers that could also take media and VIPs on rides. At each stop on their tour, a specially trained Thunderbird pilot took a handful of lucky individuals up during practice runs—one at a time, of course. It was good PR for the Air Force and a delight for the little people who only rode the wind in their dreams.

Today, a few vacationers would get the chance to experience a Thunderbird from the inside. She'd heard stories of VIPs who had pulled 9 gs during their demonstration flight. The Mayor of Tampa had even admitted to throwing up and passing out last year.

Her chest tightened. Thank God, Zack would be the one flying as a passenger today and not her. She would probably never get over her fear of flying. Just thinking about getting in one of these babies made her knees buckle.

A handful of vacationers dressed in forest-green flight suits huddled together near the two-seater, and a handful of pilots dressed in crisp, blue uniforms mingled around the group.

She strained to see, trying to pick out one of two faces. She hoped to find Zack first.

Her heart skipped when he stepped out of the crowd. He looked her way and ripped off his aviator sunglasses. His hand flew up to shade his eyes.

Her cheeks burned, embarrassed by the excitement boiling up inside her. Unable to squash her anticipation, she picked up her pace and waved. She was close enough now to see the look of surprise on his face. He broke out that Tom Cruise-like smile and waved back.

She tried to calm the flutter in her chest, knowing she must be grinning like a fifteen-year-old on her first date. Ridiculous, but fun. Okay, she had to admit it. She liked this man. She was definitely glad to see him again. More than glad. And excited she had information that might help him.

He strode toward her with that confident swagger of his. Now, this was the Zack Hunter she'd first met at Skydive Drop Zone. She laughed. God, he looked good in a flight suit. Hell, he looked good in anything. She bet he looked even better in nothing at all…

He walked faster, almost running now. Was he anxious to see her, too? She stopped, and balled up her hands to keep them from shaking.

He didn't say a word as he approached her. Instead, he pulled her into a bear hug and lifted her off her feet, swinging her around like a lover in a romantic movie.

She laughed. Or tried to. "I can't breathe."

"Good, that's exactly how I like my women. Breathless."

Before, she would have rolled her eyes at such a player line, but now that she knew his history, she beamed up at him. He was definitely not the rich, spoiled, trust fund baby she had pegged him for a little more than a week ago. Okay, he was definitely rich, with enough money to take care of her little financial problem with one simple phone call, but she'd learned at the pool the other night that his cockiness was only a shield to protect his wary heart. She clutched him back, hoping he would allow himself to experience even half of the exhilaration coursing through her own body at seeing him. He had to feel her heart racing. Was his?

"I'm glad you came back," he whispered into her ear as he set her on her feet. His arms remained around her.

"I wanted to thank you in person."

"You're welcome." His smile dimmed, only a bit. "I know you said you needed to take care of your mother's bill yourself but—"

"I'll pay you back."

He brushed away a strand of hair that had fallen over her left eye. His gentle touch accelerated the fire in her belly.

"The money came from my foundation, not me personally.

We contribute to many different charities. You don't have to pay the money back."

She dropped her gaze. "I do. I'm not a charity."

He lifted her chin up so she had to look at him again. "I know you're not. Okay, we'll work it out."

"After we find our killer."

His eyebrows shot up. "I thought you'd given up the idea of murder."

"I had." She stepped out of his embrace. "But while I was away, I dug up some new information." She bounced on her toes, having a hard time keeping her excitement in check.

"What kind of information?"

"I think I've found a possible link to Scott Fitzpatrick. Did you know that before he died he was about to stand trial in New York for ripping off investors in his company?"

The disgusted look on his face said he did know. "Yeah, real scumbag. Fitzpatrick also left thousands of employees without their pensions."

"Which means," she raised a finger for emphasis, "a lot of people could have wanted to kill him."

Zack nodded but dropped his focus to the ground. "I need to tell you something. I would have told you sooner but..."

She gently touched his arm. "Just tell me."

"Michael Flint, the guy who died diving off the east coast?"

"The waitress' lover? I remember." The man with a backpack that had a Semper Fi patch on it.

"Flint was working for New York's Bureau of Criminal Activity. He'd been looking into Fitzpatrick's death at the time of his own supposedly accidental death."

"Holy shit!" She stepped back. "Now, that can't be a coincidence."

"The FDLE is on it, but we haven't been able to find

proof of any foul play in either case."

"Which is why you're here?" It was all making sense now.

"Officially I'm off the case—too close to it, apparently. But I'm not going to stop until I find proof of what's going on here and find out who is pulling the strings." He took a step toward her. "You said you found a link to Fitzpatrick? What kind of link are you talking about?"

"Have you heard of Robert Fitzpatrick?"

"Robert? Robert Fitzpatrick?" He let out a low whistle.

Just the reaction she'd been hoping for.

"How is he linked to Scott Fitzpatrick?"

"I pulled up pictures of Scott Fitzpatrick online." She felt a little breathless as she recited her find. "Had to go through about three pages of them. Most of the pictures were court or news related, but I found one that looked like an old family picture. Like the Kennedys at Hyannis Port. Fitzpatrick had the trophy wife next to him, a couple of kids, and another man standing to Fitzpatrick's left, just behind him. Robert Fitzpatrick."

"Finally!" Zack drew her in for another hug.

"Finally what?" she whispered with the little air left in her lungs.

"A connection," he exhaled into her ear. "I did my own digging into Scott Fitzpatrick's background after my uncle died, but never investigated his family members." He pulled back and stared deep into her eyes. "Here's the connection you just made. My cousin is deaf, and I know a little sign language. My uncle signed the name Robert to the camera before he died."

Wait. "The last thing your uncle did before he died was sign the name Robert?" Her jaw practically hit the dirt.

"Yeah."

"Are you sure?"

"Yes. I assume that's who he thought messed with his

equipment—the person he believed got him killed. Or something else really suspicious. Why else would he try to tell us the name? He hoped the police would eventually get the footage from the head cam."

All this information was making her dizzy. "But why would Robert Fitzpatrick, and we're assuming it's the same Robert, kill your uncle? Did he even know Jackson?"

Zack shrugged. "I'm not saying Robert tampered with my uncle's tanks, but it's a clue and a connection we didn't have before."

"I was thinking maybe Robert might be here doing what we're doing, digging for info on why his brother died."

"Maybe, but either way, we need to talk to him. Wait a minute." Zack grabbed her shoulders with both hands. "You said *here*. Like here, right now?"

She nodded. "Robert was in sunglasses and a hat in the family photo, but there was something familiar about him. I think he might be on this adventure vacation."

Zack made a choking sound bordering on disbelief. "You're kidding."

She opened her mouth, but quickly shut it as Monica, a Thunderbird pilot, and George walked up. George aimed his video camera at them. He was probably rolling, and she didn't want him to catch anything about Robert on video.

"Ready for the ride of your life, Zack?" Monica purred as she moved between them, brushing her body against his.

Nothing like subtlety.

Zack froze for a split second, then smiled and said, "Samantha, we'll finish this conversation as soon as I'm done."

"I'm sorry, did I interrupt something personal?" Monica smiled sweetly. She might have been speaking to Zack, but she was eyeing Sam.

A ripple of worry ran down Sam's spine. Had the

interruption been deliberate? Was Monica involved in these deaths, too? What did she know about them? Or Robert?

"Why did you leave so early the other morning? You didn't even call me." Monica was speaking to Sam, but she threw a coy glance at Zack. "Did our client here hurt your feelings?"

Sam sucked in a breath. "No, of course not." Monica had a smile on her face, but venom in her eyes. What was her deal? Was she into Zack and just jealous, or was she onto their investigation?

"Samantha left at my request." Zack took a step away from Monica, who was clearly in his personal space now. "I had a favor I needed taken care of, and she wanted to check in on her mother. She was kind enough to do both while she was gone for the past two days. No big deal. She's back and we're still on. In fact—" He turned to Sam, that twinkle lighting up his features.

Uh-oh. Her hand fluttered nervously at her heart.

"In fact?" Monica prompted.

"In fact, I've been wondering how Samantha can authentically report on these adventure vacations without actually participating in an adventure herself, so I am giving up my seat on the F-16 to her."

Her stomach hit the ground. What the hell? He *knew* she didn't fly.

"Holy shit!" George's voice boomed. "This is your lucky day, girl." He turned the camera her way.

"No, no, no. I c-can't possibly let you d-do that," she stuttered.

"I agree." Monica's face tightened. "Besides, it's too late to switch now."

Zack whispered something to Monica, but Sam was standing close enough to make out his words. "An extra ten thousand dollars says it's not."

"No really, Monica is right. I don't...um..." She couldn't bring herself to say she was afraid. Make that pee-her-pants terrified. She wouldn't let Monica know she couldn't get in that jet even if ten grand—or her life—depended on it. Her feet had turned into concrete boots.

Zack, still jovial, addressed the group. "Could you give us a minute?"

The pilot, who'd been quietly watching from behind Monica, stepped forward. "Perhaps I can help you make a decision. I'm Captain Dan Dorway." He stuck out his hand toward Sam. "You're a reporter, right?"

He could probably feel her hand trembling as he shook it.

"Not just anyone is allowed to ride with the Thunderbirds. You'll need to take a thirty-minute preparation course and pass a short physical given by our Thunderbird paramedic. But still. Would you really want to pass up this once in a lifetime opportunity?"

"Yes." She dropped his hand, and raised hers in protest. "You don't understand. I don't fly. Ever."

Zack cut her off. "She'll be in the locker room in ten."

After the pilot dragged a reluctant Monica away, Sam threw up her arms. "I know you probably think this ride is a way to thank me for finding info on this Robert guy, but I don't need a thank you. We're good." She backed away from Zack. "And to think I was so excited to see you today."

"You were?" He grinned.

In her effort to put more distance between her and the jets, she teetered backward across the tarmac on her high heels.

He reached out to steady her. "Don't lose your cool. You're going to fall on your cute little ass again."

"Funny." She glared at him, hoping he could feel the fear in her stare. "You can't just throw money around and steamroll me into taking a ride I don't even want."

His eyebrows lifted. "You're serious? You really don't want to ride in a United States Air Force F-16? Are you joking? Look, I know you're scared to fly, but—"

He *did* think he was doing her a favor. *Oh boy.* She heard and felt each beat of her heart, drumming in her chest and at her temple. *Boom-boom. Boom-boom. Boom-boom.*

He pulled her into him and held her so tight, she couldn't move. Not that she could have moved anyway. She was totally paralyzed by fear.

"Okay, maybe I do want to thank you. But I'm not going to tell you what to do."

"A damn miracle." The words were muffled against his chest. She glanced up.

"My uncle always used to tell me to face what frightens you the most. And then you're free. You're always strung so tight, and that anxiety is holding you back from life. From being your best possible self."

He ran one hand up and down her back in a gesture he probably thought comforted her. Wrong. *Panic attack, here I come.*

"You can't move forward until you do this…or something like it," he murmured. "Surprise yourself. Surprise me."

"I can't." Her adrenaline must have been spiking, because she suddenly felt nauseous.

"You can't or you won't? There's a difference. Take a chance and go on this little adventure."

"Little?" she squeaked.

A firm hand jerked her out of Zack's arms. "Are you out of your damn mind?" George demanded.

Apparently, he wanted her full attention. George put his camera on the ground, and, as she backed away from both men, she almost fell over it.

"Fucking A, if your skinny ass doesn't get in that jet and fly with the Thunderbirds, I'll never work with you again, you big, fat, chickenshit." George got right up in her face. She could smell the Doritos he'd downed on the ride to MacDill. "You know how many people would *kill* for this chance to fly in a fucking F-16?"

Both she and Zack gawked at George. "Poor choice of words," she finally said. "Why don't *you* take the seat, if you're so excited?"

"You know I would." George glanced at Zack, who stood with his arms banded over his chest. "But lover boy is buying this ride for *you*."

An image of her mother lying like a corpse in that hospital bed materialized in her mind. She couldn't do it. A tremor rippled through her, and her fingers started to go numb. *Oh, boy.*

"You don't have to do this." Zack's gaze bore into her. "But you'll stay stuck in your head, in your fear, if you don't."

She wondered how he knew her so well when he'd just met her. Flying *was* her biggest mental wall. And the therapist wasn't helping. She'd always known that eventually she'd have to find a way over it. She'd never get a better chance than now. "All right." She had to physically fight back the panic. Zack was already smiling as if he knew what she was about to say. "I'll do it."

This time when he swooped her into a bear hug, she was prepared. She threw her arms around his neck and held on as he twirled her around. Her head fell back, the air rippled through her hair, and she let out a loud shout.

Ohmigod, this felt good.

A sudden thought brought her crashing back to Earth. Her feet hit the ground and she spun out of his hold.

"Samantha?" She felt him even though he wasn't touching her anymore. "What is it? Are you dizzy?"

A sick feeling washed over her. She bent at the waist and attempted to suck in air.

He put his hand on her back and kept it there until she stood up.

She turned to him, shaking. "We think someone intentionally screwed with Maxwell's parachute, and we know someone messed with your uncle's dive tanks."

"Yeah..." Zack eyed her.

She swallowed a nasty mixture of stomach content and fear. "What are the chances someone could get access to and tamper with a United States Air Force F-16?"

Chapter Thirteen

First, Sam's face flushed. Then, her fingers turned icy. "Why did I agree to do this?" she muttered.

Her heart thumped against her rib cage as the canopy on the Thunderbird closed. She could still back out. Trying to swallow the panic, it jammed in the back of her throat like a thick fist. She felt for her cell phone. In her jumpsuit pocket. Like she could call for help at thirty thousand feet.

A lock clicked. No turning back now. *Holy shit. Holy shit. Holy shit.* She blew out air in short puffs and gripped the hose attached to her oxygen mask. Her other hand grasped the edge of her flight seat as the F-16 taxied toward the runway. Even before her mom's plane crash, Sam had never had the courage to take this ride before, despite getting the offer a couple of times. After the crash, she'd refused to fly commercial, much less an Air Force fighter jet.

"Ready?" Pilot Dan Dorway's voice streamed through a speaker in her helmet, calm and controlled.

The exact opposite of her voice as it wobbled out like a baby taking its first steps. "No. I'm terrified."

"Don't worry. I'll give you a heads up before I pull any maneuvers. You're going to love it."

Yeah, because she really loved sweating, throwing up, and humiliating herself. Perspiration already beaded on her forehead, but with a helmet and flight gloves on, she couldn't brush the drops away. She couldn't believe she'd strapped into a jet that flew twelve hundred miles per hour–twice the speed of sound. How was she supposed to get through this flight without passing out? Or worse.

Could one *die* from fear? Maybe Robert didn't even need to sabotage the jet…

A robotic-sounding voice from the control tower buzzed in her helmet. "Quick climb approved. Thunderbird seven, clear for takeoff."

What the heck was a quick climb? Had she agreed to that? Was that the paper she'd signed after the so-called safety class? *Shit.* She held her breath and closed her eyes.

"Ready to hit the clouds?" Pilot Dan sounded jacked up and ready for flight.

Freaking playboy adventurers. They're all crazy. "Hell, no," she whispered, peeling her eyes open.

The pilot let out a cross between a confirmation and a whoop. The engines roared, and the jet shot forward.

Ohmigod! Ohmigod! Ohmigod!

"That's three-fifty…four-hundred…four-hundred-fifty. Here we go!"

She couldn't tell when the jet lifted off the ground. But she knew the instant the T-Bird shifted into a vertical ascent, flying straight up, climbing effortlessly into the clear, blue Florida sky.

She sucked in the oxygen being pumped into her mask as if it were liquor. Maybe it would have the same effect and numb her. *Please.*

"Wanna fly upside down?" Dan asked.

She shook her head, unable to form a word.

The jet rolled over in one smooth, quick motion.

She hung in her seat, the lap belt her only anchor to life and limb.

"That's 4 gs, right there."

She tilted her head back and managed a gasp. The frameless canopy of the jet offered a perfectly clear, perfectly terrifying view of MacDill Air Force Base. Upside down, the whole campus was laid out like a board game below her, the two long runways the only things she could actually identify.

"You okay back there?"

"I…oh! The blood is rushing to my head."

"Okay." The pilot chuckled as he whipped the aircraft back into an upright position.

The summer sky stretched out as far as she could see. Except for the muffled roar of the engine, it seemed as if the two of them were encased in a bubble of total silence, slicing through the atmosphere like a warm knife through soft Brie.

A tense laugh escaped her. A mixture of genuine fear and excitement rushed through her veins and heated her up. She'd never felt more alive than in this moment, teetering on the verge of a different type of ecstasy. She was flying again, and actually enjoying it.

She was. Enjoying it.

Right?

"How 'bout some turns?"

"I– I–"

With a *whoop*, Captain Dan rolled the jet through an escalating series of twirls and spins. The ground flashed by in a blur as if the jet itself wasn't moving, but instead the earth and sky were spinning out of control.

That was when nausea slammed into her. "Oh," she grabbed her stomach. The nasty taste of bacon coated her mouth. She swallowed, determined not to puke. Zack would never puke.

"Samantha, why don't you take the jet?"

She blinked. "Take it where?"

Captain Dan laughed. "Take control."

Did the man have a freaking death wish? She could barely keep breakfast down, and he wanted her to take over? "I don't know how to fly a plane."

"There's nothing to it, and I'm right here. Flying will take your mind off the nausea. Trust me. Grab the stick."

How did he know she felt like puking? She stared at the thin lever between her knees. Her fingers, as if they had a mind of their own, reached out and wrapped around the knob. Fine. Here goes…

"What happens if you move it forward? Oh!" The jet took a nosedive, screaming toward the earth. Her stomach stayed at fifteen thousand feet. "Shit! I'm sorry."

"Pull back. Gently. The stick is very sensitive."

No shit! She did as instructed. "I've got it." She loosened her grip. Tried to relax her cramping muscles. "I'm really flying this F-16?" Adrenaline coursed through her, but her fingers had stopped shaking.

"You are."

A moment of clarity washed over her. She had gotten through all of this without a full-fledged panic attack. Or even a sign of one.

She let out a rich, full-bodied laugh, instantly addicted to the confidence that came with this new high—literal and mental. If she could face this inner terror, she'd easily be able to get over others.

She'd crossed a line, and Zack had given her the push she'd needed.

"Want to do something your friends will never, ever do?" the pilot asked.

"What?" She had let her mind wander with her finger on the control of a multi-million dollar jet. Boy, the government was crazy to let civilians fly these babies.

"Earth to Mars. Anybody out there?"

She laughed. She was thankful Captain Dan was in the cockpit in front of her. "I'm here. What could possibly top this feeling?"

"How about this one?"

The pilot took control of the jet, sending it upward into a giant loop. "Take your glove off. Hurry."

Her glove? She struggled under the g-forces to remove one of the warm gloves issued with the flight suit. "Okay."

"And let it go…now."

The jet hit the top of the loop, flipped back over, and the glove floated in front of her as if suspended on invisible wires. *Weightlessness.* "Woohoo! So this is what the astronauts feel like." Endorphins spinning in her brain, mixed with the adrenaline coursing through the rest of her body, made her whole body tingle.

"Samantha?" Captain Dan's voice had an edge to it.

"Holy crap. Can we do that again?" She grabbed her glove from the air and put it back on.

"Samantha?" The pilot's voice dropped a notch.

"Everything okay up there, Captain?"

"Do you remember what I talked about in the Life Support Room?"

In the safety class, Dan had detailed what they would do in the air. He'd described the maneuvers he'd do, how her body would react, and most important, what to do in case of an emergency.

Shit. Her heart slammed into her chest. "Oh, God."

"Seriously, I need you to remember." He sounded distracted, as if concentrating on something else. From the backseat, she couldn't see what he was doing. Her fingers fumbled around the edge of her seat. *The ejection lever.* Where had he said it was? Oh, God, she'd been so freaked out during her brief training course, his voice had sounded just like Charlie Brown's teacher. "*Wa wa wa, wa wa wa.*"

She didn't remember, and her fingers couldn't find anything that felt like an ejection lever. Thoughts of Robert Fitzpatrick zipped through her mind. And then of Zack.

"Hold on!" the captain's voice rushed out.

She assumed it was a rhetorical order. Her mouth went dry. Before she could ask another question, the jet flipped on its side mid-air and pulled into a sharp left turn.

With a *whoosh*, her g suit instantly inflated, pushing down on her legs and chest. The pilot had told her the suit would keep blood from leaving her brain as they pulled gs. She did remember that. Without it, she'd fall unconscious. The force of the turn pushed her body back into her seat. She felt like a thousand-pound concrete ball was sitting on her chest. She struggled to breathe. Using all her energy, she forced her lungs to expand enough to budge the invisible ball and let a little air trickle in. *She couldn't pass out now.*

Not another word came from the cockpit. Something was definitely wrong.

Her arms had been rendered useless, lead appendages tied to her side by gravity. She feared her head would surely explode if they didn't pull out of this turn.

She couldn't speak. Couldn't move. Couldn't breathe. *Oh, dear God*. Could someone have really messed with this jet?

And still the jet screamed through the turn.

The color drained out of her vision. The world turned black and white. Little dots of darkness danced around in front of her like twirling disco lights.

A silent scream bubbled up in her throat as she lost her vision completely.

The last thing to go was her ability to hear. The roar of the jet, the thrashing of her petrified heart, and then—

Nothing.

Chapter Fourteen

Sam gasped and jolted forward as if startled out of a nightmare, but the lap belt kept her from moving very far. The pain as the restraint dug deeper into her flesh assured her this was no dream. She was still very much alive.

But for how long?

Jerking her eyes open, she blinked repeatedly to wash away the burn. Everything blurred, as if rain beat against her window. But at least she could see again. She opened and closed her eyes once more, trying to get them to focus.

The jet jerked. *What the hell?* She grabbed the armrests with a death grip.

This was it.

Tires squealed. Bounced. Squealed. Her heart practically leaped out of her chest as the jet slowed radically. They must have landed.

"You still back there?"

She sucked in a grateful mouthful of oxygen. "Where else could I go, Captain?" Trying her best to sound light-hearted and witty, she actually felt like an alcoholic must feel after a blackout—stunned and confused. She'd really thought she was about to die moments ago. "What happened?"

"I took you through a 9 g-force turn. You passed out." He paused. "But I won't tell if you don't."

That comment sounded like something Zack would have said. "I did *not* pass out," she groused.

He snorted on a chuckle.

Okay, maybe for a second or two. "Are you telling me you did that on purpose?"

"It's not always part of the ride, but I knew you could handle it."

For real? But she had. Handled it. *Wow.*

The F-16 was taxiing back toward the hangar where the other T-birds sat waiting.

When the jet stopped, a suction noise sounded, then a *click*. She swallowed. The buzz as the canopy opened rang in her ears. She ripped off the oxygen mask, longing to feel the hot, moist Florida air against her skin.

"Get me out of here." The words just marched out of her mouth as if they walked on their own legs. She shivered as intense sensations washed over her in hurricane-size waves.

The wait seemed like forever. She couldn't stop her foot from tapping with impatience. Finally, the ground staff wheeled the ladder to the jet's side. The same crewmember who had handed her the puke bag before the flight appeared at the top of the ladder and grinned down at her.

"Enjoy the ride?" He reached in to unbuckle her lap belt and disengage her from the equipment.

"Fucking-A, Steele! Did you barf?" She could hear George, but she couldn't see him. She attempted to stand, but her head spun, forcing her to sit again.

The crewmember reached across her body. When he stood up again, he held the empty barf bag in his hand. He waved it high overhead like a banner of honor. "It's empty!"

A roar of applause from the group gathered outside the jet brought a smile to her face. She hadn't tossed her cookies. Passed out, maybe—though she'd deny it—and you couldn't document that in a barf bag. Zack and George would be proud. Hell, *she* was proud. She threw back her head and laughed.

The grounds crew and other X-Force vacationers cheered again as she stepped out of the jet—the center of attention. Her legs wobbled, but she held onto the railing. A hot breeze blew through her hair as she moved down the ladder in what seemed like slow motion. She felt like a movie star.

Captain Dan was waiting for her at the bottom. "I have something for you."

She couldn't stop smiling. The muscles in her face actually hurt. Scanning the crowd, she spotted George immediately—his height and his red hair made him stand out. She waved. Where was Zack? She wanted him to see this.

"You've earned the 9 g pin." The pilot held up the thumb-sized pin, with a red, white, and blue aircraft on it, for everyone to see. "Not everyone who flies in my backseat earns the right to wear this." Captain Dan pinned the symbolic acknowledgement to the collar of her flight suit, provoking another round of applause.

Her gaze moved over the crowd, searching for Zack's dark head while trying to be polite and pay partial attention to the captain.

"Out of fourteen thousand pilots, and thirty-seven hundred fighter jocks, only eight fly Thunderbird F-16s. And you pulled 9 g just like the best of us."

She nodded, half listening. Where was that ex-military man? Wouldn't he love seeing this? Her heart felt like it was shrinking, despite the rush of blood pumping through it. Why did she feel this let down? She'd flown upside down and flipped around in a multi-million dollar jet. Her brain still buzzed. She should be *soaring.*

Her stomach tumbled when she finally spotted him. He appeared deep in conversation with Monica. *Really?* The two had their heads bowed together. He had missed her landing and her triumphant return. Didn't he want to see what his *ten thousand* freaking dollars had bought him? She blew out air, slapping the side of her thigh.

"Are you okay?" Captain Dan asked.

The silly grin must have dropped off her face momentarily. "Are you kidding? I'm great." She dragged her gaze away from Zack and Monica and gave the Captain a heartfelt hug. "Thanks for an unbelievable experience. Life-changing. Really, I mean that." She pulled away. Most of the onlookers had moved elsewhere or were talking among themselves. She glanced at the pilot again. "I have one more question. Why didn't you warn me about that last turn, when we did 9 g? You said you'd give me a heads up before you pulled any maneuver. Frankly, you scared the shit out of me."

"Oh, that." A playful grin lit up the pilot's face. "Just following orders. Your friend over there"—he nodded toward Zack—"pulled me aside before your flight and encouraged me to shake you up a bit. He said I needed to push you to the limit—to see how much you could take."

She whipped around to look at Zack.

The captain grinned. "I have to admit, I was intrigued to find out myself. Most reporters can't hang tough like you just did."

Zack caught her staring. A slow, sexy smile spread across his face.

"He told you to *scare* me?" she asked Captain Dan, while continuing to glare at Zack. *Feel the intent behind these daggers, my friend.* So her adventurer wanted to shake her up, huh?

The smile slid off his handsome face. Even from a

distance, he had to sense her disbelief and irritation.

She flipped her long hair over one shoulder and turned back to the pilot.

"He didn't use those exact words." Captain Dan's smile faded. An uncomfortable silence settled between them. "He is your boyfriend, right? I just thought he was having a little fun with you, I—"

She held up a hand. "No worries, Captain. The whole experience was amazing." *Except for the part where I thought we were crashing and about to burn up in a fiery ball.* "Thanks again." She shook his hand and directed her attention back to Zack.

He'd wanted the pilot to take her to the limit, huh? She couldn't wait to see how much *he* could take.

She sauntered toward him, hips swaying, as she ran her hands slowly through her helmet hair. It didn't even matter that she had on an ugly green flight suit and not her usual black skirt and high heels. Adrenaline from the flight still hummed in her veins. She felt like a woman on the edge of the world's greatest orgasm—close, but not satisfied.

Yet.

Zack Hunter had bought her a ride that wasn't quite over. She smiled inwardly. The intensity of her desire to connect with him right now scared her almost as much as that F-16, but the endorphins igniting her insides wouldn't be denied.

As she approached, Monica had her back to her and wasn't able to see her. The manager flapped her hands around as she talked to Zack. He did a double take, probably at Sam's fierce advance, and broke into the widest grin she'd ever seen. Her heart raced faster, and she felt herself grinning back like a damn fool.

Monica stopped talking and turned. Her eyebrows flew together, and her voluptuous lips drew into a thin, ugly line.

"Hello, Monica. Zack." She made sure her smile dripped

sugar, while her mind spun with thoughts of sweet revenge.

Monica said nothing, but her eyes were like weapons, sending Sam a clear warning to back off.

Try and stop me. Today, *she* was the one on a mission.

The light of appreciation in Zack's expression continued to fuel her confidence. "You look like a changed woman," he said.

"You have no idea." She let the smile stay in her eyes. Stepping between them, Sam deliberately put her back to Monica. "I need to talk to you, Zack." She paused long enough for Monica to begin speaking. Then she interrupted. "Alone."

He cocked his head.

"Don't you want to change first?" Monica jumped in, moving to wedge herself between them again.

Sam stopped her with an arm block.

The manager reached out to touch her flight suit, fingering it with obvious disgust. "It's so hot today. You've obviously been feeling the heat." Monica scrunched up her nose.

Bring it on. "You're so right. I do need to change. The locker room is that way, right?" Sam pointed toward one of the largest hangars.

Monica nodded and smiled sweetly at Zack.

Sam turned to him. "Zack, how about helping me change?"

Monica stepped back, eyebrows shooting up as her mouth fell open. But Zack's gaze glistened with desire, and that was all Sam cared about. Since she'd walked up, the gorgeous man in the green flight suit hadn't taken his eyes off her. The heat of his stare made her skin sizzle. She licked her lips.

"My pleasure." His husky voice filled with anticipation.

"Good. Let's go." She reached for his hand, but Monica stopped her by grabbing her wrist.

"Zack?" The young manager's voice revealed her

disbelief, but he ignored her.

He disengaged Monica's grip from Sam's wrist, and she slid her hand into his, pulling him along, out of reach of the woman who also wanted him.

He laughed, but didn't resist. "What's gotten into you?"

"About thirty minutes of endorphins lighting me up like the Fourth of July."

He chuckled. "And you're taking me with you into the ladies' locker room so I can share in the experience?"

"Maybe."

"Damn. I sure hope so."

She continued to pull him along, but knew she didn't need to. The energy he was putting off was just as charged.

When they reached the door to Hangar 113, she let go of his hand, but only to shove the door open. As he walked through, he whispered, "You know, I think there might be a rule or two against having sex in a military locker room."

His fingers grazed her neck as he passed by. Her hair stood up. Arching her back, she pressed her shoulders together, and moved through the door. She couldn't remember a time when she'd been so sensitive to anyone's touch. It felt like she'd ingested a drug that dragged each nerve ending to the surface of her skin. She craved to feel his hands on her. But before she gave into the electricity, she was going to have a little fun with her adventurer.

"Hmm. Is that what you think we're about to do? Have sex?"

"We're not?" He stopped, his lids heavy, his eyes dark with desire.

She pressed her lips together, holding back a smile. "Follow me." She whisked past him, barely brushing her body against his. *Wow.* The feeling of feminine power sent shivers all over her body. She almost skipped down the hall, following the signs to the women's locker room. Once inside, she quickly walked through the three rooms, shouting, "Hello? Anyone here?"

No reply.

No women.

No sounds.

No interruptions.

How lucky was that?

Her heart pumped with anticipation. She'd never done anything this bold or this naughty before in her entire life. Could they get arrested for this? She didn't even care.

Zack was right. She felt like a new woman, and she needed to do something liberating to solidify—and celebrate—this transition. Not to mention the physical release she needed. She checked the last bathroom stall and turned to look for Zack, but ended up slamming right into his solid body. "Oh!"

He had moved up behind her. She would have laughed at the skill with which he always caught her off guard, but his closeness had sucked all of the air out of her lungs. All she could see was his chest rising and falling as if he'd just run five miles. His body brushed against her nipples, sending delicious jolts of pleasure through her. *Oh, God.* She wasn't going to be able to wait.

She lifted her arms to wrap them around his neck in surrender, but he reached out and put both hands on her shoulders, stopping her. Then, as they still faced each other, he turned her around and began to walk slowly, forcing her to walk backward, one step at a time, while he held her gaze.

Sweet anticipation dripped into her, like that juicy mangosteen that had danced on her lips at the honky-tonk. Her back hit something hard, unyielding.

He reached under her arm, and she heard the *click* of a lock on a door. Her back was up against the locker room exit. But they hadn't locked the other entrance. She made a move toward the other room, but he stopped her with his frame.

"Where are you going?"

He was no longer playing. His pupils were dilated, and his face was flushed.

"Nowhere."

His hand wove into her hair and he tugged a little, just enough to let her know he meant business. Then he moved in for a kiss.

Oh, dear God, she couldn't give in this easily. She had to play out her plan of revenge. She moved her head to the side, so his lips landed on her cheek. *She* was supposed to be the one in charge, here. Placing her palms against his chest, she pushed for some space between them. "You rat. You told the Captain to scare me."

"Did he?" His hot mouth pressed a kiss into the sensitive area right behind her ear.

Her body betrayed her by trembling. "Did you?"

"Did I what?"

"Tell the Captain to scare me?"

He put one hand against the door, the other at her side, trapping her head between his large hands. He leaned forward, pressing against her hands, forcing her to use real effort to hold him at bay. "I told him to *thrill* you," he whispered.

One hand moved from the wall down to her hip. He pulled her forward into him, leaving no doubt how much she was thrilling him. *Jesus, he felt big.* She arched her back as her arms, holding him at bay, gave way.

He dragged his palm down her back slowly, lingering on the spot where her lower back met her backside. "Did it work? Are you thrilled?"

She whispered into his ear. "Not quite yet."

He sucked in a breath. "Pulling 9 gs wasn't enough for you?"

So, he knew she'd done it. A little part of her swelled. "I

must admit the ride took my breath away."

"Now I'm going to do the same."

His lips were warm as they pressed down on hers, gently but firmly. Desperate to feel even more, she bit down on his lower lip, enjoying the way his body tightened in response. She pulled him into her, as close as she possibly could, kissing him deeper. She wanted every part of her body touching his. Could he get any harder? She could only try.

"Are you wet yet?" he whispered into the kiss.

She'd been on the verge of an orgasm since that F-16 landed. "Wouldn't you like to know?"

His body stilled. He pulled back, looked right at her, and grinned. "Yes. Yes, baby, I want to know. Right now."

The way his gaze lasered into her with such heated intent scared her. She swallowed and licked her lips, thinking for the first time of backing away. This was crazy. Crazy! They'd get caught for sure. Arrested. Embarrassed. *Fired!*

His hands started roving again. One reached up and pulled at the zipper on the front of her flight suit. Slowly, he pulled it down. With his other hand, he stroked her backside, moving her back into him. A strong awareness of her own heartbeat filled her ears.

As if sensing her hesitation, he kissed her again. This time he deepened the kiss, and her shoulders relaxed, her arms falling to her sides.

She was so caught up in the taste of him, she barely noticed the flight suit slip off her shoulders, but she shuddered as the cool air hit her skin and jumped at the sound of her cell phone, in her jumpsuit pocket, hitting the floor. Holy cow, she was basically in a bra and panties. Her flight suit landed in a pile at her feet. "Zack–"

He continued the kiss, her plea lost is his mouth. His fingers found the inside of her thighs, and they dusted her skin as they traveled upward, leaving patches of tingling in their wake. She ached between her legs, and contemplated putting his fingers right where they needed to be to end this slow torture. She broke the kiss, letting out a slow moan. *Where was her control?* She had wanted to make him wait. She'd needed to tease him. *Then* taste him.

She pressed her legs together, trapping his fingers between her thighs. He chuckled and used just enough pressure to put space between them again.

A soft clicking sound pulled her out of her bliss. A grunt followed, making her jump.

"Did you hear that?" She pushed him back and searched for the source of the sound, but she saw nothing.

His eyes narrowed, and the lustful look retreated as he followed her gaze around the room. "What are you looking for?"

"Witnesses." The hair on her arms stood up. The room was crackling with a weird kind of energy, as if they weren't alone.

"Witnesses to what?" His body stiffened. And not in a good way.

She listened. *No sounds*. Shaking her head, she feared her imagination was playing with her. Her brain kept sending her mixed messages. She returned her full attention to Zack, satisfied she'd just imagined the sound. "Witnesses to my next ride."

His eyes fired up. "You haven't even told me about the first one." He glanced over his shoulder one more time.

"What do you want to know?"

"Was your heart beating?" He rested the palm of his right hand on the left side of her chest, right above her breast. "Like it is now?"

"Yes."

"Because you were afraid?"

"Because I was excited."

"I want to feel how excited you are right now." His fingers slid under her lace panties and stroked her between her folds. Goose bumps sprung up all over her arms, and her legs wobbled. She couldn't wait to step out of the flight suit pooled at her feet, and cast off every bit of insecurity, sense of responsibility, and duty, that had been smothering her for far too long. She was ready to let go. Totally.

He ran his lips up her neck. She shivered and pressed her legs together as he softly stroked her clit. Waves of pleasure began to build. It wasn't going to take her long. She was already jacked-up on endorphins and adrenaline. Her hands began their own frantic exploration of his lean, muscled back. "That feels so good."

"You feel so good."

A door slammed.

She froze.

Zack pulled away from her and wrenched around.

He'd heard it, too. "It came from that room." She gestured to a door beyond the showers. "There's a third entrance to the locker room."

"Now you tell me?" He took off running toward the door.

Heart fluttering, she quickly adjusted her panties, pulled up her flight suit, and followed.

• • •

Jesus. The wall of heat outside the locker room sucked the air out of Zack's lungs even though he was in good shape. He did a quick surveillance of the area and the people strolling past—both soldiers and civilians—but didn't see anything or anyone suspicious. So he headed back inside.

Samantha stood just inside the entrance of the ladies' locker room. She was clutching her smartphone in her hand. She stared at him, looking like a terrified child about to get in trouble.

"You okay?" His chest swelled with the urge to protect her.

When she didn't answer, he moved quickly to her side. "I couldn't find anyone. I ran outside, but whoever was in here must have slipped back into the crowd. Of course, it didn't help that I don't know who I'm looking for."

"Oh, he's here," Samantha said.

"Who? Robert?" Zack saw her shaking. He put his arms around her. It was cool in the locker room, but after the heat they'd been generating, this quaking must be due to something else.

She nodded against his chest.

"What makes you so sure? It could have been a woman who wanted to use the bathroom, and when she saw us she left." *Or Monica spying on us.*

"No. It was *him*." Samantha shuddered in his arms. "He texted me a picture. I have my smartphone with me."

He gently disengaged himself from her, dreading what he was about to see.

She handed him her cell. She'd enlarged a picture.

He held his breath. "Asshole!" Someone *had* been in the women's locker room, watching them. His temperature shot up.

He examined the image. They'd been captured in full embrace, Samantha almost naked, both oblivious to the camera. Were there other photos? Probably.

He glanced around. He didn't see any indication someone might still be hiding inside. Whoever had been there had probably left when the door slammed.

"Why would he do this?" she whispered.

"He?" Smartphone still in hand, Zack put both arms around her. Little tremors rippled through her and that made him furious. "You think Robert Fitzpatrick took this picture?"

"I think Robert Fitzpatrick is the X-Force company photographer. A guy who looked like him had a camera around his neck in that picture of the Fitzpatricks I saw online. That's how I made the connection. It was the camera."

"Robert, he's the same guy who took pictures of us at the Orange Grove Sink?"

"Yes. He's the one," she said. "At least, I think it's him."

"Look at your phone. Does it say Robert Fitzpatrick texted you?"

"No. Just a number."

"Call it," he said.

"I did while you were outside. I got a generic voicemail message."

Samantha's trembling lessened so he pulled back a little. "What motive would he have to take these kinds of pictures of us?"

"It doesn't make sense, does it?"

"Maybe Monica?" He had never trusted her. She'd come on too strong from day one. "She could have taken the picture and texted it to you. She'd have your number from the trip paperwork."

Samantha nodded. "Maybe she's just jealous?"

He glanced over her shoulder at the phone he still held in his hand. With her head pressed against the door, her long hair in disarray, and her eyes closed, Samantha looked wild and sexy. He'd bet Monica was jealous as hell. He had his lips on her neck, and his hands in her underwear. The picture wasn't quite pornographic, but was definitely provocative.

Samantha's eyes watered. "Whoever it was probably took others, and if something this graphic ever got out to the newspaper, the internet, YouTube, I'm fired. My career as a serious journalist would be over."

His stomach clenched. He didn't bother to argue the

point. This picture could screw him, too. His bosses would ask him where the picture was taken, and he couldn't lie. They'd find out he was still investigating his uncle's case despite being barred from it.

"You know what we have to do now," he said.

"Find and corner whoever did this." She gave a half-hearted attempt at bravery, pulling away from him and throwing fisted hands on her hips. "The stakes just went up."

For both of them.

Chapter Fifteen

Sam and Captain John Jacobs stood on the bow of *The Great Escape*, a live-aboard used for shark diving in the Bahamas. The seventy-five-foot charter fishing boat rocked gently, anchored twenty miles off the coast of West End, Grand Bahamas. They'd arrived yesterday, two days after that life changing F-16 flight.

Scuba divers called the area Tiger Beach because of a shallow sand bar below the surface where tiger sharks liked to feed. The X-Force Adventure Vacation Company called it Shark Heaven, the final stop on the advertised adventure vacation.

The glorious cobalt blue sky remained cloud free, and the sun cast streaks of light over the water. The rays of sunshine gave the water texture, and different shades of blue pressed out against the horizon looking like a handmade quilt.

Sam had little time to enjoy the beautiful view. She had another interview to do while continuing to keep an eye out for Robert, who had managed to hide from them—an almost impossible feat aboard a charter boat, even one of this size.

She attached a wireless microphone to the collar of Captain Jacobs's T-shirt. She and George had continued to shoot video and interviews, knowing if they did prove these accidents were murders, they'd need the footage of the adventure vacation to help tell the story. They also had to keep up their cover. So, the ploy continued.

She wrinkled her nose. Neither the breathtaking scene nor the warm breeze could clear away the smell of melting fish goo. The disgusting, oily aroma crawled up her nose and anchored itself there.

She turned to George, who was setting up the video camera on a tripod in front of the captain. "You ready?"

George nodded.

"All right. Let's get started." She stood beside George, facing the captain, so he would look at her and therefore almost directly into the camera.

"Captain Jacob, what are these adventure vacationers going to do today?" She gestured to the five guys seated topside putting on their scuba diving gear, including Zack, who looked focused and serious.

"Here's what's gonna happen." The tall, bearded captain spoke with a raspy smoker's voice. He gestured to a plastic trash can on deck. Two crewmembers were wrestling the contraption they called "the chumsicle" toward the swim platform at the back of the boat. "We lower this trash can full of frozen fish guts into the water on a float. It's gonna hover around twenty feet off the bottom, and as it melts the sharks will pick up the smell of blood in the water and come from everywhere. The idea here isn't to feed the sharks, but to draw them to the bloody bait."

"What keeps the divers from becoming bait themselves?" Sam asked.

"Good question. They have strict instructions to stay at least twenty-five feet away. Sharks, especially tigers, don't like to compete for food."

She wondered how you would judge that kind of distance underwater. She wouldn't be caught dead putting as much as a big toe in the water that close to sharks.

Her plan was to stay on the boat and try to dig up some incriminating evidence on Robert the photographer or Monica the manager. Maybe see if either had left their smartphones on board or had a digital card with more pictures.

The captain had mentioned that Robert had boarded late last night, right before they departed West Palm Beach. The creepy guy had managed to avoid her and Zack by taking to his bunk in the bow almost immediately. They couldn't very well barge into his cabin and cause a scene. *Patience*, Zack had said. And they still had no evidence on Monica, either. Sam thought it best to let him handle Monica.

"Captain, how do sharks usually act around the divers?" She continued the interview even as her mind wandered.

"They will be all over the place, but they'll be thickest by the chumsicle. They'll bump and sniff the bait while the divers observe and take pictures from a good distance."

"What happens if a diver moves in too close?" George intended to dive with Zack, and she wanted her daredevil cameraman to have all the facts before jumping in.

The captain paused and gave her a cool stare. "You get bit."

George's head popped out from behind the camera. "Thought that didn't happen much."

"The sharks will warn you if you get too close, especially the tigers," the captain said.

George met his gaze incredulously. "*Warn* you? What, these sharks have manners?"

A roll of laughter moved through the small group of divers watching the interview.

"Funny guy, aren't you?" The captain walked straight up to the camera, so close his hot breath left a foggy imprint on George's lens. "Want a physical example of what happens if a smartass like you doesn't heed the warning?"

George mumbled from behind the camera. "Sure."

The captain turned around so his backside faced the camera. Then he dropped his trousers. His white ass stuck out against the rest of his tanned body. In the center of his right butt cheek was a large scar, ragged and red.

A chorus of groans and one whistle washed over the deck.

"I told Sharon Stone to kiss my ass, and this is what I ended up with. Twenty-five stitches. I almost bled to death before the rescue chopper could get here."

"Sharon Stone?" Sam asked, puzzled.

"We name the ones we can distinguish after movie stars. Especially the ones that leave their mark." The captain pulled his pants up.

"But this is usually safe, right?" She feared for Zack and George already.

In dramatic fashion, Captain Jacobs threw one foot up on a bench next to him and glared into the camera. "Sixteen hundred people a year are attacked and bitten in New York City." He paused and glanced around the top deck. "By other people."

Sam also glanced around the deck. Most of the divers had stopped to listen. "Okaaay."

"Four hundred people a year die from falling objects. Nine people a year die trying to get money out of vending machines."

"You're making this shit up," George said.

The captain shook his head. "Seven people die each year from shark bites."

"His point is..." Zack walked front and center, fully dressed in his wet suit. Looking sexy as hell. "Shark diving is really a very safe thing to do, if you follow the captain's directions." He focused on George.

Point made. Thank you, Zack.

"Thanks, Captain." Sam took off his microphone.

Out of the corner of her eye, she caught Monica watching them from a seat at the helm. Determined to act as if nothing was up, Sam turned away, not even acknowledging her.

"Nervous?" Zack asked George.

"Hell, yeah."

"Good."

"Why good, dude?"

The two men stood face to face. Zack's shoulders appeared high and tight in the black scuba outfit. "Nervous people pay more attention to what's going on around them."

She took a few steps closer so she could hear better. Zack must have sensed her. He turned so quickly her breath caught in her throat.

"But I'm also worried about the two-legged predators. Be careful, Samantha. Even on deck, it could be dangerous."

She swallowed. "Don't worry. I intend to keep my clothes on," she whispered. "I'm safe on board with the staff around. Robert is diving, right?"

Zack shrugged. "I assume it's his job to take pictures for the company."

"You know, I've been thinking. Robert was the one who first told me about your uncle."

"So?"

"So, he was working here as a photographer even back then. Doesn't that strike you as odd? His family is rich."

"Scott Fitzpatrick used to be rich. His funds were frozen once he was arrested." Zack ran a hand over his chin. "But, yeah, Robert being here for so long is odd."

"Zack, man, I'm ready to gear up. Can you go over my equipment with me?" George's voice had lost the cockiness and now had a nervous ring to it.

As Zack and George walked over to where his stuff lay on the deck, Sam decided to check out Zack's gear. He already had on his dive suit, but his tanks, mask, and regulator still sat on the other side of the deck.

A short, squat man drifted toward Zack's tanks.

Holy shit! Her heart stilled. "Zack, I think that's him. Hey!" she yelled across the deck, taking long strides toward the guy.

The X-Force photographer had his back turned, but she thought it was Robert by the shape of his body. What the hell was he doing? He was standing right in front of Zack's gear. "Don't touch anything."

The man backed off the dive gear as if he'd heard, but he didn't turn around to acknowledge her.

She huffed across the deck. Glancing back, she saw Zack right behind her.

She reached the man first. "Hey, what are you doing?" She pulled on his arm. His skin felt unusually slick and cool.

His body stiffened, but then, as he turned, his muscles appeared to relax like a snake slithering out of an uncomfortable situation.

"Are you Robert Fitzpatrick?" She blew the words out before stopping to think if this was the best course of action.

"Fitzpatrick? You must be mistaking me for someone else."

She squinted. The sun made it hard to get a good look at his face. In the picture she'd pulled up online, Robert Fitzpatrick had on sunglasses and a hat. She glared at the man. "I thought…"

Yes, this man had the same body type, but his head was shaved and his face seemed fatter. She couldn't be certain…

"What's going on here?" Zack demanded. She felt better now that he was standing next to her.

A flurry of questions flew out of her mouth like anxious butterflies. "What is your name, then? Where are you from? How long have you been taking pictures for the company?" Zack put a hand on her back. She took a breath as his dark eyes drilled into the man in front of them. Forget his subtle warning to slow down. She had to ask. "Were you messing with his tanks?"

The man's emotions remained shuttered by calm features. "I'm sorry? Messing with whose tanks?"

"Mine." Zack knelt at his gear and examined each piece.

"I'm Ian Fredricks. We've met before, Samantha."

She noticed his long skinny fingers, and the smell of expensive cologne. Who wore cologne on a dive boat? The sunlight caught his irises, turning them into an unusual shade of gray. *Cold eyes*, she thought. The hair on the back of her neck crept into a standing position.

"Everybody knows you. You're on TV." The man's lips curled up into a creepy, satisfied smile. "And people will know you even better soon. I've been busy snapping some very candid shots of you and your friend here. I intend to post them online when I get a chance."

Zack stiffened. "I want to see all pictures first. You won't post anything with us in it without permission."

"But both of you already signed a release. Remember the pictures I took of both of you at the Orange Grove Sink and MacDill Air Force Base?"

Her throat constricted. He had taken professional pictures of them at both locations, but she felt certain he'd also taken that picture in the locker room. But she needed proof, and she needed to make sure he didn't have any other photos before scaring him away.

Zack rose to his full height and towered over the man she thought was Robert Fitzpatrick. "I'd like to see those pictures, Ian." He hit the name like he probably wanted to punch the man. Hard.

But Ian remained cool and crisp in his white cotton polo. “Fine. I’ll be glad to show them to you both. After the dive.”

What did that mean?

“I need to change.” The snake slithered below deck.

“What do you think? Is it him?” Zack asked as soon as the man was out of hearing range.

“I can’t tell. He looks different than in the Fitzpatrick family picture. Older. Rounder.”

“It’s him.” Zack continued going through his gear methodically. “I can tell by his energy. He’s practically taunting us.”

“Should we go after him?” She half wished he’d say no. The guy gave her the heebie-jeebies.

“No. He can’t escape. We’re on a boat. Surrounded by water. Besides, I have a different plan.”

Chapter Sixteen

"Put your regulator in and take a few breaths, George."

Sam watched Zack place one hand on the bottom of George's tank and put his other hand on her cameraman's regulator. Then Zack tried to shake the tank up and down. It didn't move much. "Tank is secure."

He was an ex-Army Ranger, so he had to know what he was doing. Right? Worry shimmied down her back as George tested his air supply. Zack looked at a gauge and tapped George on the back. "You're good."

"Zack, I don't think you should go. What if Robert—Ian, whatever his name is—what if he did mess with your stuff?"

He stood up straighter. "You just watched me check it all out."

She cocked her head at him. "So did Maxwell."

"I didn't let anyone else prep my gear."

A twinge of guilt rocked Sam. She shouldn't have let Maxwell hand off his gear to do her interview.

"You got a good look at this photographer guy?" George asked her, fiddling with his mask. "Is it him?"

"I think so."

"What does that mean, Steele? You *think* or you *know*? You're a reporter, for Christ's sake." George's eyes looked bloodshot and tired.

Maybe he shouldn't dive, either. "It means I can't be sure it's the same guy I saw in the Fitzpatrick family picture. But he was hovering over Zack's dive gear. I'm just a little concerned about what he might have done. We are investigating suspicious deaths, remember?"

Zack smiled at her with what she supposed was reassuring confidence. "I've double-checked the gear. I promise. But I'm glad you're so worried about me. It's nice."

Smiling, he brushed a hair away from her cheek. He always did that to distract her. It wasn't working. She could tell he was nervous, too. And that made her even more worried.

"I promise I'll keep my attention on Robert while he's diving with us, and I will be extra careful."

She wanted to knock some sense into him. "I know you think you're Superman, but—"

George groaned behind her. "Will you chill the hell out? You're making me nervous, too."

She glared at him. "Why don't you stay out of it? You weren't there when we were talking to that snake."

"I was rushing to get my camera. You couldn't even keep him talking long enough for me to get him on video."

Zack smacked a fin against the side of the boat. "Stop it. Both of you. People are watching."

As if that would keep her from speaking her mind. After doing 9 gs and surviving, she refused to be that scared girl anymore. "Fine. Ignore my warning." They *would* listen. "What do you think you'll find down there besides frenzied sharks? Hidden clues to one of the murders? Michael Flint died here a year ago. There's nothing left to find."

Zack knelt to grab his fins.

Damn him. If she thought she could move fast enough, she would have thrown the fins overboard. Childish maybe, but they weren't taking her seriously.

Zack walked to the back of *The Great Escape*. A series of steps led down to the dive platform, almost even with the ocean. The rocking of the boat splashed cool salt water onto the standing area.

Not only was Zack diving, he was going first. Watching him made her a little dizzy. He sat on the top step and slipped his fins over his feet. He motioned for her to sit next to him. She hoped he could feel the exasperation rolling off her body.

When she sat down, he whispered, "Calm down. I'm diving with George so we can keep our cover." His voice was low and reassuring. "I want our friend Robert to take the bait and follow."

She looked behind her, not spotting the photographer, but she did see a few vacationers watching them with interest. A vacationer from Texas wandered their way, fins in his hands.

"If he dives, that leaves you on board with access to all his personal belongings," Zack whispered. "He's not going to dive with his smartphone. Go see if you can find it and prove he actually took the picture. Then delete it and any others."

She dropped her gaze, cheeks burning. Just the thought of what else might have been caught on his camera made her so damn mad.

"While you're poking around, look for anything else that ties him or Monica to any of the deaths."

"Like what?"

"You're the reporter." He grinned.

She'd grown to love that smile, but today it didn't wipe away her dread. "I can't change your mind, no matter what I say, can I?"

He shook his head and lowered the mask over his face.

Zack was still acting like the Lone Ranger. She wondered

if he'd ever change.

George went down the steps, carrying the underwater casing he would use to shoot video of the shark dive. He threw her a thumbs up.

Reluctantly, she got up and moved to a bench on the side of the boat near the stern, out of everyone's way. *Oh, boy.* Why couldn't she shake the bad feeling? Zack did know what he was doing.

A couple of the vacationers gathered at the back of the boat watched her with genuine interest. Word had spread that she and Zack were more than just reporter and subject. The day on the tarmac at MacDill Air Force Base had pretty much confirmed that. She didn't really care about that. She just didn't want to stir up any other suspicions. Not when they were stuck out on a chartered boat with a possible murderer and very few places to run and hide.

"Ya'll ready?" The captain, who was also the dive master on this trip, went past her to the bottom of the stairs and onto the swim platform. Water lapped at his finned feet.

George circled around, looking a bit concerned. "Hey, Zack, I didn't check the buoyancy control device."

Zack didn't even flinch. "I checked the BCD earlier. It's working. Let's hit it." He stepped out into the water, and with hardly a splash disappeared into the crystal blue sea.

Sam's rapidly beating heart sank with him.

She stared at the brilliant blue water. Stars of sunlight danced on the surface, making the sea look happy and peaceful. The consistent roll of the waves mesmerized her but didn't wash away her worry as the other divers followed.

"How's it going?"

Monica's sultry voice pulled her out of her trance. She had to get up and go below deck, do her job.

"Samantha?" Monica's voice went up an octave, into that zone of irritation. "I asked you how it's been going."

She was standing in front of Sam, a young brunette glued to her side. Sam placed a hand above her eyes and squinted. She couldn't tell if Monica was being serious or sarcastic, and frankly she didn't care. "Are you getting everything you need?" Monica was smiling, but she had her arms crisscrossed over her chest.

"Everything is great, thank you." Reluctantly, Sam turned her attention away from the water where the red and white dive flag had been buoyed. "George is shooting video underwater right now." She forced a smile. "I'm sure he'll catch great moments of Zack flirting with whatever dangerous sharks show up."

Monica sat down next to her.

Terrific. The woman wanted to hang out.

"When will the story air?" The young girl next to Monica remained standing, as if waiting for her boss to give her permission to sit down, too.

"That depends," Sam told Monica. "Hi," she said to the girl. "I'm Sam Steele."

"Oh, I know. I'm from Lutz, near Tampa. I watch you on the news all the time." The young girl's voice bubbled like a teenager's. "I'm Jenny."

"Nice to meet you." Jenny was a younger version of herself, she thought, with dark eyes and dark hair, about the same length as hers. "Hard to know when it'll air. We have to wrap up this trip. Then my cameraman and I have to get the footage back to the station. I have to log the video, pick out sound bites, then decide which clips we want to use. So far, we have a lot of great stuff to work with." She smiled at Monica. "I could fill a documentary."

Monica nodded, a Cheshire cat's grin on her face. "Of course. No company puts on adventures like we do."

Of that, I am sure. "Then I'll have to write the story, and George will edit the video. That could take a few days."

"You should have enough video already." Monica didn't even fake a smile this time.

Was the manager trying to get her to leave? "Well, the vacation isn't over yet." And how the hell could they leave anyway? Sam turned her attention to Jenny, "Do you work for X-Force?"

"I'm the cook," Jenny answered.

"In that small kitchen down below?"

"You don't think these uppity men cook for themselves, do you?"

Sam laughed. "Good point."

"You have such a great job." Jenny sat next to her on the other side. "Working in TV news must be exciting."

Jenny's vibe was so positive—a much-needed change from the tension Sam had been feeling from Monica the last few days. She dropped her shoulders a notch. "For the most part, reporting the news is exciting. At least it's different every day." She'd loved her job, before the panic attacks had made each live shot a struggle.

"Do you always enjoy the fringe benefits of the job?" Monica asked coldly.

"Excuse me?"

Monica smirked. "Obviously you and Zack are—"

Sam cut her off. "Are what?"

"You're both *enjoying* this assignment." Monica stabbed her with a knowing look.

"Why, yes we are." She gave Monica her back. "So, Jenny, where did you learn to cook?"

The dark-headed girl shifted on the bench. "Who says I can actually cook?"

Her shy smile warmed Sam, and she laughed.

Monica gave her shoulder a persistent, pissed-off tap. "Isn't that an ethical violation?"

"What? Pretending you know how to cook?" Sam asked.

"No, sleeping with the subject of your story."

"I'm sorry?" Sam couldn't believe Monica had the nerve.

"Oh, I bet you're not sorry." Sarcasm laced Monica's words.

Jenny shuffled her feet on the deck and cleared her throat. "Um, I think I'll go check on what I can throw together for lunch."

Monica's gaze had locked with Sam's. "Good idea," Monica said.

In the past, Sam probably would have been the one to give up in this game of chicken. But now, she had no intention of letting Monica make her feel guilty for her relationship with Zack. What the hell did Monica care anyway? Unless she wanted Zack for herself.

The sun rained down on them in drops of intense tropical heat.

Sam pushed her chin out and stared directly at Monica. "Do you have a problem with me?"

The woman pulled her blond hair behind her, twisting it into a knot, but she never broke their eye-lock. "No, I just wanted to give you a friendly warning."

"Oh, I'm feeling your good intentions."

Monica's eyes narrowed. She snorted out a laugh.

"I don't know why you need to warn me, Monica. I'm not the one swimming with the sharks today."

"Think you're not? I've been working these vacations since we started them three and a half years ago. These adventure seekers are like sharks. They're predators drawn to excitement, like the tiger sharks are drawn to the chum. They're not like other men you've dated."

"What's that supposed to mean?" Now Sam was totally confused as to where Monica was going with this conversation. Was this about Zack? Or something else?

The woman's gaze drifted away, over the water. "They're

adrenaline junkies. Thrill-seekers. Nothing is *ever* enough because their brains are wired differently. They need constant excitement and stimulation. And most of them are lone wolves, doing what they want all the time without much regard for the wishes of others."

"People say most reporters are adrenaline junkies, too. I'm a big fan of excitement and stimulation."

Monica scoffed. "These guys will sweep you off your feet, say all the right things, and woo you until you give in. But don't be fooled. It's the chase they love, not you. Once they've captured you, they move on to the next big adventure, and they'll abandon you, leaving you wondering what the hell happened." Unexpectedly, she dropped her gaze and her voice. Sam had to lean in even further to hear her. "They'll scar you."

Was she talking about Zack? Impossible. Dehydrated from the heat and the fact she'd hadn't eaten anything today, nothing moved down Sam's throat, even when she swallowed. "You know this from personal experience?"

Monica smiled, but her gaze looked guarded, as if they held a sad secret. "You should stay away from Zack. In fact, you should leave. I can call you a helicopter lift."

Sam sensed something other than jealousy motivated this woman. "I'm a big girl. I can take care of myself." She glanced at the water. No sign of any of the divers yet. She still had to find Robert's bunk and go through his stuff.

When she turned back, Monica was staring at her again with that unreadable gaze. Sam needed to make up an excuse and get away. "I've got to…got to go to the bathroom. Thanks for the enlightening conversation." She rose to leave.

"I blew off the warnings as well." Monica's grip on her arm stalled her. "Then I met Michael Flint."

That name and the anger in her voice stunned Sam. She plopped back down. "Michael Flint?" The undercover cop who died while diving with the sharks on his adventure vacation a year ago. “You were lovers?” Might as well get right to the important question.

“I loved him.”

Wow. Didn’t see that coming. Why were Monica’s eyes full of fire instead of sadness? “You don’t seem very upset about his death.”

“It was a while ago.”

Monica’s reply sucked the air out of her. “Okay.” What was the deal with the freaky employees on this trip? And did Monica know she’d been sleeping with an investigator?

Her cheeks did look flushed, but it was hard to tell if that was a developing sunburn or real sentiment.

“It was over, anyway.” The manager’s voice iced over. “Michael betrayed me.”

Now they were getting to the real story. “With another woman?” Sam already knew the answer to that question. Rita, the cute waitress from North Florida.

“Obviously, I wasn’t enough for him.”

What does one woman say to another after that? Sam studied her. Monica stared out at the water, her eyebrows furrowed and her mouth set in an angry line.

So, Monica had been sleeping with a man who was investigating the X-Force Adventure Vacation Company. If criminal activity was going on and she was also involved, if she’d found out the man she was sleeping with was on to her, maybe Michael Flint’s death wasn’t an accident, either.

But how could Monica—or anyone—ensure that a shark in the wild would bite a particular diver? That was how Michael reportedly died— from a shark bite. Whoever was pulling the strings here was good. But *that* good?

“Must have been a horrifying way to die.” Sam threw out the bait to see if Monica would take it.

“He bled to death right here on this deck.” She shivered

and looked down at her feet.

So, that was how they had done it. "Michael Flint bled to death while you watched?" Maybe they didn't initiate the bite, but once it happened, maybe they'd chosen not to call for help right away. Michael could have bled out while they'd turned their backs on him. That would mean more than one person was involved. And Sam was stuck on a boat with them.

She hoped her theory was wrong.

Monica pulled her gaze away from the water. "Help got here too late." Her eyes clouded over. Sam scooted down the bench, away from her. The look in Monica's eyes made the hair on the back of her neck stand up. A sick realization washed over her. Monica had re-directed her romantic attentions from Michael to Zack. Zack had blown her off more than once. Was Zack her next target? Was *Monica* the crazy killer? Or their ringleader?

Sam's gaze shot back to the water. The warm liquid gently lapped at the back of the boat where the swimming deck reached out into the sea. What the hell was going on down there?

She shook her head because she had no control over the situation now, no matter what happened below the surface. And Monica knew it. Whatever plan she may have set in motion must already be unfolding.

And there wasn't a damn thing Sam could do to warn George or Zack.

Chapter Seventeen

The divers knelt, shoulder-to-shoulder, in an eerie semi-circle on the ocean floor. Zack looked up. A dozen predators circled overhead, not like vultures, but like objects dangling from a mobile high above an infant's crib.

A handful of smaller sharks swam belly to the sea bottom, flirting with the group of six men, but so far, the beasts made no move to swim through them.

A sea turtle lumbered by, and a school of silver baitfish danced above Zack's head in a symphony of light and movement, but he couldn't actually enjoy the beauty of the moment.

His breathing, which should have been rhythmic, was ragged and too fast. And he couldn't push Samantha's warning into the back of his mind. Even though he'd double-checked his gear. Including the mix in his tanks—which he hadn't let out of his sight after filling them himself. Whatever had happened to his uncle's air supply was not going to happen to him.

He inhaled deeply of the oxygen mixture. He had to be

alert and prepared for whatever came their way, be it finned or not. Thank God Samantha was safe on deck. One less thing to worry about.

The dive master had armed him and the other men with pieces of metal pipe, each about three feet long. If a shark got too close, he'd simply hit the animal's snout with the pipe and force it back, far enough away that damage or injury would be improbable.

A snort escaped him, sending a slew of bubbles toward the surface. *Right.* Tell that to Michael Flint. Zack's blood pulsated through his veins. He glanced around, hoping to spot Robert among the nearly identical divers. If the photographer was here, he was hidden behind a standard mask and X-Force wet suit, like all the others.

A tiger shark, at least eight feet long, brushed past George, who was shooting video from a spot directly across from Zack. The shark circled around and nudged George from behind. The kid jumped, and almost lost his grip on his underwater camera.

Zack's gut clenched. How fast could he get to George?

The kid stumbled backward over a patch of coral on the sea floor. By the time he had steadied himself and flipped around, the powerful shark had passed by.

The tiger had its eye set on the lollipop of fish guts floating about fifteen feet off the bottom, to the right of George's head.

The cameraman's chest rose and fell in fast, furious motion. He had no problem imagining the cuss words flying through George's head.

He'd warned George to control his breathing. If he got too excited and sucked in air, he could end up quickly depleting his air supply. Made for a short dive, and a disappointing day. Of course, he should talk… He gestured for George to take it down a notch, determined to heed his own advice.

Once George was back on solid ground, knees to the sandy ocean floor, looking at the monitor of his camera, Zack once again began scanning the other divers, looking for anything to set Robert apart. Hard to tell.

After a few minutes, his focus was drawn back to the sharks. One with dark spots and stripes covering its body had a rusty hook stuck in the right side of his snout like some rebellious teenager. A lone hammerhead whipped its end fin back and forth aggressively, as if taunting the divers into a fight. Who would have the balls to do that? None of these guys appeared to have the desire to do anything risky.

Zack, however, was a different story. A nagging need for danger tugged at him. Like his uncle, he had a hard time resisting life-threatening, endorphin-producing experiences. Unfortunately, he'd promised Samantha he would be careful.

But when a smaller lemon shark slid past him, he couldn't resist. He put one hand on the sensitive snout of the seven-foot long beauty. The sensation caused a dizzy lightness in his chest. He was so close he could see the pores on the animal's pointed nose.

Be careful. Don't cross the line.

Almost of its own volition, his other hand gently grasped its dorsal fin, effectively hypnotizing the creature. His heart pounded, and he relished the power of the moment. He was controlling a man-eater. He rubbed the shark's snout. Its silver-dollar size eyes rolled back, and the creature became docile, as if in a trance.

A surge of chemicals lit up his brain. He'd read about this phenomenon in sharks, but had never thought to experience it. Biologists believed the tiny metallic chain links in the dive gloves, placed over the electromagnetic sensors in the shark's snout, hypnotized the animals into compliancy. Every nerve fired as he ran his gloved hand over the hard, leathery skin.

Damn. His uncle would really have gotten off on this.

He glanced up to make sure George was catching this on video because he had to admit, he wanted Samantha to see it.

He let the animal go. An uneasy feeling swept through him as the current of water from the lemon shark's tail signaled his exit. He'd been so lost in the ecstasy of the dive that he'd forgotten to pick Robert out from the group. He dragged his gaze over the divers. Most of the men were photographing him.

A few of them moved like little kids on a playground, sliding in and out of the gray wall of sharks. Zack's gaze swung from one man to the next. He knew the importance of keeping an eye on the enemy. But today, like a giddy schoolboy, he'd lost his concentration and begun to play.

How in the hell had he let himself get so caught up in the dive he'd forgotten the mission? Lapses like that could get a man killed.

Where the hell was his suspect?

He swung around.

No one behind him.

The X-Force photographer was supposed to be down here. Zack never did see the bastard jump in, but documenting this adventure was part of his job.

Of course a killer wouldn't really care about that. He'd have more important things on his mind than keeping his job.

Like murder.

Damn!

What if Fitzpatrick *wasn't* along on the dive? Zack had no way to warn Samantha if their suspect may still be on the boat.

He heard a gurgling sound. He flung his body around.

George was dangling dangerously close to a fifteen-foot tiger shark that must have weighed a good twelve hundred pounds. He had his back to it, still looking through his camera.

The shark opened its huge mouth.

Shit.

Zack feared even a ship's hull would be no match for this slayer's serrated teeth, each bigger than a dinner plate. He grabbed his tank banger, a rubber band with a metal ball attached to it. He pulled it back and let go. The ball hit his air tank, sending out an unmistakable warning sound.

George turned around, searching for the source of the sound. Instead, he found the shark. He froze.

Zack kicked his way to George's side, holding his metal pipe in front of him, and pushed the shark away. His chest hurt from the exertion.

The shark reared its head, appeared to growl, and snapped its razor-sharp teeth down onto his pipe, jerking on his only weapon. The pipe was whipped through his dive gloves, despite his best attempt to hang onto it. *Damn it.* The friction burned like liquid fire.

The tiger eyed him for a split second before dropping the pipe and swimming away.

Wow! Now who was sucking air?

George still hadn't moved a muscle. But his insides must have been quivering. That was too damn close. A former dive master had once told Zack that one had a higher chance of surviving an attack by a great white than a tiger shark. Tiger sharks weren't picky. They'd eat anything, and would just as happily chow down on your calf as a sea turtle's head.

He sank to his knees, glad to feel the sandy bottom.

The fun was over. Time to surface. Time to check on Samantha.

He felt a ripple in the water.

He spun around.

The tiger had returned.

George faced the predator. The animal bumped the port of George's underwater camera casing with its nose, as if challenging the cameraman to a duel. George didn't have a pipe to defend himself. He was using both hands to hold the camera casing.

Zack had never seen a shark act this aggressively before on any dive.

George followed the shark's movement, keeping the camera between them. Like that would do him any good. Zack's stomach muscles clenched. George was doing the right thing. He just had to move slowly and not panic. He made three turns with the shark in a kind of death waltz. Zack kicked over to help him. Out of the corner of his eye, he saw two of the other men swimming for George, too.

Just as Zack got close, the tiger shark raised its blunt nose and opened its mouth in an obscene grimace of warped teeth. Then it closed the membrane over its eyes and thrust its jaw at George.

It happened in a second.

A single, horrific lunge.

A vicious, slashing bite.

Zack sucked in air and kicked harder.

An unexpected hissing sound forced him to spin around. Air was inflating his vest.

No fucking way!

He twisted to get vertical and flung his arms out as his body shot toward the surface. He had to stop his quick ascent. He flipped upside down and kicked his fins as hard as he could, reaching for the sea floor.

His ears popped as he continued to rise like a cork. His body picked up speed as the ocean floor receded. Shooting to the surface at this rate would give him the bends. Just what he needed—an air embolism in his brain that could explode.

Motherfucker! He'd *checked* his gear.

His numb fingers found the BCD control device on the end of the inflator hose. He pressed the manual deflate button. It wouldn't depress. What the hell! He struggled to breathe. *The asshole had tampered with his BCD valve.*

No time to get pissed now.

He reached behind his vest for the dump valve on the backside.

His last resort.

His fingers found the string attached to it. He pulled. The string broke. The valve didn't budge.

He screamed inwardly, his vision beginning to blur. He looked up. Light filtered down, like God's fingers reaching out to greet him.

What a perfectly good way to kill someone.

What a fucking shitty way to die.

Chapter Eighteen

Sam's heart flip-flopped as she tiptoed down the narrow hallway leading to the cabins in the front of the boat. *The Great Escape* barely slept twelve people. It was a tight squeeze, with not many places to hang out or hide. That made sneaking around and investigating a bit of a problem.

She swallowed and glanced behind her. No one followed her. Good. After she'd extracted herself from that weird conversation with Monica, she'd gone down the companionway into the center of the boat. Jenny had been working in the kitchen, which smelled of freshly baked chocolate-chip cookies.

Sam hurried toward the bow. She had no idea when the men would resurface. She needed to move fast. Which bunk was Robert's? Her hand shook slightly as she pulled aside the curtain shielding the top bunk.

A black athletic bag had been pushed into a corner of the bed. Stepping onto the lower bunk, she hauled herself up. Stomach against the rail of the top bunk, she reached across and for it. As she unzipped the bag, the smell of dirty feet hit her. Shaking off the foul odor, she plunged her hand inside. She was looking for a smartphone. But she was also hoping to stumble across more proof of Robert's identity, or of his guilt. Anything that might help their investigation.

After some digging, she found nothing but toiletries and clothes.

Dammit. Wait. She felt a wallet.

For one moment, guilt at digging through another person's possessions assaulted her. Then *that* image of her and Zack popped into her head. She pulled the wallet out and flipped it open. The driver's license read Stephen Souto. He was the software engineer from Austin, Texas. She dropped her shoulders. *Damn.*

Quickly she hauled herself back up to the top bunk, threw the wallet into the duffel, and pushed it back into its original position.

Her heart raced as she pulled aside a second curtain. A flashlight would have helped, but even without one, she could make out camera equipment laid out across the bed. *Bingo!* Nerves on fire, she plowed through a camera bag.

Nothing unusual. And no phone.

She checked under the pillow. Nothing.

She lifted the front of the mattress so she could slide her hand between it and the bottom board. As her fingers grazed an object, her breath caught. She pulled it out, and in her excitement, forgot the mattress, which crashed back down. She froze. But heard nothing in reaction to her loud mistake.

She'd found the photographer's smartphone. And since it was password protected, she pocketed it for now. Its disappearance would alert Robert, Ian, whoever he was, to someone being here, but she didn't care. What else did the asshole have hidden under his mattress?

She forced the mattress up and brushed her hand over the entire length of the bunk board. In the back right corner, her fingers found leather again.

She smiled. It took all of her control to keep from whooping.

Wallet out and open, she stared down into the face of Ian the X-Force company photographer.

But the name on the driver's license was Robert Fitzpatrick.

I'm right. Hell yes!

And now she had the bastard's name and address. Not really evidence of any criminal activity, but proof he'd been lying.

She took the license from the wallet. As she removed it, a folded-up paper fell out. She shoved the license into the pocket of her shorts and knelt to pick up the paper. It was a newspaper clipping. She rubbed her thumb over the worn surface, wondering how many times Robert had folded and unfolded it. It was soft as tissue, so it must have been hundreds.

She was tempted to stop and read the article, but electricity shot through her like an omen. She forced the wallet, minus the license and newspaper story, back into the corner.

The mattress fell.

"What are you doing?" a male voice accosted her.

She froze. *Robert!* He was supposed to be diving.

"I asked you a question." His angry tone grabbed her like rough fingers.

She pushed away from the bunk and faced him. Shoulders squared, eyes on fire, she barked back at the enemy. "Hello, *Ian.*"

"Samantha." He spit out her name.

Remain cool. He didn't know what she'd just found. "I thought you were diving."

"Dying?" Robert's eyes narrowed, but the corners of his mouth moved up into a creepy smile.

Her stomach lurched. "Diving." *Asshole.*

"I decided to stay on board. I thought I might catch something much more interesting up here." He took a step toward her.

She scooted to her left, closer to the door, but he was blocking her exit. "Is this Zack's bunk?"

"Wouldn't you know?"

She swallowed. "Well, I'm looking for something he borrowed, so if you'll excuse me, I'll just—" She started to edge around him.

He held out a hand. "It's *my* bunk."

He still wouldn't let her pass. "Really? Wow, I'm sorry." She gestured toward the hallway. "Do you mind?"

His snaky gray eyes narrowed. "What were you looking for?"

"My Tylenol." Her voice shook. *Get hold of yourself.* "I have a headache."

Just like a serpent, he struck without warning, grabbing her head in a vise-like grip. "Want me to fix that?"

"Ha ha." She forced her voice to sound light. "I wish you could." *Smile, Sam. Or better yet, scream.* She reached up to pull away his hands, but couldn't budge them.

He applied pressure, and then started to roughly massage her. "Do you?"

"Stop it, Robert." The name slipped out in a nervous rush.

He dropped his hands. "What did you just call me?" He cocked his head to the side.

"I'm sorry? I—"

He moved closer, so close she could smell his hot breath. "You called me Robert. Again."

"Right." She stumbled backward. "Wow, my head is really pounding." She had nowhere to run.

"You should have stuck to your original story."

"What story is that?" She sensed a change in him, as if the animal instinct to kill had blinded him to any type of rational thinking. *Change tactics. Do something!* "I think the story *you* have to tell would be much more interesting."

"Too bad you won't ever get the chance to hear it."

"Why not?" *Keep him talking.* "We could get George to—"

"What did you find in my bunk?" The hot demand battered her.

"Nothing." *Deny. Deny. Deny.* Her heart slammed against her ribs.

Robert snorted. "My phone? Did you find it?" He placed his hand on her chest as if he were about to caress her left breast.

She sucked in air and batted his hand away. But it boomeranged back and stopped right on top of her bosom.

"Your heart is racing. You found the pictures, didn't you?" He sneered at her. "The photos make my heart race, too."

Sick bastard. She smacked his hand away again, this time as hard as she could. "Why did you take those pictures?" She struggled to keep her voice calm.

He laughed at her. "Besides the obvious? They were good."

"Good for what? Jerking off?"

"Good for blackmail."

"That won't work." *Screw this!* She tried to push past him.

With one sweep of his arms, he stopped her. "I know. And I'm sorry about that." He shoved her up against the bunk.

"Stop!" She grunted as she hit the solid wood. Something sharp spiked her upper back, sending a searing heat through her flesh. She flinched and yelped.

"Be quiet," he ordered, running one cool finger down her

cheek.

She cringed, her back still burning.

"You still have no idea what's going on, do you?"

Fury beat the words out of her. "Did you kill Maxwell Wentworth?"

He didn't seem surprised by the accusation. "How badly do you want to know?"

He ran his finger down her chin to her throat and pressed against her carotid artery. "Your heart gives your fear away. Let me ask you something."

She didn't respond. She could barely breathe. Terror nearly suffocated her. Did he want to kill her? How was he going to pull off *this* murder and make it look like an accident?

"Don't you hate these rich fuckers who have it so easy?" He let up a little on her artery.

She blew out a breath. "I don't think about it." *You piece of shit.*

"Sure you do." He backed off just enough to look into her eyes. "How's your mother?"

A chill shimmied down Sam's spine, paralyzing her. She couldn't answer.

"When was the last time you checked on her?"

Her bottom lip quivered involuntarily.

Robert shook his head. "I know. Too emotional to speak." He sneered. "Money would solve so many of your problems. Mine, as well. Yet we have none, and they"—he gestured above him—"they have vast wealth and waste it on foolish things, like diving with sharks."

She struggled to find her voice. "So, you kill them?"

His hands shot around her neck.

She screamed, but his grip cut off the sound as he constricted her airway.

"Only doing what I'm told," he said. "Trying to say something?" He lessened his grip.

"I...can't...breathe," she croaked as she struggled to loosen his hands.

His eyes narrowed, and he squeezed harder. "Where you're going, you won't need to breathe."

"Hey, Samantha? Where are you?" Monica's voice advancing from down the hall.

Thank God! Who'd have thought she'd ever be grateful to hear that voice?

Robert released her and stepped back.

She fell forward, her hands on her knees as she braced herself, dragging in oxygen.

"Whoa! What's going on? Ian?" Monica asked suspiciously.

She stood in the doorway. Sam stood up and reached for the bunk bed to steady herself. Still short of breath, she struggled to speak. "Monica, this man just tried to—"

"Help her with her mother." Robert stepped in front of Monica, blocking Sam from the manager's view. "She's ill, you know, and I was offering Samantha some sound advice on how to keep her mother healthy and alive."

Her mouth dropped open. He had just tried to *kill* her, and now he was threatening to kill her mother. Was he bluffing? What did he know about her mom? Had he done anything to her already?

Automatically she reached for her cell phone. *Crap!* Not on her. And she couldn't get a signal out here, anyway. Until she could call and check on her mom, she couldn't risk exposing the son of a bitch.

Monica twisted a lock of her hair. "Look, there's something you need to know. Zack just surfaced. He's had an accident."

Sam's blood pressure plummeted. A light-headed feeling washed over her. "What? Is he okay?" She sat on the bunk to keep from swaying.

Monica shrugged. Her face white, she didn't look Sam in the eye. "He looks okay, but I'm not sure. The doc is about to check him out. And George..."

"What about George?"

"A tiger shark attacked him." The words flew out like arrows, piercing Sam in the heart.

"Oh, my God!" She addressed Robert, wanting to kick the shit out of him. "Did you know about this?"

"How could I?" he said. "I've been down here playing with you."

Asshole.

"Are you coming up?" Monica's voice shook.

As Sam's stomach somersaulted, she got to her feet and sprinted toward Monica. "Let's go." Sam tugged on the manager's arm. "Is George alive?"

"I don't know. The team is pulling him up right now."

Chapter Nineteen

Sam bolted up the companionway, two steps at a time, making it to the deck of *The Great Escape* breathless and dizzy. She blew past Monica, almost knocking her down.

Her brain cells fired an electrical storm of bad thoughts, and she couldn't tell if the burning sensation in her chest came from her heart or from oxygen deprivation. Either way, her gasps of air barely carried her around the corner of the wheelhouse and onto the main deck.

She searched the deck, desperate for a face she recognized. The topside buzzed with activity, a flurry of feet, and a sea of dark wet suits mixed with frequent flashes of bare skin.

Two crewmembers helped a diver over to a bench. He was still in full gear except for flippers. His body shape was familiar, but he wasn't George.

Her gaze darted across the bow. Where was George? There was no sign of the tall, lanky redhead. She quickly pushed through the bustling bodies and made her way toward the diver on the bench.

He pulled off his mask.

"Zack." Sam took a knee at his side. "Ohmigod, what happened down there?"

He didn't look at her.

Her heart stilled. That wasn't right.

The two other crewmembers unstrapped Zack's tanks. Odd that he would let them. He did everything for himself. The deck hands pulled his arms out of the black harness and vest, and moved the tanks away from his body. The whole time he seemed to be dazed.

"Zack?"

She touched him. His body convulsed. He stared right through her.

"Come on buddy, stand up." The crewmember on the other side of her helped him into a standing position. Another person pulled down the zipper on the back of his wet suit and helped him out of it. Once he was stripped to his swim trunks, he sat back down, and his head crashed forward into his hands.

She held her breath. What the hell was wrong with him?

"Breathe in some of this, mate." A man she recognized as the doctor handed him an oxygen mask. It was attached to a portable machine.

"Why does he need the oxygen?"

"In case he's got the bends."

She looked at Zack, who now stared at her above the mask. His eyes were red, but at least now they'd started to look focused. When he threw her a slow wink, she knew he'd finally recognized her.

That small movement brought a lump to her throat. She blinked back hot tears and smiled, placing her hand gently on his arm. She'd heard of the bends, but didn't know much about the condition other than it could kill.

The doctor knelt down in front of Zack. "Feeling short of breath? In any pain?"

Zack shook his head. He wasn't talking, maybe due to the oxygen mask, so she sent a slew of questions the doctor's way.

"What happened to him down there? Were you there? Did you see it? How did he get the bends? Is it dangerous? Is oxygen going to cure it? Where's George? He was diving with Zack."

Zack pulled the oxygen mask away from his face. "Relax, I'm fine. I can tell you what happened."

"No, you can't. Put the mask back on." The doctor forced the mask back onto his face.

Zack flinched.

"You know the routine. If you have nitrogen bubbles in your bloodstream, you're in trouble, mate. You don't want an embolism in your brain. Breathe in."

The doctor's words sent another rush of anxiety through her. "Will the oxygen stop that from happening?" Her chest started to tighten.

"The pure oxygen helps the nitrogen bubbles dissolve. But he may eventually need treatment in a hyperbaric chamber. We won't know for 24 hours. In 95 percent of cases, symptoms show up within a day."

"Where's George?" Zack had the mask off again.

"You don't know?" She stood up, and her gaze quickly swept the deck. No sign of him, but she did spot Monica standing close by. Her arms were crossed against her chest, and a frown tugged at the corners of her mouth. Why didn't she come over and check on Zack?

"George? That's the tall, red-headed guy?" the doctor asked.

"Yes."

"He's coming up. Probably on a decompression stop." The doctor gestured to Zack. "Unlike your friend here, who just shot to the surface."

Zack pushed the mask away again, obviously irritated. "My vest inflated. I had to use my dive knife to cut the damn hose."

"You saw George? He's all right?" she asked.

"He'd just beat off a tiger shark when I started to surface. I don't know if the tiger got a piece of him, but he was still alive last I saw."

She searched Zack's face for any information he could add. He wouldn't look at her. "Go check on him." His voice sounded hoarse.

"Okay." She hesitated. He didn't look so good. Maybe she shouldn't leave him. But George could be in even worse shape.

"What a freak accident," the doctor said as she got up to leave.

She froze. "Accident?"

"His vest inflating like that."

"They don't usually inflate?"

"Not unless you inflate them on purpose." The doctor sounded impatient.

"I'm a reporter, not a diver, Doc."

"Right." He held up a hand, an apology in his eyes. "The vest is a glorified life preserver. It lets you float on the surface, but also gives you neutral buoyancy underwater. You control the amount of air in the vest." He directed the next comment to Zack. "Why didn't you just press the manual deflate button?"

"It didn't work," Zack mumbled through the mask.

"Did you try the emergency dump valve?"

"That didn't work, either."

The doctor rocked back on his heels. "Holy shit, mate, you could have died." He shook his head. "Like I said, freak accident."

Her gaze locked into Zack's. He shot her a look that said

We'll talk about this later.

"If you feel any numbness, tingling, or paralysis, let me know right away," the doctor said.

Zack took off the mask again. "I know what the symptoms of the bends are. I don't feel anything but aggravated that my vest failed, and pissed off because no one will tell me what the hell happened to my dive partner."

Jenny appeared in front of them, wide-eyed, wet, and dripping blood. "That TV guy is in the water getting ready to come aboard."

"Jenny! What happened to you?" Sam knew Jenny hadn't gone scuba diving. The girl was still in her shorts and company tank top, but they were now wet, her shirt clinging to her like a spring breaker in a wet T-shirt contest.

The cook had both hands covering her nose, but the cloth she held there couldn't stop the flow of blood leaking through her fingers.

"I think I broke my nose." Jenny mumbled through the wet towel. "They told me the doc was over here."

"Sit here." Zack made room for her on the bench. "I'm so sorry that happened to you. Jenny jumped in to help me. When I cut the hose with my dive knife, it deflated the vest to stop my ascent, but once I surfaced I could barely stay afloat with all the heavy gear."

"I saw you struggling. I didn't really think about it. I just jumped in." Jenny appeared to blush under all the blood. "I landed on his tank. My bad. I was trying to save him, and he ended up helping *me* get to the boat."

"Luckily, another diver surfaced and helped us both. Thanks, though." Zack nodded at Jenny. "Seriously. Does it hurt much?" His voice still sounded shaky.

Jenny tried to shake her head, but had trouble moving while holding off the nosebleed. Zack flipped the oxygen mask back onto his face.

A wave of guilt sloshed through Sam. She should have been up on deck waiting for him. She could have helped. She wanted to let Zack know she would have, but at the time, Robert Fitzpatrick had his fingers wrapped around her neck like a boa constrictor.

Instinctively, her hand moved to her shorts where she'd stuffed his phone and driver's license. Despite her mad dash up the stairs, they were still there. She searched around. Too many people stood within hearing range. She couldn't divulge what she was hiding, and it wasn't the time or place to share what had just happened to her.

Zack stared at her with a question in his eyes. "You okay?" he mumbled through the mask.

She offered him an unsure smile, her pulse fluttering.

Without a word, the doctor who had tended to Zack began working on Jenny. He told her to keep her head back and called for tissue and his medical bag.

A flash went off.

The unexpected light caused Zack to squint and Jenny to flinch on the bench.

Sam knew what was happening and whipped around to face the enemy, the hair on her neck standing on end.

Robert's smile spread across his alabaster face.

The asshole was taunting her. He knew she wouldn't call him out in front of all these people, especially now that he'd threatened her mother's safety. She feared what Robert could do to her mother, even from this far out at sea. Maybe he wasn't working alone, and someone back on shore could get to her mother easily. Hadn't he said something about just following orders?

Her muscles tightened with worry. Zack must have sensed the energy shift. He tried to stand, but swayed and sat back down.

The doctor glanced at Zack. "Mate, I wonder if we should

call the Coast Guard? You aren't looking so great."

"No way. I'm not leaving." He had the mask in his hand as he flashed a look at Robert, who still snapped shots of the group. "*Enough.*" His tone left no doubt of his intentions if the jerk kept taking pictures. Then to the doctor, he said, "I'll hit the hyperbaric chamber when we get back to West Palm Beach."

"All right mate, you've got a few days," the doctor said.

The photographer took one last photo.

"I said enough." Zack rose and took a step toward Robert.

"Hey, George is up!" another diver yelled from the back of the boat.

Sam swung around toward the voice in time to see her skinny friend pull himself up the dive ladder, flip over the side of the boat, and crash onto the deck with a loud thud.

"Holy balls!" George's voice boomed. "That was sick!" Her cameraman landed belly down on the deck with his arms stretched out in front of him and the dented camera casing above his head. His forehead rested on the floor, but his words bounced off the wood and reverberated across the stern. Tentatively, he rolled to one side, his tanks still strapped to his back.

Another diver, just off the ladder, slapped him on the butt. He put his hands under George's armpits and pulled him to his knees. "Unbelievable, man. I thought you were a goner." The vacationer, the guy from Los Angeles, dropped to his knees in front of George. They pulled off their masks at the same time. "That was one big fucking shark." The two exchanged a high five, then struggled out of their gear, their mouths moving faster than their hands. The doctor rushed over to George.

Sam's shoulders dropped in disbelief. "He's fine."

"I can see that." Zack attempted a grin, but only managed to get halfway there before he grimaced. She grimaced with him.

"Want to go check on him? I'm headed below deck to change." He stood up, still a little unsteady on his feet.

She worried about this bends thing, but knew better than to baby him, especially in front of all these people. He was the last man on earth who wanted to be coddled.

She moved closer to him. "I need to talk to you."

"About Robert? You talked to him?"

She nodded, and stood on tiptoe so she could whisper into his ear. "He confessed to taking the picture, and I have proof he lied about his name. It is Robert Fitzpatrick. I have his driver's license."

Zack's eyes seemed to light up, but his face was still ashen. "Good job. Very good."

There's more, she wanted to say. *He tried to kill me.* Would attempted strangulation be enough to convince the police that the crazy man was also a killer? But instead, she remained quiet. There were still too many people standing nearby.

George was summoning her by cupping his hands around his mouth. "Holy shit, girl, you will never believe what just happened to me. Get over here."

"Go on." Zack gestured for her to join George. "Go find out what happened to that wild friend of yours."

"Okay," she said reluctantly. "But you still need oxygen."

"I'll change and come right back up."

She nodded, still not moving.

"Sam?" His eyes narrowed.

She knew she had to shake it off and let him take care of himself first. Then she'd fill him in on what had happened to her below deck. She shivered. "I'm fine. Go." She waved him off.

Zack struggled to smile and headed below deck.

She watched him go, rooted to the spot until he

disappeared from sight, her heart aching to go with him. She wanted to wrap herself in his strong arms. By the time she made it over to George, her cameraman looked like the popular kid in class telling dirty stories during recess, with all the wanna-be kids gathered around him, staring in awe.

She pushed her way to him. “So, I hear you got attacked by a twelve-foot tiger shark.”

“I did.” George grinned, his curly wet hair standing up in unruly waves. Red sunburn obscured his youthful freckles, but not his larger-than-life smile.

“I thought you were *bitten* by this tiger shark.”

“Ha! You think I’d be standing here shooting the shit with you if a tiger shark *bit* me? Hell, no. He was no match for *this* dude.” He tipped his thumb at himself.

A chorus of rude comments and laughter rippled through out the group.

“Whatever.” She mimicked George’s favorite comeback. However, inside, a real sense of happiness spread through her. Thank God he was okay.

“The sucker swam straight at me, intending to bite my head off I’m sure, but I put this expensive armour-coated camera casing in front of me like a shield. This badass Gates EX-1 housing unit is worth every damn penny the station paid for it. It’s like something fucking Batman would use. Or Aquaman. They can add shark-proof to the label.”

She surveyed the large dents all over the casing, amazed the shark’s teeth hadn’t done more damage.

“He wrapped his jaws around this mother and tugged. But I wasn’t letting go.” George’s eyes widened as he relayed his story to a fascinated audience. “This camera has some great video in her, and the station would probably make me pay for the damn thing if the shark destroyed it, so I—”

“You were really thinking about how much your camera cost while you were staring a shark in the mouth?” She didn’t believe it for a second.

"Truthfully?"

"Yeah."

"Actually, I was peeing my wet suit."

Laughter exploded around her, and she couldn't help herself. She laughed, too. "So, you won the tug of war with the tiger?"

"Damn right!"

"Why did he pick on you?"

George pointed to his left ankle. His wet suit had been slashed, and he was bleeding.

"I stumbled over some shit on the ocean bottom and cut myself. The cut isn't bad, but I guess the blood was enough to make that big baby come sniff me out." He turned away from her and addressed his fans. "I'm dying to see video of the attack. I don't know if my camera was still functional at that point. Anyone else shoot video or take pictures?"

She stepped back through the crowd. George obviously didn't need her help. He was a rock star, and she'd let him have his fifteen seconds.

"Hey, Sam."

She whipped back around.

"How's Zack?" George asked sheepishly.

"Oh, *now* you remember your dive partner?"

His skin was already so red it was hard to tell if he was blushing.

"He's okay, right? I saw him shoot toward the surface. Couldn't tell what was wrong, and I was a little preoccupied at the time."

She waved him off. "He's fine and ready to hear your big shark story." Both men had faced death and survived. And there was no obvious way to tie either incident to Robert, or any other potential killer, and yet—

She felt his gaze before she actually saw him. Robert

Fitzpatrick stood across the deck, eye behind the camera, snapping pictures of the group of men behind her. Or was he shooting pictures of her? The muscles in her upper back tightened.

Slowly he moved the camera down so his face could be seen. A lopsided, sarcastic grin uglied his already distasteful face.

She couldn't fight off the shivers. She could just call him out right here, right now. Tell George and the handful of men behind her what she'd found out about Robert. He was lying about his name. He'd snapped intimate pictures of her and Zack with the intention of blackmailing her. He had tried to kill her.

But she didn't have enough proof to tie him to the murder of Jackson Hunter, Michael Flint, or Maxwell. Hell, maybe he'd killed Scott Fitzpatrick, too. Robert had said he hated the rich and Scott had been rich beyond her wildest imagination. Maybe his rich relative had refused to share the wealth. That would be motive. And killing Flint would have been necessary if he'd been onto Robert.

The snake continued to stare at her from across the deck. His eyes had narrowed to slits, and his bald head shone in the fading afternoon light.

An uneasy feeling washed over her as she caught him exchanging his camera for what had to be a satellite phone. She'd already found out cell phones didn't work way out here. So, that was how Robert was communicating with the mainland. Her stomach dropped, thinking about her mother's safety. Who could he be talking to? Her mouth went dry as she remembered one of the things he had said to her below deck.

"Only doing what I'm told."

Her fingers flew to her throat. Who had told Robert to put his hands around her neck and squeeze until she couldn't breathe? The person he was talking to right now? Or had he made the decision to kill her on his own?

Unconsciously, she rubbed her throat. Identifying him was clearly only the first step to solving this mystery. But whether he was the ringleader or not, he was obviously ready, willing, and able to commit murder.

Forget about killer sharks.

She was trapped in the middle of the ocean with a *real* monster.

Chapter Twenty

"Man overboard!"

That was the captain's voice. Below deck, Zack stopped dead in his tracks. His stomach dropped. Spinning around, he bolted for the galley, where he'd last seen Samantha. He knew she was likely safe with George, but a growing concern drove him forward. He shouldn't have let her out of his sight, not even for a minute. The last time he'd let a partner wander off—

"Hey, George." Zack bumped into several vacationers as he tried to reach the cameraman. George was in the line of men heading out of the salon where they'd been watching the shark attack video. "Where's Samantha?"

She should have been hugging George's waist or holding his hand, dammit. She had told him what that asshole Fitzpatrick had attempted when she'd checked on him a while ago. It was no longer safe on board for any of them.

George stepped out of the fast-moving line. "I thought she was with you."

The two men stared at each other for a short, meaningful moment. Zack's throat felt like it was closing up. *Shit!* They both bolted toward the companionway. On deck, the glare of harsh white spotlights forced Zack to squint. The sun had set and a strong night breeze blasted him with sea salt. Blinking back the burn, he allowed his eyes to adjust and took in the situation. The captain's assistant stood on the dive platform. The man's back was straight as he pointed toward an object in the water. Zack wasn't close enough to make out what was floating. He shoved his way through the crowd.

In the circle of a spotlight, a body floated face down. Female. But it was her white T-shirt with distinct lettering across its back that caused his heart to seize.

"No! Fuck!"

The University of South Florida T-shirt was the one Samantha had been wearing earlier.

"Shit, that can't be Sam." George pushed to the front.

"Not sure." Zack's knees felt as if they'd give out on him.

"She's not moving." George's voice cracked.

"I'm going in."

"Me, too."

Zack headed toward the lockers that held the dive gear.

"Wait. The boat is powering up." A crewmember grabbed Zack with a firm hand. "The captain will maneuver closer to the body."

The body. Zack closed his eyes in absolute disbelief. *He'd failed again.* The pain searing his center was just as bad as when his uncle had died. He ripped the crewmember's fingers off his upper arm. "I said I'm going in."

"You can't," the crewmember ordered. "It's too dangerous while the boat's moving. We'll need hands to lift her onboard, anyway."

"Plenty of people on deck to do that." Zack looked back at the rippling ocean. "She's drifting too fast." The spotlight had already lost her to the darkness. "I'll stay with her while you bring the ship around."

Again, a firm grip cut into his skin. "I can't let anyone go in. Captain's orders."

Another crewmember approached. "Head count shows two missing."

"Two?" George frowned. Running a hand through his unruly mop of red hair, he turned toward the crowd. "Sam!" he yelled. "Where the hell are you?"

The buzz of the men topside died down temporarily, but Zack didn't wait for a response. Instinctively, he knew there'd be none. Sprinting across the deck, he opened a locker and pulled out the scuba gear he'd used earlier.

He knew attempting a rescue this late at night, while the ship's engines were on and the propellers spinning as the captain maneuvered closer to the body, was suicide. But what else could he do? He swallowed down the acid taste of bile and bitter guilt.

No time to react with emotion. He suited up quickly, the layers going on like armor, shielding his heart from reality. He had been wrong to let Samantha follow him undercover, wrong to let George dive with him, wrong to let himself care about Samantha, and wrong to enjoy seducing her. Wrong on all accounts.

Guilty as charged.

And because of him, she could be dead.

• • •

Sam heard the *man overboard* call. She knew it couldn't be George. From the bathroom, she could hear him holding court in the salon. She couldn't believe these men were still watching the video of his wrestling match with the shark. Alcohol must be involved. They'd already watched it twice.

But the video had suddenly silenced, and there were running footsteps on deck. She poked her head out of the bathroom to see what was going on. Just in time to see Robert Fitzpatrick slip effortlessly in with a few stragglers heading topside. She almost went after him, but stopped as a plan flashed into her mind. She checked left. *No one.* Right. *No one.* Everyone was up on deck. If her heart would stop smacking her chest, she might be able to do this without getting caught.

Moving quickly to the center bunk she knew was Robert's, she searched the area, looking for one thing—his satellite phone. She needed to call her boss and fill him in on what was happening. And she wanted to make sure her mom was okay.

She also intended to call Stuart Johnson and let him know about the attempt on her life. She'd give the Pasco County detective Robert's full name and address and see what he could dig up. Contacting law enforcement would not only point a finger in case something happened to her, George, or Zack, but it would relieve some of the culpability she was feeling. The three of them knew too much. If someone else got hurt, or God forbid died, she would hold herself partially responsible for not disclosing important information just so she could get an exclusive news story and keep her damn job.

Her fingers found a hard metal box tucked into a corner below Fitzpatrick's bunk. *Jackpot.* She paused and listened, half expecting Robert to suddenly appear as he had yesterday. When she heard nothing suspicious, she pulled the box out. It wasn't locked. Odd...

Before going on this trip, she would likely have been feeling a full-blown anxiety attack by this point, too scared to search Robert's stuff again. Now, she felt like a stronger woman, more self-assured, not as afraid, ready to do what was right, no matter the cost.

She opened the box and found the phone inside. She smiled in triumph. Zack would be so proud of her. Now they could call for backup.

• • •

Three-foot swells in the pitch black sea made finding Samantha impossible. The spotlight continued its dance across the black blanket of water, but the crew couldn't hold the light on her body due to the angry tossing of the waves. The winds were kicking up something fierce.

Zack was tiring too quickly because of his accident earlier in the day. His muscles screamed with exhaustion. He was starting to feel dizzy and disoriented when a good-sized wave tumbled him. Rolling over and over in total confusion, he knew his only chance at survival was to use what strength he had left to swim back to the ship.

He had failed her, failed himself, and the self-loathing made his stomach sicker with each watery toss.

He should just let go. Join her in this dark abyss, and never have to worry about failing anyone again. He started to relax, his body giving in.

No. No! His conscience screamed at him.

He couldn't do it. He had to get back on that boat and finish what he'd started. The anguish he felt over losing Samantha would be his punishment, a lifelong pain branded on his heart.

He kicked and began to swim. With the waves smacking the side of the ship, it would be hard to get back on board. Looking up at the blurry faces of the men leaning over the side, Zack wondered if fate would have him die here tonight in a watery grave with a woman who had started to trust him.

A woman who had finally convinced him to start trusting himself.

The woman he had started to fall in love with.

• • •

Sam pushed her way through the men topside, searching

for George and Zack. It didn't take long to locate George. The crowd moved aside to let her through, whispering in her wake. Why were they parting like the Red Sea and looking at her like she was Moses?

She got to George and tapped his shoulder. He jumped as though she'd shocked him with a police Taser.

"Where's Zack?" she yelled above the wind.

"Sam! Jesus Christ!" George pulled her into a tight hug, squeezing her until she couldn't breathe.

"What is wrong with you?" She struggled to speak against his chest. She had to shove him to get him to let go a little. "Why is everyone acting so weird?"

George's eyes glowed like white saucers in the night sky. "We thought the man overboard was *you*."

She stepped back, and the rocking of the ship almost knocked her sideways. Reaching out to grab George, she righted herself. "Why would you think that?"

"Because the man overboard is a *woman*. Wearing a USF T-shirt." George hugged her again. "I saw the body bobbing in the ocean before the spotlight lost it. She even looked the same size as you. I can't believe you're alive."

Sam froze. "Omigod. Jenny!" Her heart sank at the realization that the sweet young girl had fallen overboard. Or had she been pushed? Maybe someone thought Jenny had been her.

"Jenny?" George was yelling to be heard above the roar of the water and wind.

"The cook who jumped in to help Zack and got a bloody nose. She was soaking wet and I gave her my shirt."

"They said two people were missing." George yelled, turning to face the sea again, an eerie slump to his body.

She fell against him, guilt assaulting her. *Jenny was dead.* A dark object bobbed in the water below them, in danger of being smashed against the stern by the waves. "Wait. That's not Jenny."

"No," George yelled. "It's Zack. And we're having trouble getting him back on board."

• • •

Zack's body had been battered repeatedly in the effort to bring him on board. He felt like he'd been run over by a tank.

They finally flipped him up over the rail, and he rolled on the deck until his tanks, heavy on his back, stopped him from moving. A sharp pain hit him under his right lung. He held his breath. He knew he was close to passing out.

Hands all over him expertly removed his scuba gear.

"Zack?"

Now he was hallucinating Samantha's voice. Would that sound be stuck in his head forever? The guilt would kill him if this last dive didn't.

"Answer me."

Or maybe he'd died and this was heaven. Though it sure as hell didn't feel like puffy clouds under him.

"Are you okay?"

Someone finally removed his mask, and he blinked several times to clear the sting and the blur.

"You jumped in to save me," she said.

Samantha! But how?

His breath caught when her lovely, pale face came into focus. She was on her knees next to him, very much alive, peering down at him with those big, beautiful, brown eyes. He opened his mouth, but nothing came out.

"Thank you. Oh, thank you." She threw herself onto him, cradling his wet and shivering body in her arms.

Her body was shaking, too. He wanted to hug her back and squeeze her until she was just as breathless as he was, but his arms felt like heavy logs.

"It was Jenny." Her warm breath was at his ear. "She fell overboard, not me."

He managed a small nod, feeling guilty at the joy rushing through him. He tried to move his mouth again.

Her voice was still right at his ear. "What? I can't hear you."

"Where were you? Why did you leave my side? Never, ever leave my side again," he whispered.

"I'm sorry." She kissed him on his forehead, and her warm lips on his chilled skin caused him to shiver. "I found Robert's satellite phone."

With a curse, he hauled himself up onto one elbow, stars dancing before him. "Help me up."

She shook her head, a firm hand on his shoulder pushing him back down. "Lie still a minute. Let the doc check you out. You almost drowned."

He struggled onto his side and then to his knees. A chorus of voices chimed in, but he couldn't understand any of them. His attention was focused solely on Samantha. "Have you used it yet?" he whispered to her. "The sat phone?"

"No. I couldn't figure out how."

"Good."

"Good?" She frowned, offering a hand to help him up. "Did you hit your head?"

"Hey, are you okay?" George joined them, squatting down to help by putting his hands under Zack's armpits. "I'm going to help you up slowly, man. Let me know if it's too much."

As he was lifted, a sharp pain ignited his right side. Not fucking good. He'd probably bruised a rib. He held his breath, but it didn't assuage the fiery pain. He let out a curse.

"I'm putting you back down." George started to lower him.

"No." Zack wobbled on his feet, but did manage to stand

on his own. "I need you to get me to my bunk."

"I think the captain wants to talk to you first," a voice rang out. "And the doc."

Great. He gestured for Samantha to come closer.

"Who did you plan to call?" But Zack already knew the answer.

"The authorities," she whispered. "Someone needs to know what's going on out here. Especially now that Jenny has died. This is crazy. You almost died twice today."

She tried to touch his face. He pulled away. He had to make her understand. "The captain already called the Coast Guard." He swung his arm around George's shoulder and motioned him to start walking. The crowd that had gathered around them made way.

"Well, I'm calling my detective friend, too," she said over the chattering of the crowd.

Zack checked around to see if anyone had picked up on that, but it was hard to tell. "You can't do that," he said with a ferocity he hoped would stop the conversation for now. Jesus, she was about to blow it big time.

"Why not?" she demanded. "You're a cop yourself."

"Can you say that a little louder?" he ground out. "Not sure everyone heard you."

"So?" She wasn't even trying to hide their conversation.

"So, there's something you're forgetting." He braced for her reaction.

"What?" She threw up her hands.

"Can we *please* take this below deck so we're not causing a scene?" Even talking hurt like hell, let alone walking. What happened to the woman who was cradling his head like he was her dying lover?

"Fine." She blew past him.

"Oh, boy. She's pissed," George said.

"No shit." With George's help he struggled down the

stairs, his legs weak as boiled noodles, his muscles burning from overuse.

At the bottom of the stairwell, she planted herself in his path. He swallowed and leaned on George for support. They were alone, but wouldn't be for long. He spit out the truth. "You can't call the cops because my superiors don't know I'm here."

She fisted her hands on her hips. "Well, I think it's time we told them. We need backup. Robert tried to kill me. If we find solid evidence that Robert killed other vacationers, how do you plan on bringing him to justice, if the Florida Department of Law Enforcement can't even know you're here?"

Zack held her gaze. "The Coast Guard could take him into custody. I wouldn't have to be involved."

Tears crested her lashes. "I can't believe this. Jenny just died! You know what I think? I think someone pushed her off this boat because they saw her in my shirt. It was dark out. She's my size, has my hair color. We're all in danger here. We need backup."

"I need you to trust me, Samantha."

"I can't trust you to keep us safe if you're dead."

"The Coast Guard is on the way to escort us back to land. The game has changed now that Jenny is dead. Please, I'm asking you to wait to make any calls until the Coast Guard arrives. Give me that time to find some proof, because once the Coast Guard takes over, our access to this boat and everyone on board is over."

He was right, and she knew it. They were getting closer, ruffling the feathers of those involved. She could feel it. "If I wait, we stay together. You do not leave my side Zack Hunter, not once."

Relief flooded his tired eyes. "Deal."

"I mean it." She looked at Zack, and then at George. "We three stay together to stay alive."

Chapter Twenty-One

Zack sat in the front seat of the rented Ford Focus. He'd parked in the lot of a low-rent strip mall across from the Sailfish Marina in West Palm Beach. It was almost midnight, and his attention was focused on the ramp exiting *The Great Escape.*

The air hung heavy despite the car's air-conditioning. By morning, all the X-Force crew and clients would be gone, and with them would go any remaining clues to his uncle's death.

"How did you manage to get us off the boat before anyone else?" Samantha said from the backseat. They were the first words she'd spoken since they'd disembarked about twenty minutes ago. "Detectives were making everyone pack up their gear and wait topside to be interviewed. They wanted to question each person about Jenny's death. Why not us?"

"I told the lead detective I was with the FDLE, on vacation, and that I have the bends and have an appointment to get into a hyperbaric chamber at West Palm Memorial. He's familiar with the bends so he told me to get going."

Sitting in the driver's seat, he gripped the wheel, wishing

this shit would go down already. He was getting nervous they'd missed their suspect.

George sat next to him in the front passenger seat with his video camera perched on his shoulder and his eye glued to the eyepiece, ready to catch anything interesting.

Samantha wedged her body forward into the space between the two front seats. "I get the professional courtesy thing, but why didn't they question us?"

She was releasing her nervous energy by bouncing her knee, rocking the back of his seat. Over and over. It was pissing him off. "I told the detective you were documenting my trip, not actually a lie, and the hyperbaric chamber would be part of it. I told him I'd bring you back to him to interview later." He took a deep breath, pausing before he continued. "And I promised him that if he let us go right now, you'd let him have the video George shot over the past few days."

Her hand slapped the back of his seat. "You what?"

"Samantha—"

"You can't promise him that! You're going to get me in trouble."

"We're already in trouble," George said. "The fucking news director has been blowing up my phone since I got a signal again. And he's left a ton of messages. We're fucked, no matter what."

Thank you, George, for taking some of the damn heat off me by shifting her attention.

Samantha sat back forcefully, the backseat creaking as her body connected with it. "Stan is blowing up my phone, too."

"Listen, let's focus on the positive." Zack had to redirect his team. "We're off the boat. Robert can't touch you anymore. You've called to check on your mother and she's fine. We still have a few hours to try and dig something up on Robert. When he exits, we follow him."

Samantha made a disgruntled sound.

Just as he suspected, not the right answer. He sighed inwardly. She would always be a challenge. He knew that. But he didn't mind. It seemed…right to have her by his side. "Let's just focus on the plan."

God, he would miss her when she left.

"The plan. Right." George wiggled around in the front seat, probably trying to get the blood moving in parts of his long body that had been still for a while. "I wish to hell those cops would wrap their shit up and let everyone go, so we can get going on this *plan*. My shoulder is killing me. And I'm seriously hungry."

"I've got a protein bar," Samantha offered.

"Chocolate?"

"No, blueberry."

George shifted in his seat. "You know I like chocolate. Who the hell eats blueberry protein bars? Gross."

She made a clicking sound. Zack couldn't see her but imagined the roll of her eyes.

"You want it or not?" she said.

Family, Zack thought as he listened to them bicker. They sounded like brother and sister. That kind of intimacy was exactly what he'd longed for since leaving his uncle's house. And he had found it in the most unlikely of places—on a stakeout, in a shit-smelling car, next to a stinky dumpster in some low-rent strip mall. He smiled.

"Action." George sat up straighter, banging his head on the car roof. "Ouch!"

Zack tensed, his fingers tightening on the wheel. A few people were now leaving the ship.

Samantha leaned forward again. "We're too far away to make out who it is."

Zack squinted. He could make out bodies, but no faces.

"Not a problem," George said. "The camera can zoom

in."

"Do it." Zack held one hand on the ignition key, should they need to move quickly.

"The detective is the first guy," George responded. "The dude from Texas and his doctor buddy are walking off the boat next. Monica is with them. I see…"

"Who? Don't even blink, George." Samantha sounded breathless and pissed. "That snake has a bad habit of slithering away before you can stop him."

"I've got him," George said. "Robert Fitzpatrick just walked off the boat, and he's headed toward the parking lot."

Samantha craned forward. "Follow him with the camera."

"Yeah, thanks, Sam." George snorted. "I almost forgot what I was doing here."

"Sorry, I'm just nervous."

George adjusted in his seat. "He's– Oh shit, I lost him."

"George!" Samantha's voice squeaked as she smacked the back of George's seat.

"Come on, man, find him." Zack's own tone surprised him. His military training helped him remain calm, even in the most stressful of situations. Once you'd survived being shot at, not much else could raise alarm. But tonight, he wanted—no, he *needed*—to nail Fitzpatrick with something, even if it was only attempted murder for what he'd done to Samantha.

"I think…no, shit. That's the doctor." George let out an explosion of expletives.

"Use the zoom," Samantha said. "Find him."

"Yeah, I know how to work a camera. You are getting on my last nerve tonight."

"Let's all take a deep breath," Zack ordered, wanting to keep this train on the right track. They had only seconds before their chance would be lost.

George shifted in his seat, moving the camera to an odd

angle in Zack's direction. "I've got him!"

"Thank God," Samantha whispered the words he was thinking.

"Yeah, he's getting into a red Impala. Give me a second. Zooming in. License plate is ZKY45O. Florida plates."

A familiar burn ignited in Zack's belly. "Yes! We're back in this, people. Robert is on the move. Let's see where's he going and who he might lead us to."

Chapter Twenty-Two

As Zack drove, the highway lights rolling past splattered harsh white images across his face. His skin was pale and his cheeks drawn.

He looked like he was about to collapse. Sam could relate. She was definitely miserable. They'd been following Fitzpatrick north on Interstate 95 as he maneuvered in and out of traffic for a couple of hours now.

She checked out George. His head rested awkwardly on the headrest, and he held his camera on his lap. His eyes remained partially open, almost like a dead man's, but the rhythmic breathing from his half-opened mouth told her he was asleep. How he could sleep right now, she could not fathom. Nerves were keeping her wide-awake.

Robert Fitzpatrick continued to dodge slow cars in the fast lane like a man on a mission. She sighed, wishing he'd just get to wherever the hell he was going.

Zack glanced back at her. "You doing okay?"

She glanced up in surprise. They hadn't spoken much since the trip started. She'd been focused on gathering some info with her smartphone now that they were on land and she had 4G again. She hesitated to answer. He sounded weary, too. Why worry him? "I'm fine. Just a little hungry, that's all." The protein bar hadn't satisfied her cravings, nor had it stopped the rumble in her belly.

"Me, too. Any more snacks up your sleeve?" he asked.

She dug through her big black bag, but her stash was spent. "No, but I have a Flintstone vitamin and two Altoids. Oh, and half a piece of Big Red."

Zack released a sound that could have been a grunt or laugh. "I'll take an Altoids. Hey, George snores."

"Yeah." She stopped to listen. "Never did learn how to turn that off." Her gaze flickered back to Zack's chalky face. "Are *you* feeling okay?"

"I've been better."

"How long can you wait to get treatment if you have the bends?" His ashen face told her he could pass out at any moment. That fear kept her awake. She should be driving not him. But he'd said no. He was fine.

"I don't have any symptoms, really. I'm just tired. And even if I do have the bends, I've got about 10 days to get into that hyperbaric chamber. No rush. I'm not going to die tonight."

Funny. "What happened down there while you were diving?"

He shook his head. "I'm not sure." His shoulders rolled. "And that really pisses me off. The bastard must have messed with the BCD valve on my vest because the damn thing inflated on its own for no reason. A BCD valve can theoretically malfunction, especially if it's old, but the vest was nearly new and I checked it thoroughly before I put it on. How he pulled that off, I'll never know, but one thing I do know."

She sat forward. "What's that?"

"I know how the asshole stopped the manual deflate button from working."

"How?" She held her breath.

"Superglue."

"Huh?"

"The jerk glued the button in place so it wouldn't depress when I tried to dump air out of the vest. I could feel the hard edge of the glue when I reinspected the vest after the dive. Think how easy it would be to spread a few drops in all the right places."

"When I saw him near your gear. Damn. I *knew* he was up to something."

"I should have listened."

That statement should have sent a sense of power surging through her. Instead, relief washed over her with such intensity her heart skipped.

"I pulled the cord to open the dump valve in the back of my vest—the last resort safety device—and the damn cord broke."

"He superglued that, too?" she asked, gooseflesh creeping up her arms. How could a person be so deviously sinister?

"It's insulting."

"Why?"

"How simple his plan was, and how well it worked. I should have—"

"You couldn't have foreseen a few drops of superglue *after* you checked your gear."

He nodded, but his jaw was set in a hard line. "I should have checked again." He exhaled. "Anyway. You never did tell me what else you found in his bunk while I was diving."

Just like him to steer the subject off himself. "Well, we've both been a little busy." She cleared her throat. "I found his phone as you know." She'd filled him in on that earlier. "And his license. When I pulled his ID out, something fell on the floor."

"A signed confession?"

She laughed. "Could we be so lucky? No, a newspaper article."

He frowned back at her in the rearview mirror. "About what?"

"It was about a reporter in New York who died in a freak accident." She shuddered. "It gave me the heebie-jeebies."

His gaze locked into hers in the mirror. "*Another* freak accident?"

"Or not." Her stomach fluttered as she eyed the Impala. The traffic was finally letting up, and it was one of the few cars left on the road this late at night. "Don't follow too closely. He'll pick up on us."

"I've trailed a car or two in my career."

"Right. Sorry," she mumbled. They were all so tired. "Anyway. The article said this reporter and photographer were covering a story on the Upper East Side three years ago. They had a microwave truck parked on the street, and they'd sent their mast up for the live remote."

"Like a giant antenna, right?"

"Yeah. It sends the signal with the video and sound to the TV station."

His forehead pleated. "Let me guess. Struck by lightning?"

"Close. Going up, it hit an electrical wire. Both the reporter, who was getting something from inside the van, and the photographer, who was raising the mast, were electrocuted on the spot."

"Jesus."

"Our managers make us take safety classes every so often, but that kind of accident does happen from time to time. Employees get careless. But I can't help but think..."

"That it could have been deliberately set up?"

"It did happen about the same time Robert's uncle, Scott Fitzpatrick, was appearing in court on charges. And this reporter had exclusive information on where Scott had been hiding his money. I've been reading a couple of her old online reports on my smartphone while you've been driving. Sounds like a motive for murder, don't you think? Kill the reporter who exposed you?"

Zack released air in a long, slow whistle and met her gaze in the rearview. "Robert carried that newspaper article around with him for *three years*?"

"Even weirder, right?" A flurry of movement in front of their car caught their attention. "Hey. What's happening?" Her pulse kicked up.

The car jerked as Zack floored it. "He's turning."

She sat back and held on. "Do you think he knows we're behind him?"

He ripped the wheel to the right. "Hope to hell not."

Fitzpatrick took the exit off I-95, but she couldn't read the sign in the passing streetlights. "I think he turned east, right? If so, he's heading for the beach."

"You sure?"

"I've lived in Florida all my life. He's going toward…wait. I see a sign. Port Orange."

"Where the hell is that?"

"Between Daytona Beach and New Smyrna Beach. Turn! Turn!"

He did, so sharply George fell sideways into the door.

"Hey, what the—" George wrenched up in the seat, clutching his TV camera as the car sped around the corner.

The Impala continued east on a two-lane road through a residential neighborhood.

"What the hell is he doing in suburbia-land?" George, now very much awake, peered out the window at the cookie-cutter houses.

Zack glanced his way. "Good question."

"It's where normal people live," Sam said. "Nothing exciting ever happens here. Look. He's turning." She pointed.

"I can't get too close. He'll see us."

The streetlights thinned out as they traveled further away from the main drag and down a narrow street.

"What a perfect place to hide," she muttered.

"If you're a murderer." Zack said quietly.

The red Impala crossed over a bridge from the mainland onto a peninsula, and made a turn onto the A1A, the highway that ran along the coast.

George yawned. "Why am I not surprised we're back near the ocean?"

"Hey." Zack slowed down. "He's turning into a marina. Can you catch the name?"

She checked to her left. Bathed in glow of a streetlamp, she read the sign. "How appropriate. Adventure Yacht Harbor."

Zack cut the lights as he eased off the road into a parking lot across from the harbor. He drove into a dark corner and put the car in park, but left it idling.

The Impala was parked in a handicap spot close to the marina's entrance. A restaurant sat right next to the gate, directly in front of them.

Fitzpatrick jumped out of the car and took off walking with purposeful strides.

"You have to get me closer," George mumbled. "It's too dark and too far away to make out details. I won't be able to follow in the viewfinder if he walks much farther."

"If I move the car now, he might pick up on us."

Sam glanced at the car clock. Two thirty a.m. The night was dark under a half moon and simple street lighting. Only a handful of people buzzed around the restaurant. Otherwise, all was quiet.

The marina had four long docks, and almost every slip was occupied by either a sailboat, live-aboard, or in a few cases, small yachts. If Fitzpatrick took a stroll down any of those docks, George would lose him. He would have to get out of the car and track him on foot—without attracting unwanted interest.

"I think we may be in luck," George said with a grin.

She pushed forward so she could see what he was talking about. Fitzpatrick was walking toward a yacht moored at the jetty alongside the marina boardwalk.

The vessel, which might be able to sleep five or six, had elegant lincs. Even in the minimal light, Sam could tell it was either new or very well maintained. She sucked in a sharp breath at the name painted on the hull.

Catch Me if You Can.

"Someone has a sense of humor," Zack said dryly.

"Or maybe the owner is just an arrogant bastard," she muttered.

George sat up in his seat. "I've got someone. Top deck, near the pilothouse."

A door opened and a man walked out. He stood against the railing of *Catch Me if You Can*, a cigar in one hand and a glass of liquid in the other.

"The guy is wearing sunglasses. What's up with that?"

"Yeah, I'm zooming in. Hey, I got Fitzpatrick, too. He's on board."

Fitzpatrick now stood next to the man in sunglasses. They were fairly close in age. And height. And…

A thought suddenly smacked her in the head.

No. Impossible. It couldn't be.

Nevertheless, she strained to see more.

George let out a long whistle. "Who do you think Mr. Sunglasses is?"

And yet, it would make perfect sense. And answer a lot of

their questions about motive.

"The boss." Zack's hands gripped the wheel.

How he'd managed to pull it off would be a whole other question.

She sat up straight. "Guys. I think I know who it is. Keep shooting video, George. Give me a second."

She reached for iPhone. Her heart cartwheeled inside her chest as she opened her web browser. She typed in a name. *Holy shit. Holy shit.* "Holy shit!"

"Sam?" Zack glared back at her.

"Give me a minute." But she couldn't stop looking at the pictures popping up on the screen.

"They're talking. Looks like Fitzpatrick is doing some explaining, and the sunglass man isn't happy about it," George said.

"Get me a close up on the new guy's face," she ordered excitedly.

Zack kept glaring. "Samantha..."

George made some quick adjustments and rocked the camera to his other shoulder. She leaned forward and looked through his eyepiece.

"I knew it." Her heart galloped like a Kentucky Derby winner crossing the finish line as she double-checked the photos on her smartphone.

"Do you have an ID?" It was the first time Zack had really sounded like a cop. He turned to look at her, his dark eyes hidden in the shadows.

"Yeah, I..."

"Who. Is. He?" Zack's voice dropped into a lower register. He sat perfectly still. The air around them crackled.

George broke the tension. "They're gone. They went inside the yacht." He hauled the camera off his shoulder and dropped it onto his lap.

She handed her iPhone to Zack. George leaned over

to stare at the screen, too. "Hot damn, that looks like Mr. Sunglasses, all right."

Zack was still glued to her smartphone, his face a mask of intensity. "Scott Fitzpatrick."

"Yeah." She sat back and nodded. "A dead man walking."

Chapter Twenty-Three

Zack let out a low whistle. “If Scott Fitzpatrick is on that yacht…who is buried in his coffin?”

“He faked his own death?” George asked, incredulous. “Can you really do that?”

“Apparently. I guess if you have enough money, anything is possible,” Samantha muttered. “Robert must have helped him.”

Zack could hear the satisfaction in her voice. He felt it, too. Together, they’d found the killer—or rather, killers. Because now, there really wasn’t any doubt. An itchy feeling of anticipation spread throughout his body.

“Now we need to find out why,” George said.

“Scott’s motive is pretty obvious,” Zack said. “Fifty-eight federal counts of fraud, money laundering, and conspiracy is powerful motivation to disappear. Robert’s…not so clear-cut.”

“I bet you a million dollars it also has to do with money.” Samantha leaned forward. Her breath hit his ear in warm bursts.

"Any theories?"

"When Robert was choking me he spit out something about rich people and hating them for spending money on stupid things like adventure vacations. I bet Scott held the purse strings, and Robert did whatever he said, but secretly resented Scott for it."

"Good reasoning. Makes sense." Zack loved the way her sharp brain worked. "But then why help Scott fake his own death and help hide him?"

"Money of course. Without Scott, Robert might have nothing. My guess, anyway. Let's go see if I'm right."

Her car door opened.

The smile dropped off his face. In half a second, she had jumped out. Where the hell did she think she was going? He ripped open his own door and followed. "Hey, what are you doing?"

"*Ssh!*" Her finger flew to her mouth as they both eased the car doors shut.

He took a quick look around. The Fitzpatricks were still inside the yacht. The parking lot was empty and dark. The few people across the street at the marina restaurant probably couldn't see them in the limited light. He hoped they hadn't blown their cover when the car's overhead light had switched on and off.

He pulled her into a darker area behind the Ford and got right up in her face. "What the hell are you doing?" He fought to keep his voice under control.

"I'm going to interview Scott Fitzpatrick."

"Like hell you are." Her confidence while making that comment sucked the wind out of him. *This* was the same woman who had panicked when the camera was on her less than three weeks ago? He liked the change, and wished he could let her go bust Fitzpatrick's balls, but it was too dangerous. "Not without backup."

She wagged a finger at him. "You don't have backup."

"Neither do you."

"I only need a cameraman. And I've got one of those. Do you know how many uncertain situations I've walked into?"

"None like this, I'm sure. The man's a murderer."

"He won't dare touch me. You want to know why?"

"It doesn't matter." He reached for her hand.

She smacked him away. "Because no one is stupid enough to commit a crime with a TV camera in their face."

"Unless they kill you, too, and smash the camera." Zack shook his head and grasped her firmly. "Forget it. I'm not letting you do this."

"You can't stop me."

He tightened his hold, so tight he could feel the pounding of her pulse. "I just did."

She tugged to get away. "Don't you want to know what Robert Fitzpatrick's motivation is?"

"Of course. But we need to regroup and come back with a plan."

"I've learned from years of experience as a reporter that you stand a better chance of getting a bad guy to talk if the element of surprise is on your side."

"You honestly think if you walk over there in your sexy little shorts, Scott Fitzpatrick will invite you onboard his yacht and spill his secrets while sipping expensive wine with George's camera rolling?"

"Why not? You did."

Ouch. Zack's faced flamed. She was on fire tonight. He wished he knew exactly what emotion, or hormone, was fueling this feistiness. "Get your story right. It was Grey Goose."

She smiled and he felt the tension go out of her wrist. He relaxed his grip. Instantly, she bolted around the back of the car to the other side. "George, let's go."

Un-fucking believable. She was going to get them caught. Or get herself killed. Where was all this newfound courage coming from?

George jumped out of the car. When Samantha hurried up to him, much to Zack's surprise, he put his right arm out and stopped her. "I happen to agree with Zack."

"Thank you," Zack said, storming over to her.

"You're going to let him get away?"

"I have him on video," George answered. "That will prove he's alive. We know where he's hiding."

"Not if he heads out to sea, taking Robert with him." Even though George towered over her, Samantha's energy made her seem just as tall.

"The three of us can't corner him." Zack pointed to the yacht. "If we go over there right now, they could kill us all and nobody would ever be the wiser."

"How? We'll be videotaping him. He's in a public marina. People will hear." Samantha's voice vibrated with frustration.

"He'll take us out to sea, where he'll throw my camera overboard, right after he dumps our bodies."

"He's right." Zack fingered the cell phone in his pocket, anxious to make a call. He needed to get both George and Samantha back in the car and out of the line of sight of the men on the boat.

"You didn't even tell our news director where we were going tonight," George pointed out.

"How could I? I didn't know where we were headed until we got here."

"I didn't tell anyone either." George glanced at him. "Zack?"

"Let's take a breath." He walked around the car front to stand next to them. "Do you realize what we just got on tape?"

"Yes. But it's not enough. What do *you* propose we do?"

she asked.

"I have a few friends in law enforcement…"

"But they don't know you're here. And you can't tell them."

Sarcasm again. "What's with you tonight?" Zack asked.

"Hey, hey." George stepped between him and Samantha. "Is this high school, or what? I say we find a hotel and sleep for the night."

"Are you serious? You're giving up?" Her exasperation was evident.

"No, but my camera batteries are. We've got to recharge them. How are we going to confront Robert and his dead uncle if the camera batteries are dead? Besides, I need to pee. And I need to eat. I need sleep, and about a hundred aspirin. If I have to kick some ass to save yours, you're in big trouble. I can barely move."

"I can't believe this." She shoved past George.

What a little hellcat. Zack reached out to stop her. "We'll come back first thing tomorrow morning. Before the sun comes up."

"They'll be gone."

"No, they won't. I'll make sure they don't go anywhere. All it takes is one phone call."

"What phone call? To who?" She walked up to him, stood on tiptoe, and put both hands on his chest. If she was trying to distract him, it was working. He could feel the heat where her palms lay flat against his clothing. "How do you know that?"

"Know what?" He stepped away from her. *Focus, man.*

"That Robert and Scott Fitzpatrick won't leave before we have a chance to talk to them."

"It's almost dawn and they haven't slept. Look at the yacht. They just turned all the lights off. They won't be up for a while."

A twinge of guilt dug into him. He'd already decided to

call the local PD and ask for their assistance. They'd have no reason to check his credentials overnight. They could keep an eye on *Catch Me if You Can* until dawn and assist if there were any problems in the morning. In fact, he might even call his superior at the FDLE and ask for backup. What could they say when he told them he'd located a dead man with fifty-eight criminal indictments who'd cheated prosecution.

"You heard George. You don't even have a camera to record anything. What else can you do tonight?"

Samantha looked at the yacht and lifted both hands in surrender.

Thank God. Gently, he put his arms around her, giving her a comforting squeeze. He moved her around as if slow dancing, so he could take another peek at *Catch Me if You Can.*

An overwhelming sense of contentment washed over him. Finally, he knew who had masterminded the murder of his uncle. All he needed to know now was why. And he had to keep Samantha from revealing what they'd uncovered to the rest of the world until he had a chance to prove it, and arrest Scott and Robert Fitzpatrick and anyone else involved.

At the same time, a rush of yearning heated his blood. He knew exactly how he'd distract her, so she wouldn't brood about it all night. Or call her boss and get the media frenzy rolling.

He buried his head in the nape of her warm neck so she couldn't see him smile. Who needed sleep, anyway?

Chapter Twenty-Four

Sam threw open the door to room 106 of the Sandcastle Suites on A1A in Port Orange, her temporary home for the night. She was glad that Zack and George intended to share a room because, frankly, she was still pissed at both of them for forcing her to wait to confront that snake and his uncle. Zack might have his answers, but she still desperately wanted to know what Maxwell Wentworth had to do with all of this. Why her friend had died was still an unknown, and she intended to get that answer. And she needed to get some justice for Jenny. She couldn't help but feel responsible for her death.

She reached into her dark room, fumbling for the light switch. Where the hell was it?

Suddenly, strong fingers curved around her waist and warm breath tickled the back of her neck. She recognized the spicy masculine scent of him. She stilled. "Zack?"

"Hi," he whispered, his voice husky and hot.

A little tremor raced down her back. "I thought you'd gone with George to your room."

"He's taking a shower." Zack gently pushed her forward before she could flip the switch on. "I'm giving him some privacy."

The muskiness that had settled on his skin on their long drive up the coast touched off a visceral response in her. He smelled like such a *man*. She closed her eyes as intoxicating warmth rushed into her middle. "Um…how about you give me time to take a shower, too?"

"I like it dirty." He chuckled.

She pushed against him. "Funny." She walked into the dark room, unable to see a thing. "Zack?"

The door shut, followed by silence. Was he here? Did he leave? God, her nerves were shot, but every part of her was tingling.

She couldn't even hear him breathe. But she could feel the energy he was putting off. The hair on her arms and neck sizzled with the anticipation. She stood still, waiting.

The floor creaked in front of her. The air conditioner clicked on. Maybe the hum of the unit would drown out the beating of her heart, because it was pounding so loudly. "What are you doing?" she whispered.

"Wild guess." His voice was right in front of her. Reaching out, her fingertips grazed his chest. He pulled back.

She stepped forward and searched for him, wanting to touch him again. Nothing. She shook her head, a bit dizzy. "Can you turn on the light?" she murmured. "I want to see you."

"We don't need light to do what we're about to do."

"Then why are you making me wait?"

"For what, baby?" His finger found its way to her mouth. His rough skin brushed against her bottom lip, igniting a wave of heat that rushed through the rest of her body.

Feeling wicked and a bit out of control, she pulled his finger into her mouth. Slowly, she sucked the tip and then stroked it with her tongue.

He groaned.

His free hand moved into her hair and he bunched up a handful. "I need to tell you something." He tipped her head back with just enough force that her scalp throbbed in an almost orgasmic wave. He knew just the right amount of pressure to bring her right to the point where pleasure met pain, but pleasure still won.

She swallowed, suddenly wary. "What?"

"I need to thank you," he whispered.

Relief flooded through her. "There are so many ways to do that. Can I show you the ways I prefer?" She didn't want to fight with him anymore. Not when he'd barely touched her and already had her body throbbing with need. "You can start by kissing me."

He laughed but never released the grip on her hair.

"We found the murderer." He sounded a little drunk, even though he hadn't had a sip of alcohol.

"We did." She barely got the words out. His tongue teased the sensitive skin behind her earlobe. The wetness of his kiss traveled across her jaw. She ached for more. "Let's celebrate." She reached for him.

He brushed her hands away. "Oh, I intend to." His lips moved up to meet her mouth.

She opened her lips to greet him. Just the touch of his tongue on hers made her shiver with need. She wrapped her arms around his waist and tugged his body up against hers, kissing him deeply.

He didn't resist.

She couldn't remember a time she had wanted a man more. She ached physically to connect with him. But it was about more than just that. She'd fallen in love with this man.

The realization stilled her.

He must have sensed her hesitation, because he whispered

her name into their kiss. He stepped forward, urging her backward. The back of her legs hit the bed. She let herself fall. Landing on the bedspread, the rough, thick material did nothing to stop the hard rush of desire ripping through her. He followed her down, covering her with his body.

She pushed up and into him. She was so high on adrenaline and need, she thought she'd have an orgasm without even taking her clothes off.

He made a guttural sound and slowly rocked his hips, grinding his hard cock into her. "You drive me crazy."

"I'm the one who's going crazy right now." Anxious to feel his flesh against hers, she reached down to undo his fly. His hands met hers. Together they battled, quick and clumsy, over the metal buttons.

Moaning an incoherent medley of words, he jumped off the bed. He pulled off his shirt, his shoes, and pulled down his jeans and boxers, reaching into the pocket before tossing them aside and sheathing himself.

The moonlight filtered through the drapes, allowing her enough light to make out his muscular arms and chiseled chest. Another wave of desire rocked her flesh with goose bumps. His abs were ripped and his thighs muscular, but it was his cock that had her breathless. Jesus. She clamped her legs together, her muscles clenching with desire.

She followed his lead, tearing off her clothes in fast, furious movements, while never taking her attention off his body. She tossed her clothes over the side of the bed.

He crawled back onto the bed and pulled her to him. She rolled on top, mesmerized by how hot his flesh was. Her goose bumps melted into liquid fire, warming her from the outside in. She leaned down for a kiss—achy, wet, and needy. "Please touch me now."

He laughed a hot breath into her mouth, denying her what she longed for, and rolled her onto her back. He pulled her arms high above her head and gathered both of her hands into a vise hold, rendering her helpless.

"Zack, you're such a control freak." Her heart fluttered, scared by the wave of vulnerability washing over her and, at the same time, high from the way his actions pushed her closer to the point of release.

"*You*, my dear, are the control freak."

She bucked against his hold—part in play, part in earnest. He held her wrists with his left hand, while his right hand tickled its way down her side, fingers moving across her stomach, walking over her hipbone. She squealed as he hit a particularly sensitive spot.

She wiggled beneath him and struggled to free her hands. Not that she wanted to get away, but the intensity was almost too much to bear. She shut her eyes and arched her back, straining against him. With a sigh, she melted into the bedspread, ready for him to take her.

"Not so fast," he whispered.

The lingering was like torture. "Why not?"

He nuzzled her neck. "What's your rush? On deadline tonight?"

"Always on deadline."

"And always so demanding?" Zack let go of her hands and spread her legs wide.

The sudden and brazen move shocked her. She'd never felt so exposed.

He ran one finger over the most sensitive part of her, now swollen. She bucked up at the bliss that little touch caused.

"Is this what you want?" He stroked her, his fingers expertly massaging her, until the tide within her began to swell and rise.

She couldn't hold back much longer. She moaned. "Yes. That feels so damn good."

"You're so wet." He sounded pleased.

She pushed against him, wanting more. "More. I can't wait."

"Greedy little..."

She grabbed the back of his head and pulled him down, forcing his mouth back onto hers.

This time he didn't fight her. As his mouth consumed hers, he moved his body over her and thrust into her. He was huge and the friction of his entry sent a tidal wave of pleasure over her. When the length of him filled her completely, she cried out. "Zack!" Grabbing the bedspread with her fingers, she closed her eyes as the delicious rippling of a slow orgasm overtook her. Oh, God, she'd needed this.

He moved slowly at first, but she clawed at his back, wanting it harder and faster. She couldn't get enough of him. She needed to feel him. She'd been starving, and hadn't even realized it, but this was the feast she'd been craving all her life.

"I love you." She whispered the words against his moist skin as she savored the pleasure.

His body froze.

So did she.

Omigod, I didn't just say that.

He lifted his head. "Samantha, I—"

She waited. Her heart trilled against her chest like fast fingers on a flute. *Oh, please.* An unexplainable ache roared through her. *Say something. Anything.*

He bent down to kiss her, and she tasted salt on his lips. "Please, let me in" she said. "Tell me what you're feeling. I need to know."

He answered with another deep kiss—slow but strong enough to keep her from forming any more words. Her body pulsated, waiting for him to start moving again, to pick up the intensity, to get back to where they were before she'd thrown out those careless words and doused the raging fire.

But her heart was also desperate for him to return her sentiment in words, not just actions.

• • •

Zack sensed her emotional withdrawal. She wasn't kissing him back with the same abandon as before. He wanted—no, he needed—her wet, hungry, and wanton as she'd been just seconds ago.

Just tell her, the voice in his head screamed.

But loving words had never come easy for him. He had to find a way to *show* her he loved her. He reverted to the way he knew best, the thrill of physical pleasure.

He continued to kiss her, not letting her speak again. Her lips, swollen from their rough kisses, had proven her passion.

Now he was going to prove to her that she couldn't live without him, because he knew now he couldn't live without her. He was going to make her cry out with uncontrolled pleasure. Make her his forever. Leave that mark on her like he'd told her back at the Orange Grove sink. He stroked her, slowly and deliberately. He also rocked his hips, picking up the pace again. He knew how to hit her spot internally. Once he did that—

"Zack," she moaned and arched her back.

His heart swelled. He loved the way she moaned his name and pushed against him. He had plenty to give her. He'd been waiting all his life to find the right person to receive the love he'd bottled up.

Her hands grasped his head and tugged at his hair.

She was close.

He intensified the speed. She was so fucking wet, and that was all the proof he needed that she was his. First, her thighs stiffened, then her back arched again, and she let out a sound he couldn't describe. Just watching her joy pushed him over. He lost himself in the ripples and tremors of her muscles as they gripped his cock. He threw his head back and came with her.

Tell her. Tell her.

His heart beat against his ribs. If he didn't, she'd think it was just sex to him. He glanced down at the woman still physically connected to him. Her hair was spread across the white sheets in dark waves, her eyes were closed, her chest rose and fell.

It's now or never. Don't think. Just do.

He whispered in her ear, "I love you, too, Samantha. I do." A cramp seized his chest. "No matter what happens next, don't forget that."

• • •

He loves me.

The hot, pulsating water from the showerhead beaded up on Sam's shoulders. Her fingers were waterlogged and wrinkled, but she couldn't move. She just wanted to stand in the searing heat and revel in the euphoric sensations still humming through her body. But she knew if she did, she'd probably pass out from the heat and sheer exhaustion, so she finally stepped out of shower.

She reached for a towel, a slow smile spreading across her face. For the first time in days she felt weightless, high on endorphins. She wrapped the soft terry cloth around her body and stopped to listen. Was Zack calling out to her? His voice filtered through the closed bathroom door. No. He was talking on the phone. Who could he be talking to at three thirty a.m.? Quickly, she tiptoed closer to the door. She put her ear against the wood. Her heart pounded out an unsteady beat as she listened, hating herself for being so suspicious, but unable to let the reporter in her go.

Or the wary lover.

"I know. I agree. Look, I've got to go."

She held her breath. He stopped speaking, but she heard other people talking in the background. What was going on?

"Okay. I don't know." Zack's voice again. "I'll try. She's pretty determined."

Was he talking about her? A slow burn spread through her. She threw open the door.

He had turned on a table lamp. He sat on the bed, head resting on the backboard. He put down his smartphone in one smooth motion. Then he smiled at her. Perfect. Casual. Charming.

"Who were you talking to?" She didn't care if she sounded suspicious.

"George."

"George?"

"That's what I said. How was that shower? You look… hot."

"Funny."

"What's wrong?" His eyes widened, but he didn't really look surprised.

"Why were you talking to George? He's not asleep?" She noticed Zack had thrown on his boxers.

He was still smiling. Confident. Sexy. "I was asking him about the video."

"What video?"

"The one playing on my laptop. George brought me the video card." He turned his laptop so she could see.

The images George had shot at the marina played full screen. Robert and his uncle were talking on the deck of the yacht. That was what she had heard? The video?

"He set that up for you? When?"

"While you were cleaning up." His eyes, red and glassy, twinkled. "You take a long shower."

She bit back a smile. That explained it all. The voices she'd heard. They were the voices of Robert and Scott Fitzpatrick playing on the video.

Zack raised his eyebrows then patted the bed next to him.

She smiled. "I need to put on my—"

"I want you to sleep naked."

She tilted her head to one side. "So, you don't want me to sleep at all?"

He shook his head slowly, his smile wicked. "Not really."

An uneasy thought still nagged at her. She put her hands to her hips and her towel slid down over her breasts. Quickly she grabbed it and covered herself. He watched her with definite interest.

"Why did you ask George to set up the video so you could watch it if you had more sex on the mind?"

He shook his head again, but this time his energy had changed. "I just needed to see his face."

"Whose face? Robert's or his uncle's?"

"I needed to see a close up of the man who orchestrated my uncle's murder."

She examined the screen. The two men were talking, but she couldn't read lips, and since they hadn't had microphones near the men at the time, it was impossible to hear the conversation. So, it couldn't have been them she'd heard from the bathroom.

"What do you hope to see? It's not like he has his motive typed across his forehead." She regretted the comment as soon as the words left her mouth. She hoped the contrite look on her face would work as an apology.

"That was rather nasty." Zack stretched his arms above his head.

His abs rippled like sand dunes in the Sahara. What a distraction.

"I intend to find out the motive, but not tonight. Come to

bed." He winked at her, thankfully not upset at her insensitive comment.

Wanting to make it up to him, she walked over and slowly spun around, dropping the towel.

He didn't have to say a word. His body did the talking for him.

She smiled.

The room emptied of all sound except the drone of the air conditioner. She took in the sweet smell of sex and approached the bed with her best Victoria's Secret runway walk. "Sorry, but this is not my idea of a romantic movie." She closed his laptop and placed it on the dresser.

He rolled over to one side and shut off the table lamp. She settled into the bed behind him. His body was already familiar, her knees fit into the curve of him like perfect pieces of a puzzle connecting.

She wrapped her arms around his waist, inhaling his male scent, and whispered sexy words in his ear until he turned toward her and answered her back. His fingers spoke another language between her legs. Her eyelids fluttered as she fought off the urge to drift away into a blissful, orgasm-fueled sleep.

The low buzz of his phone vibrated against the countertop.

"George calling?"

"Ignore it."

Oh, God, his fingers moved like magic.

"You're much more important."

She arched her back as the waves of a powerful release swept her away for the third time that night.

• • •

The chill woke her. She shivered under the little blasts of arctic air delivered by the air conditioner. Shivering, she reached for her human heating pad.

One long sweep with her arm turned up nothing.

She sat up. No light filtered through the window. What time was it?

Zack had piled the sheets high on his side. Frowning, she wrapped a blanket around her body for warmth. "Zack?" The light in the bathroom wasn't on. "Are you in there?"

The whiny air conditioner rattled her, as did the fact the room felt so empty.

The clock on the nightstand read five a.m.

Her heart picked up speed and she reached over to turn on the lamp. Glancing at the nightstand, she saw his cell phone was gone.

"Zack?" This time she said it louder, with just a hint of irritation. And fear.

He was coming back, she told herself firmly. Trying hard to believe it.

Hell, she didn't even know his cell phone number. She'd forgotten to ask. Maybe George had his number.

Maybe he went to get coffee…

No, Zack probably took off to meet up with his cop friends and bust Fitzpatrick on the yacht. And he'd left her behind

So she wouldn't video it? Or maybe so she'd stay safe.

Either way, so much for them working as a team. "Damn it!"

She rolled off the bed and took the blanket with her. Checking the dresser for a note, her gaze landed on the empty spot where she'd left Zack's laptop.

No, he didn't. But he had.

Her heart fell ten stories.

He'd taken his laptop and George's video card, too.

The evidence. Zack had taken all the evidence George had shot.

And abandoned her.

No note, no nothing.

Just like her dad had abandoned her mother.

She shook off the thought, knowing it wasn't nearly the same thing. But she couldn't stop the anger and disbelief that coursed through her.

Digging through her purse, she pulled out her cell phone. "George, wake up. Zack left with the video card. We've got to get back to that yacht."

"Huh?"

"Right now. Before both the snake and the cop get away with our story."

Chapter Twenty-Five

At 6:20 a.m., Sam and George arrived at the Adventure Yacht Harbor just as the red glow of dawn barely peeked out above the horizon.

George carried little gear, just the camera, a microphone, and a fanny pack. Sam had her cell phone in her jeans pocket, a small purse over one shoulder, low heels, and a hidden secret weapon—their undercover camera worn under her shirt, barely poking out of a buttonhole.

Her heart thumped as they approached the marina. A few cars were parked in front of the restaurant. The lights were on inside, and a waitress moved around the dining room. Could anyone inside see them? Would they notice George's video camera and run out to see what was going on?

She grabbed George's wrist. "I'm nervous. You?"

He halted. "Ya think? This was your call, hotshot."

Yes, it was. Just a few weeks ago she wouldn't have made this kind of gutsy call. She slid her hand into George's and pulled him along, away from the restaurant's window. "Let's just do what we came to do, and get the hell out of here. Don't look at anyone. Don't make eye contact. Don't stop. Just follow me. We're not messing this up."

"Yes, general."

She tiptoed down the sidewalk, praying her shoes weren't making too much noise. Before she could count to ten, they stood next to *Catch Me if You Can*.

Her heart was no longer fluttering. It was now galloping inside her chest. God, she should have left her boss a more detailed message. Maybe even talked to him about this first.

"Okay, the yacht is still dark," she whispered, stopping behind a utility shed. "We'll just camp out here and wait until they come out." She took a seat on a rock and squirmed to get comfortable. It was no use.

George scrunched down in front of her, his tall body barely hidden by the shed. "Man, you are brave these days." He was peering around the corner at the yacht as he spoke.

Brave and a bit reckless. Acting more and more like Zack? She wrinkled her nose at an odd smell, almost like smoke, curling into her nostrils.

She tried to clear her head of the odor. A sound right behind her left ear sent a chill rippling down her spine. It was a metal *click*, followed by two more. She recognized those sounds. *Holy crap!*

George whipped around. His camera was still in his hand, but he didn't lift it. In fact, he didn't move a muscle. Nor did he take his eyes off what was behind her. "Sam, he's got a gun."

Chapter Twenty-Six

Robert Fitzpatrick shoved her into the doorway, using the hard steel of the gun barrel at her spine to force her forward. She stumbled into the salon of *Catch Me if You Can*. Her gaze darted around in a hasty inspection, looking for doors, windows, stairs, or any avenue of escape.

Two couches with big throw pillows faced each other, and a long black lacquer coffee table stretched between them. No space to run between the furniture.

"Keep moving." Fitzpatrick shoved her forward. She tripped, her breath rushing out of her. Barely keeping her balance, she stumbled ahead, wishing he wouldn't keep shoving the gun into her spine.

It looked like the only other door was at the far end of the salon. It was closed. And locked? Probably.

"You should have gone home when you had the chance, Samantha Steele." Her captor's voice, so close behind her, made the hairs on the back of her neck rise. "Bad move to follow me."

She wanted to throw out some lame reply to sound brave,

but thought better of it.

"Sit down. Both of you." Robert moved to stand in front of her and George.

Her cameraman hadn't spoken a word since warning her of Robert's presence outside. That was highly unusual. But then, they'd never been in this kind of situation before—forced at gunpoint by a madman onto a yacht owned by another murderer.

They sat on one of the couches, their butts sliding back on the cool leather almost simultaneously. George set his video camera down on the floor, the lens facing forward.

Was it on? She didn't see a red tally light. But that didn't mean he hadn't pressed the record button.

"So, what happens now?" she asked.

The killer's eyes narrowed into scary slits. "What do you think?" He pointed the gun directly at her.

Stall him. "I'd like to interview you."

He snorted. "Like I'd tell you a damn thing, you nosy little bitch reporter."

"I just want to know why." *Keep talking. Keep him talking.* "Why did you start this whole adventure vacation thing? Why murder the people? Why Maxwell?" She was running out of breath. "What was the motivation? Why did you—"

"You ask too many questions for a woman about to die." Robert's disgust flew at her.

She rubbed the burning center of her chest. "If I'm about to die, why not answer me?"

Silence.

Was Robert growing nervous, too? Or maybe he was fighting with himself over the urge to spill the beans. *Appeal to his warped ego.* "Come on. Aren't you dying to tell me how you masterminded this whole plan? It was brilliant." She stroked him with a complimentary tone.

His eyebrows shot up, and the corners of his mouth rose.

"I came upon the plan by accident, actually. And a nosy little bitch-ass reporter like you inspired me."

The newspaper article. "Go on."

George reached down to pick up his camera.

"No. No camera," Robert hissed.

The camera back on the ground, George flipped her a worried look.

She wished she could reassure him that she had his back. She adjusted a button on her shirt, trying to let him know the undercover camera had been switched on.

George's eyes lit up with understanding.

"Go on, Robert," she continued.

He lowered the gun to his side. "Scott was having an affair with some female investigative reporter. Prissy, like you. She'd strut around my place in high heels and a tight black skirt as if *she* owned the place. I couldn't stomach it. Most of the time, I just left her there waiting for my uncle. They'd fuck each other silly, and then they'd both leave. For six months my apartment reeked of sex."

Sam cringed at the way Robert's eyes filled with hate.

"Scott always screwed around. When he got tired of that bitch, he dumped her. But this cunt was smart. While she was waiting for Scott at my place, she'd been digging into my files. Financial files. Scott had put me in charge of hiding his money. He'd been bilking the company profits for years. I had a record of it all. But I'd locked all those records up. I have no idea how that fucking reporter got to them."

Wow. Scott Fitzpatrick had been betrayed by a reporter. No wonder Robert had it out for her.

"There's nothing more dangerous than a bitch scorned," Robert continued.

She crossed her legs, hoping to provoke more out of him. "And your uncle Scott blamed you," she said.

Robert nodded, his cheeks flaming red. "But he gave me

a chance to make it up to him," he said angrily. "We'd been ostracized by all of our friends, even by the assholes who once benefited from Scott's financial tips and inside information. The government froze Scott's assets, including the money I'd been hiding. He was going to prison. That fucking reporter had ruined our lives."

"So you killed her," she whispered, her hand resting on her throat.

"Oh, it wasn't easy."

Robert went on to explain in detail how he'd followed the reporter and her crew around for weeks, until the opportunity presented itself. He'd been able to convince a shop owner to direct the news team to park in a lot with low power lines, difficult to see at night. When the mast had been raised into those lines, the reporter, who'd been sitting on the steps of the truck, and the photographer, who been raising the mast, were both electrocuted. And killed. Instantly. "You could smell their charred flesh. Think of burnt meat on a greasy grill."

"Jesus Christ," George spat. "You are a sick fuck."

She gagged and leaned down to bury her face in her hands.

"You think you're a genius, when actually, you were just damn lucky to have pulled that off." George scoffed.

The snake's gaze slid off her and moved over to George. The mad man chuckled. "I admit fate was on my side, but the fact that it all worked in my favor justifies my actions, don't you think? It's called karma. That bitch burned. She got what she deserved."

"And their deaths were ruled accidental." *Concentrate on getting him to confess.* "And that's how you got the idea to fake Scott's death and make it look like an accident?"

"Exactly. When I told him how I'd killed the bitch, we started to brainstorm other scenarios. Before all the mess with the reporter, and the indictment, he'd talked to me about bidding on and winning an adventure vacation at one of those charity events his wife always made him attend. The company was called the X-Force Adventure Vacation Company. We were both certified divers."

"And you applied for a job as a photographer with the company to get on the inside?" Sam asked.

"Righto, reporter. Scott couldn't buy the company. Couldn't leave a paper trail. So, I had to infiltrate it. Once I was an employee, I could get down in those underwater caves before Scott arrived and map out a strategy. A man could easily get lost in those caverns and die, if he didn't know exactly where he was going."

"He sure could." George must have been having a flashback to his own close encounter with the Grim Reaper.

"Or Fitzpatrick could escape through a different exit." Sam was catching on now. "So who did you kill and leave in the sink for the police to find?"

"A man who was about the same size and build as Scott. Some pothead with no family and an insatiable thirst for drugs and money. I paid him to go diving with me, and then I tangled a guideline around a rock formation and left him down there to die when he ran out of oxygen. The tanks were empty when they found him, so it looked like an accident. Monica was called in to represent the X Force Vacation Company. I was the family member who responded. We both identified the body. Case closed. I had the body cremated the same day."

So Monica was involved, just as she'd suspected. The plan was rather ingenious. And it had worked. "It was the least you could do after messing up your uncle's life by letting the reporter read all those files." Sam froze, realizing she'd said her thoughts out loud, and waited for Robert's reaction.

"You little bitch!"

She'd pushed one final button, and it had been the wrong one.

Robert's eyes flamed. His finger hovered over the trigger of his Glock 23.

Sam's breath stalled halfway up her windpipe.

She heard George's labored breath, but dared not take her eyes off Robert and the gun.

The killer took aim. "To bad you'll never get to report that story live at five. Because now I'm going to kill you. Any last words, Samantha Steele?"

Chapter Twenty-Seven

A gargled half groan escaped Sam's lips. She didn't even recognize her own voice. She closed her eyes. *Think. Think.* She could charge Robert, or maybe push George down if he fired. She jumped at the ring of her cell phone.

"Don't even think about answering." A different voice came from the other side of the room.

Sam wrenched around to see who it was.

Scott Fitzpatrick's large frame filled the open doorway. "Say 'hello' and it will be the very last word you ever utter."

Her phone clattered against the coffee table as she set it down with shaky hands. Immediately it buzzed again, and then went to voice mail.

"You said there were three." Scott strode into the living room, a trail of pungent cologne following in his wake.

"What?" Robert shuffled a few steps back.

Interesting. She thought the two were supposed to be close, but after being in the room with them for less than ten seconds, she had no doubt Scott Fitzpatrick was actually in charge, and held little affection for his nephew.

"You said you were following a team of *three.*" Scott stood before the two of them, then leaned over to pick up her cell phone. "The reporter." He nodded at her. "And the cameraman. Where's the Army Ranger?" He pointed her cell phone at Robert. "Of the three, he's the one we should be most worried about." The older Fitzpatrick opened her phone. "Where is he?"

Was the man talking to her?

His heated gaze shifted her way.

She flinched. "I don't know." She tensed, waiting for him to erupt. "Really."

"Was that the Ranger calling?"

"No."

"I can check."

"Be my guest." *Asshole.*

Scott's black eyes narrowed. They were a stark contrast to his shockingly gray hair, which sprang out from his head like angry lightning bolts.

He glanced down at the phone and pressed a button. Had to be redial. He placed the phone to his ear. After a moment, "Who's speaking?"

Sam knew who had answered the call. Even if she survived this kidnapping, her boss would probably fire her.

"I asked you a question." Fitzpatrick's voice was low, demanding, but still very much in control.

She could only imagine the words and attitude coming from her boss on the other end. Stan was a former New Yorker with a temper, and he didn't like being questioned.

"There's no Samantha here."

Her boss knew better. Stan had issued her that cell phone for work. Plus she'd left him a message this morning, right after waking up George. Now he would know something was really wrong. But his help would get here too late.

"You must have dialed the wrong number earlier. Who

is this?" Fitzpatrick scowled and held the phone away from his ear.

A slew of curse words exploded from the cell.

She shot George a knowing look. He lifted his eyebrows, acknowledging he heard it, too. This was the first time she'd actually appreciated Stan's lack of a filter.

The older Fitzpatrick abruptly slammed the phone down. He stared at her for one long, uncomfortable moment.

She swallowed, her skin tightening.

"I imagine your boss will be looking for you now." Scott walked toward Robert. "The clock is ticking. We have to make a move. But we need all three of them. What's the Ranger's name?"

"Zack Hunter," Robert offered.

"Where the hell is Mr. Hunter?" Scott slammed a fist onto the bar next to the doorway.

She jumped.

When no one answered, he stalked back toward the couch. "All right, let's work a little trade." The big man sat down next to her. She fought the urge to turn away. "You tell me where the third member of your little party is, and I'll tell you why I had Robert kill Maxwell Wentworth."

Her heart slammed against her ribs, but Sam struggled not to scoot away, even though her knees were knocking together. *Fitzpatrick was offering her a confession! And she was recording!*

On cue, Robert shoved his gun at her temple.

She swallowed heavily. "Last I saw of Zack, he was at the hotel. I woke up this morning, and he'd already left."

"And you came back here?" Scott Fitzpatrick asked. "Big, brave girl to come without your military man."

"I thought maybe Zack was actually working for you guys." She looked Scott Fitzpatrick straight on, hoping he wouldn't notice her right eyelid twitching.

"That's a lie."

She could feel the man's hot, rancid breath on her cheek as he spoke. This time she couldn't stop herself. She scooted back. "I don't really know Zack Hunter. And he lied to me at every turn. I found out about his uncle's death from Robert." She looked to Robert to back her up. "Ask him."

Robert nodded. "It's true."

"I used Zack Hunter as my cover to go on the adventure vacation because I wanted to find out if Maxwell's death was really an accident. I found myself sexually attracted to Zack so I slept with him." She shrugged, trying to play it off as casual. "Where he is now, I couldn't say. Probably gathering a large contingent of police to come arrest you."

Scott studied her for a moment. "I think she *is* telling the truth, which doesn't make me happy." The big man stood. "Wake up the captain. Tell him we shove off in less than fifteen minutes or he's fired. And you know what *fired* actually means."

"Where are we going?" she demanded.

Did she really want to know? Not really…

The former dead man peered down at her and smiled, but there was no laughter in his cold eyes. "Doesn't really matter. Wherever we end up, you and your friend are shark bait. But I'll be sure to have Robert shoot pictures, so your death makes the top of the evening news."

Chapter Twenty-Eight

The hum of the yacht's motor forced Sam's pulse up. The captain was pulling away from the dock. She couldn't look at Scott Fitzpatrick, afraid he'd sense the panic in her eyes. He'd probably enjoy that.

Her seat vibrated as the motor kicked up a notch. Each passing second took her farther away from escape, but oddly not any closer to a full-out panic attack. Instead, she was concentrating on finishing off the job at hand, getting a confession recorded, before either Fitzpatrick could finish her off. She was scared, for sure, but oddly she still felt in control.

Stall him. Talk to him. "I've told you about Zack and me. You promised to tell me about Maxwell Wentworth. And I also want to know what happened to Jenny."

"Jenny? Who is Jenny?" Scott Fitzpatrick asked.

"You told me to kill the fucking reporter." Robert sounded agitated. "I thought that bitch Jenny was this fucking cunt."

"You were wrong, asshole." Jenny had died because they

looked alike. She would have to live with that guilt. Forever. But at least, if she survived, she could make sure Robert did time for Jenny's death. "Tell me about Maxwell." Part of her seized at her callousness, her ability to put Jenny's death into a compartment and move ahead with the plan. The map they had to follow to survive.

A flash of appreciation flickered in those hardened eyes. "Maxwell Wentworth. Now there was a man who made many enemies."

"Yes, much to my surprise." After Maxwell's death she'd done her homework, unable to believe the hometown hero who'd helped her could make an enemy ruthless enough to kill him. "I recently found out Maxwell was having an affair with the wife of his company's vice president. So, he had a scorned wife, a pissed off business partner, and a trophy mistress who wanted to become his new wife." She counted them off with her fingers. "Not exactly the Maxwell I thought I knew, but not the first man to cheat on his marriage. So, those are his enemies, but which one wanted to kill him?"

Scott actually smiled at her. "Which would you put your money on, Samantha?" But his eyes remained cold and reminded her of a serial killer she'd interviewed in prison in Daytona Beach.

"If I were a betting woman, I'd say...the ex-wife."

"Good guess, but you're wrong. The ex-wife didn't want him dead. She wanted him alive so she could keep taking his money. Bitch liked her monthly alimony."

"Okay, then, the new girlfriend?" George leaned forward. "Women are so fucking greedy."

Fitzpatrick lifted a finger. "But she also had everything to gain by keeping him alive. His name, his house, his money."

"So, it was the vice president," Sam whispered, totally appalled she was participating in this verbal banter with an arrogant killer...but also undeniably interested.

"Bingo," Scott said.

The mystery of Maxwell's death had finally been solved—another man who'd fallen victim to lust and revenge. Sam had put Maxwell on a pedestal, but in the end, he was just another vulnerable man controlled by his baser human urges.

"They all had motive for murder." Scott Fitzpatrick reached out and grasped her wrist so tightly the blood supply to her fingers stalled.

She fought back the urge to yell and jerk away.

"But only his vice president had the balls to follow through." The big man slanted forward. "Maxwell's vice president financed his murder. And I paid Robert to execute it by messing with Maxwell's parachute at Skydive Drop Zone."

Her body tensed, but she tasted victory. A confession at last! A jury would hear how proud the asshole sounded as he described how he'd orchestrated the deadly plans. If she survived. "How did the VP find you to hire? I mean, I don't get the connection."

Fitzpatrick backed off a bit, but didn't release her wrist. "I had an employee troll charity events for possible clients."

"Monica." She'd been right not to trust the woman. Monica had been in on it from day one.

"Yes, beautiful Monica could throw on a long gown and fake diamonds and fit right in with the rich and powerful. The inebriated fools who flirted with her never realized she was nothing more than ambitious trailer trash doing my bidding for cash."

Selling her soul to the devil was more like it. "So, Monica hung out at charity events and asked drunk, rich people if they wanted anyone murdered?" She hiked her brows at the absurdity of the idea.

"Stretch your mind a little, Miss Reporter. What do most of these charity events include?"

George snorted. “Besides wealthy, whiskeyed-up people?”

Curiosity overpowered her terror, if only for the moment. “There’s always a band, and a rubber chicken dinner.”

“Amusing. Before that.”

“A silent auction with—” The match finally fired, and she made the connection. She met Scott Fitzpatrick’s smug eyes. He’d let go of her wrist and was now gripping the gun in his other hand.

“You offered Adventure Vacation packages as silent auction items at charity events.”

“That’s right. In Wentworth’s case, it happened at the St. Francis Society Gala in Tampa. By that time, Wentworth’s affair was public knowledge. He and his vice president were already circling each other like wolves, trying to figure out ways to ruin one another. I provided them with a clever way for them to compete, bidding over our popular vacation.”

The sound of metal hitting something hard outside made her jump. Someone was out there. Robert stuck his head out of the doorway to check.

Fitzpatrick was too carried away in the story and didn’t notice. “Wentworth’s ego got the best of him. He couldn’t let his rival win the adventure vacation. A bidding war ensued.”

George faked a cough.

Sam assumed that was a hint and glanced around the room. She checked out both doorways. Robert had disappeared from the one doorway leading to the deck. No one else was around, at least that she could see. Every nerve in her body went on high alert.

“Wentworth won of course, which made his death look even more like his own fault.”

She shook her head, sickened. “So, Maxwell actually paid for his own murder.”

“And his business partner paid me another seven-hundred thousand dollars to make sure it looked like an accident." Fitzpatrick thrust his chest out as he said it.

Sam's jaw nearly hit the deck. This man had made almost *a million dollars* on Maxwell's death. No wonder he continued his murder for hire scheme. It probably funded his secret, underground lifestyle.

"That's the going price for a CEO?" George asked.

Fitzpatrick smacked George on the back of his head, sending him flying forward. "Yes, but I'll kill *you* for free. Does that tell you what you're worth, camera boy?"

George finally snapped. He jumped up from the bench and dove at Fitzpatrick, body-slamming him onto the floor. Scott's gun sailed across the carpet.

The gun! Get the damn gun!

"Fucker. You want to kill me? Do it with your hands in a fair fight," George yelled as the two rolled and wrestled on the carpet.

Sam dove for the gun, her heart galloping, but Scott kicked it away.

"*Ahh*!" George yelped, and the gun slid to a stop against the far bulkhead.

Could she still get to it? If so, could she actually use it?

George let out another grunt, and she flinched at the sound of something slamming against a wall.

"Don't move." A familiar hiss stalled her going for the weapon. Once again, Robert stood at the door, his gun pointed at her. His finger moved to the trigger, deadly intent gleaming in his eyes.

Hell. This was it.

"Nobody move!" A different voice rang out from the other side of the room. Calm. Cool. In control.

Oh, thank God.

Zack!

Chapter Twenty-Nine

Sam wanted to run and hide behind Zack, but Robert stepped in front of her with his damn gun pointed at her head.

Scott Fitzpatrick and George must have stopped fighting because the grunts and groans had ceased. She could hear George's labored breathing. Risking a quick glance backward, she swallowed. The big man was holding George in front of him like a human shield, one arm tight around his neck.

Silence swept through the room, leaving nothing but her crazy heart pounding in her ears.

Zack took a few steps closer, but he never stopped glaring at Robert.

Her mouth turned dry and chalky. She figured she had about half a second to make a move, or her destiny would be sealed.

She raised her hands in surrender. "I don't have a weapon. I'm not a threat to you."

"Samantha," Zack warned.

She zeroed in on Robert. "I just need to know one thing before I die." She took a small step to the right. She had to get around the coffee table to reach him.

"We're all done talking." His stare hardened.

"Just one more question." She took another small step and saw his hands were shaking again. "Who paid for Jackson Hunter's death?" She had to do this. For Zack.

"Shoot her," Scott commanded. "She's stalling for time."

"Wait!" Sam took another step toward Robert, holding out both hands like a school crossing guard. "Answer the question. I have a right to know everything before I die." The air in the room crackled with electricity. She inched closer.

"His own brother paid," Scott snapped. "Now kill the bitch, Robert!"

From the corner of her eye, she saw Zack standing frozen in shock. *Damn.*

Her heart flipped erratically. "Robert, why are you doing this? Why kill all these people for your uncle? *You're* the one who'll pay if you're caught."

"Revenge, okay?" Robert wiped his brow. "Now, shut up!"

"Jesus." Scott's voice thundered through the room. "Fucking *kill* her. She's playing with you, fool."

George wheezed as Scott's hold tightened around his throat.

A *click* sounded from Robert's gun. The hair on her arms stood.

"Revenge against whom, Robert?" she said desperately.

"Move another millimeter, asshole, and I will happily shoot both of you." Zack's voice was calm but chilling.

Robert's frantic gaze darted to Zack.

Just the break she needed. She lunged forward, diving toward Robert's short, stocky body.

Bang!

Oh, shit. Body in motion, she tensed, waiting to feel the searing fire of a bullet penetrating her flesh.

Instead, Robert's hand jerked. He screamed and the gun

clattered to the deck just as she crashed into him shoulder first, bounced, and then tumbled to the floor.

White-hot pain shot through her body. She started scrambling to her knees. *Where was the gun?*

"Get down!" Zack shouted, and she instantly obeyed.

Bang. Bang. Bang!

George let out a bellow that sounded like it came from hell itself.

Oh, God! He'd been hit!

"Take cover!" Zack called.

She glanced around and rolled toward the solid wood wet bar near the door. A hand grabbed her ankle.

Robert. He was dragging her back into the open. The heat of carpet burn ignited her skin. She dug her fingernails into the rug but couldn't get a grip. Fear tore at her heart.

She kicked, then kicked harder. Her right foot found flesh and bone. Robert squealed. She drew in a deep breath and kicked with all her might, letting out a mighty yell as she flipped over.

His hand on her ankle relaxed just enough for her to break free.

She scampered behind the cover of the bar.

Where was Zack? And George? *Oh, Jesus.*

More explosive gunfire erupted. She scrunched into a ball, her spine hitting the bulkhead behind the bar.

"Fuck," came a deep growl. "I'm hit!"

Ohmigod! "Zack!"

Chapter Thirty

Sam heard Zack fall to the floor with a moan.

Her muscles went weak. “Zack!” She peered around the corner of the bar. No one had a gun pointed her way, so she bolted out toward him.

She almost stumbled over a body. Robert was sprawled across the floor, bright red stains soaking into the beige carpet under him. His eyes were open and glassy.

Oh, sweet Jesus. He was dead.

“I had to shoot the fucker.” Zack’s voice was weak, but at least he was still conscious.

She let out a rush of air as she reached him, dropping to her knees. “Where are you hit?” She touched his face first, her heart racing. She ran her fingers down his body. He was putting off waves of heat, but no blood was pumping onto his shirt.

He struggled to sit halfway up, resting on his elbows. “I’m okay. The fucker was dragging you away. I had no choice.”

Her gaze locked into a hole in his shirt on his left side. He pushed up and ripped open his shirt. He was wearing a

Kevlar vest.

The air whooshed out of her lungs. “Oh, thank God.” She threw her arms around him.

He tumbled backward. “Ouch!” Despite the sound of protest, his arms wrapped around her, squeezing tight. “Damn. My ribs will never be the same.” He rolled her over so she lay by his side. “Be gentle with me.”

Tears welled up as she nodded. “George?” She sat up and scanned the room.

“Over here.”

He was sitting with his back against the opposite bulkhead, looking dazed. Scott Fitzpatrick was slumped over in a heap next to him. Dead?

“Are you okay?” she asked.

“Never better.” He cocked a brow and chuckled.

“Really? This is funny to you?” Freaking men.

“Fucking-A. Did you see that? Zack nailed the bastard while he was still holding onto me!” His eyes shone with hero-worship as he looked at Zack. “That was frikkin’ *awesome,* dude.”

She just shook her head, and glanced at Scott Fitzpatrick, who was apparently still alive—his breathing was shallow and raspy but steady. Zach crawled over to secure his wrists with zip-ties.

“What do we do now?” she asked.

“Backup and paramedics are on the way,” Zach told her.

She let out a sigh of relief. “So, it’s over.”

“I wish we’d been able to take both Fitzpatricks alive. They both deserve to swing.” Zack stood, both hands on his hips, looking angry but focused.

George pulled himself up off the floor. His tall, lanky body didn’t make it all the way vertical. Still bent at an odd angle, he groaned. “My back is shot. No pun intended.”

She rolled her eyes. “Glad to see you still have your sense

of humor."

She waited for a reaction from Zack, but he was pacing the room. "What are you looking for?"

"Won't know until I find it."

"Yeah, about that confession you wanted?" Sam couldn't help the smile that spread across her face.

"Thanks for asking about my uncle." Zack stopped dead in his tracks, turning to look at George. "Please tell me you managed to get that on video." His voice held such hope.

"Sorry, no. They made me turn it off."

Zack resumed pacing around the cabin.

"However," she said with a rush of satisfaction and joy. "I got the entire conversation on my undercover mini button cam."

Chapter Thirty-One

Sam had around thirty minutes before *Catch Me if You Can*, now captained by a U.S. Coast Guard Petty Officer, returned to dock in Port Orange. Thirty minutes to get cleaned up, get her shit together, get her story straight, and get her plan to fix her mess of a life in order.

Only her life no longer felt so disastrous. Zack was alive, and she had him with her.

At least figuratively.

Standing on deck alone, the warm wind whipping through her already tussled hair, she wondered what would happen to the two of them once they made shore. Would he have to leave her? He had just shot and killed a man. There would be an internal investigation.

Would she have to leave him? Her heart ached at the thought. "How are we both going to get out of this situation without being fired? Or arrested?" she asked herself out loud.

"Sam, I have a plan."

She jumped at the sound of Zack's voice behind her.

He'd just called her Sam. He'd never done that before. He

had always called her Samantha. She looked up into his eyes, longing to put her questions behind them. "You always have a plan. Most of the time the plan involves something dangerous and even illegal."

"If I spell it out for you, will you stop worrying?"

"Are we negotiating?"

"Jesus, Sam." He pulled her to him, locking her lips with his. His kiss was intense and way too short. When he pulled away, his eyes were on fire. "Here's your scoop. When we get back to Port Orange, the local police department will be waiting for us. When I called them last night, they almost creamed their pants at the thought of such a high-profile bust. They will arrest Scott Fitzpatrick, with the assistance of the Coast Guard and the FDLE, of course."

Her heart sped up. "Your bosses know you're here."

"Confessed last night."

"And you still have a job?"

"I told them I wanted to check out the vacation my uncle went on and I ran into a hot young reporter who'd uncovered some important clues the FDLE missed. Okay, maybe I didn't say hot. I did tell them I'd been tailing you and your evidence and keeping it safe until we could get back to shore. That explains why I was on the yacht, and why I had to use force."

"You told them all that and they didn't fire you?"

"Haven't yet. But they're very interested in seeing what evidence you have."

She dropped her gaze. "Including the evidence you took from me."

He lifted her chin.

Something in his gaze shifted.

This new vulnerable look tugged at her heart.

Then he pulled George's video card out of his jeans pocket. "I should be turning this evidence over to my superiors. But I'm giving it back to you." He handed her the video card.

Her heart swelled. "Why?"

"When I first met you my goal was to keep you from splashing any evidence you uncovered all over the evening news. Now, that's exactly what I'm asking you to do."

"I don't follow."

"I'm trusting you to make sure this video and the confession you videotaped get into the news before prosecutors and defense attorneys get involved. I want the public to hear the truth, and I want them to hear it from you."

Her breath stilled. He was trusting her with one of the goals most important to him—justice for his murdered uncle. "I have evidence that will guarantee Scott Fitzpatrick will be charged with murder, on top of all those other fifty-eight counts."

"And you have the power to follow this story and make sure it doesn't die, that he doesn't get off by paying off some greedy judge or financing a get out of jail free pass."

"Not going to happen. I promise. Not on my watch. I'll see this through for you."

"One more thing."

"Anything."

"You can't use my name or face in any of your stories," he said. "I have to remain an anonymous source, and I'm trusting you not to reveal my real part in this investigation. If you do, I will get fired."

"Protect my source. I can do that."

"And don't worry. You'll get your exclusive."

She threw her arms around his neck.

"Which means you'll keep your job," he huffed as she continued to squeeze the air out of him.

Zack Hunter was a changed man. Maybe she'd changed him. Maybe finding the truth about his uncle had worked, too.

Whatever it was, he was now trusting her with the two most important things in his life. His honor and his reputation.

But she still didn't know if he was healed enough to trust her with his damaged heart.

Chapter Thirty-Two

A wave of warm, tropical air blasted Sam as she stepped off *Catch Me if You Can*. They'd docked again at the Port Orange Marina, and police officers moved onboard as she and Zack tried to get off the vessel.

"First ones off the boat?"

She jumped at the sound of Stan Delamonte's voice. *Her boss? Here?* Her heart flip-flopped. *Shit.*

"Hear you've got a hell of a story, Sam." *Yep. That's Stan.* She stumbled.

Zack steadied her. "Watch that last step."

"Well?" Stan asked when she reached his side. "Are you going to introduce me to—"

"Zack Hunter, this is Stan Delamonte. He's my boss at the news station." Before the men could even shake hands, she faced her boss. "What are *you* doing here? How did you find us?"

Stan stepped around her and shook Zack's hand. She noticed the firm grip and the hard shake. *Men.* "You left me a few pertinent details on your voicemail. I used to be a reporter, remember?" Then to Zack, "I understand you saved my reporter's life today."

Zack shrugged off the compliment. "Your reporter solved the mystery the FDLE has been investigating for months. I guess we can call it even."

Stan acknowledged Zack with a knowing look and turned his attention back to her. "You and I need to have a little sit down."

"Stan—"

"And we will, right after you do your live shot at noon."

Her eyebrows shot up. "You brought a live truck?" She didn't need him to answer. A satellite truck, from their sister station in Orlando, sat about fifty feet in front of her, ready to beam video from Port Orange all the way to Tampa. *Oh boy.* She waited for the familiar tightening in her chest to begin. But this time it didn't. "Where's George?"

Stan pointed. "George, who obviously still has his mind on *work*, already shot the ambulance taking the injured guy's body off the yacht. The Medical Examiner is here, onboard still I think. George got his arrival as well. And now he's over in the sat truck dubbing that undercover confession video so he can send it back to the station." Stan shot Zack a look. "Don't even bother. Some other FDLE guy already asked. I need a court order to share that video." Her boss placed a hand on her shoulder. "It's eleven fifteen. Say good-bye to your...partner. You've got forty-five minutes to get your shit together and tell the world about the incredible plot you've just uncovered."

"I..." She swallowed, glancing from Zack to Stan, and then back to Zack.

"You're wasting precious time, kid." Stan's facial muscles twitched.

"You trust me, Stan, to walk in front of that camera and start talking about what has happened over the last couple of weeks? You don't want me to vet this information through you first?" The thought did make her a little uneasy. She knew what a big story she and Zack had uncovered. A lot of highly paid lawyers were likely to pick through every word that came out of her mouth.

Stan shook his head. "We don't have time. And I do trust you. Just stick to the facts. Interview your partner here with the FDLE. You've got a solid source in him."

She flipped a look Zack's way. "I've got an anonymous source. And he's going to stay anonymous."

"Why?"

"Because I gave him my word, that's why."

"You can't make that kind of deal without consulting me. Your *anonymous source* shot and killed one man and injured another. You can't keep him out of the story."

"My *anonymous source* is not the story, Stan. The videotaped confession I have is the story, and the shootout that was also videotaped by my undercover camera will tell its own story. I'm keeping his name out of it. Masking his face if he's in the video."

"Not if I tell you otherwise."

"If you tell me otherwise, I will quit. Before your noon newscast and before you can get your exclusive for the TV station." Wow. She couldn't believe she'd said that. Her chest puffed up.

"Is that a threat?"

"Stan," she sighed. *Take it down a notch.* "I don't need a source for this story. I was a witness myself, and the video will back up every word I tell the viewers. I need you to trust me on this."

"You're not going to freeze up on me?"

Figured Stan would get a last jab in. Sam lifted her chin. "Not ever again."

• • •

Sam went in search of Zack, who had disappeared into the main building of the marina looking for a place to clean up. Down the main hallway, she heard a man groan. Not just any man. *Her* man. The moan came from within a single bathroom next to the main office. She held her breath.

Zack had left the door open a crack.

She peeked in, trying not to make a sound.

Zack was facing the mirror, his shirt off. One arm was lifted above his head as he ran fingers over the left side of his chest.

Watching him move took her breath away. He was physically perfect. Lean waist, rippled abs, no body fat. She just wanted to savor the sight of him for a few moments, before he saw her.

What a different man Zack Hunter had turned out to be than she'd first thought. He wasn't the arrogant party boy she'd met at the drop zone, or the hard-assed ex-military cop he wanted to appear. She had fallen in love with the wounded, recovering soul she'd uncovered beneath the façade.

He lifted his other arm. She'd explored his body a few times, but always in a rush of passion. Now she took her time and drank in his lean form, savoring each ripple of flesh over muscle.

He leaned over the sink and splashed water on his face. He straightened and groaned again, his hand shooting to his chest. A large purple and red mark splashed across the left side of his flesh, like a child's messy painting.

"Oh, my God." The words whooshed out. "That must really have hurt."

He whipped around, then his body relaxed and his eyes lit up. "Spying on me?"

She gave him a little smile. "Well, I *am* Bond. Samantha

Bond, right?"

He chuckled.

"Are you okay? Those bruises look pretty nasty."

He tilted his head. "Hmm. Maybe you better check me over to make sure…"

Her heart fluttered like a drunken butterfly's wings. Excitement spilled through her veins. "Oh. I guess I could do that."

"Shut the door behind you." He leaned back against the vanity. "And lock it."

Her insides danced. "I take it you're feeling pretty good."

He looked at her with dark, lust-filled eyes. "You tell me."

She closed the door and moved toward him, taking slow, measured steps. She didn't want to look too anxious or too needy, but she was desperate to grab hold of him and touch her fill. Carefully, of course.

In front of him, she traced a finger across the vicious mark where a bullet would have blasted a hole in him. He winced a little. Swallowing a painful lump, she realized how close she'd come to losing him.

He touched her face.

A rush of raw need swept over her. Once this day was over, who knew what would happen? Zack still hadn't talked about the future. Their future. She blew out a breath and disengaged herself from the heated circle of his embrace. What if she never saw him again?

"Sam?" he asked in a husky voice.

"I have to know," she said.

His eyes narrowed. "Now is not the time to play reporter." He put his hands on her waist and pulled her back to him.

She resisted the strong urge to press into his rock hard body, to feel how much he wanted her. "I'm not."

"Good." He tugged harder, until she lost her footing and fell into his chest. He wrapped his arms around her, and his warm lips found the sensitive spot of flesh between her shoulder and her neck.

Instinctively, her shoulders hunched up.

He forced them back down and began nibbling her so gently the hair on her nape sizzled. He was so damn good at this.

"Stop," she moaned.

"Stop what?" he whispered, his breath hot and demanding on her skin. He ran his fingers through her hair and pulled her head back until her neck was totally exposed. "Are you glad I'm alive?"

"Of course."

"Why?"

"Because—" She hesitated.

"I want to hear you say it."

"I—" The words clogged in her throat.

"I *need* to hear you say it." His voice dropped a register, deep, low, and needy. He ran his lips up her throat until chill bumps erupted all across her skin.

With the last ounce of reserve she had left, she placed both hands on his chest and put distance between them. "I need you to answer a few questions first."

He stepped back and looked at her through suspicious eyes. "You're kidding, right?"

"No."

With a grunt of disbelief, her handsome lover leaned back against the counter, putting cold air and distance between them. "We almost died today, both of us. Can't we forgo the questions and get right to the—"

"No. You left me on the morning after the best night of my life, and I have to know why."

"It was? The best?" He raked her with a bad boy smile. "Really?"

Sam gave him an unrelenting stare. "Cut the crap. Open

up to me. For real. It's now or never."

His smile faltered and his laughing eyes slowly went serious. After a forever-like pause, he said, "Okay. I left you because I had an appointment at the local hospital to get into the hyperbaric chamber. I didn't want to wake you for that. And I guess I was a little embarrassed about needing the medical help. When I got back to the room, you were gone. I knew exactly where to find you. You scared the shit out of me. I barely made it to the marina in time to jump on the yacht undetected. That was ballsy of you, Sam."

"But you took my video evidence with you. Why?"

"Couldn't risk you flashing it all over the news before I could make an arrest." He jammed his hands in his pockets. "I was determined to nail the person who murdered my uncle. You knew that from day one."

"At any cost?"

"We've already had this conversation. We've both admitted we used each other. In the beginning."

Her stomach flip-flopped. "And now?"

"And now things are different. We've gotten to know each other. Both seen past the walls." Gently he placed both his hands on her cheeks, cradling her face, making it impossible to look away. "All my life I wished for someone to care about me the way I see you care about your family. Your sister and your mother. And George."

All she saw in his eyes was sincerity…wrapped in a blanket of vulnerability. Emotion choked her, straining the muscles of her throat. She could only manage a squeak. "Really?"

"Why do you think I paid your mother's bill? I hoped it would bring you back to me."

"But you had no way of knowing it would. You gave me that money with no strings attached. That was the moment I think I started loving you."

He smiled, unlike any smile she'd seen on him before. "I'm not sure I heard you right." The joy in his face went deep, and his eyes danced with the mischief she'd grown to expect and to desire more than anything on earth. "What was that last part?"

"Oh, boy." She rolled her eyes at him, even as a wave of happiness cascaded over her. She used to think Zack Hunter didn't need anyone. He'd probably even thought that himself. But no longer. "I love you. And I'll say it as many times as you need to hear it." She raised a brow and looked up at him expectantly.

He laughed. "My turn, eh?"

"Ya think?"

His eyes softened. "I started loving you the moment you agreed to ride in that F-16. I knew you were terrified. But any woman who could face her fears like that, she's the kind of woman I wanted to—"

She gently placed her hands on his bare chest. "I know what you wanted to do with that woman." His skin felt moist and hot.

"Nothing's changed, Sam."

A knock on the door.

"Steele. Five minutes until airtime. Finish brushing your hair. Or whatever the hell you're doing in there. And get out here. Now."

Stan. Her news director. Always blunt and bold.

She exhaled, looking up at her perfect man. "I've got to go."

"So go." He smiled. "I'm not going anywhere. We're going to finish this…conversation."

Her heart swelled.

That mischievous look entered his eyes. "Do something for me."

Uh oh. "Anything."

"Nail that live shot." Zack smoothed a wayward strand of her hair. "Are you nervous?"

"No." *Holy shit*. She really wasn't. She placed a hand over her heart. Regular rhythm. She hadn't even given a thought to what she would say. She should be in a panic. But she wasn't. She laughed out loud. "I think I'm just going to pull a Zack Hunter."

He pulled back, cocking his head at her. "What the hell does that mean?"

"I have a plan."

"Uh oh." He mimicked her favorite saying, just as she'd copied his.

"I'm just going to take a giant leap of faith…and wing it."

• • •

Ice Queen.

How could anyone look so hot and be so frigid?

Zack laughed out loud. He recalled his first reaction to Sam performing her duties as a TV reporter at Skydive Drop Zone, right after Wentworth had died. That moment seemed so long ago, when in reality it had only been a couple of weeks. So much had changed since then. Now, Zack knew how much her job could actually pain her, and how seriously she took her work.

Her face appeared animated yet solemn as she spoke to the camera in front of her. She and George set up their camera in front of *Catch Me if You Can*, while a stream of investigative personnel still moved on and off the yacht.

Zack wasn't close enough to hear her words, but this time he didn't fear what she was saying. He knew she'd keep her word and keep him out of the story.

Despite the bruise, the rest of his body felt light, almost

weightless. A heavy responsibility had been lifted off him. With Robert's death and Scott's impending arrest, he'd completed his personal and professional assignment.

Samantha pulled the earpiece out of her ear, smiled, and high fived George. She acted like she was proud of their accomplishment. As she should be. She was the one who'd put all the different pieces together.

She glanced up and caught him staring.

Unlike the first time she'd done that, this time Zack didn't look away.

She cocked her head to one side and grinned.

A new emotion rocked him. He felt like a schoolboy with an overwhelming crush, warmth rushing through him.

She started walking his way. After such an intense morning, followed by an intense few minutes alone with her in the marina's cramped bathroom, all he wanted to do now was have a little fun.

She stopped in front of him, placing her hands on her hips as if challenging him to say something, just like she had a few weeks ago when they first met. So, she wanted to play as well. He grinned. "How can you do that?" He mimicked his words from Skydive Drop Zone.

"Do what?" She raised an eyebrow, but the wicked smile on her face told him she knew what he was doing and planned to follow along.

"Turn your emotions on and off like that? One minute you're crying over me because you think I'm dead, the next you're this indifferent journalist reporting on a death and a couple of shootings as if we were all strangers to you."

Her eyes widened. "It's my job. It's what I have to do, like it or not."

"It's cold." He knew he was pushing her buttons, but this time instead of trying to hurt her, he was engaging in some foreplay. He couldn't believe how turned on he was. Again.

"Cold? Really? Well, some of us—"

Before she could finish her sentence, he swooped her into a bear hug and planted a fierce kiss right on her lips. He heard her gasp, and that natural reaction sent desire pulsating through him. He kissed her slowly, passionately, moving her body up against his in an unmistakable way.

"Wow." She sounded breathless. "You're making a very public statement with that kiss."

A few law enforcement officials had stopped to stare at them. Stan, her boss, fired off a death glare at him. Zack merely chuckled. Nothing could ruin his mood or his plans. "Good. I'm done hiding, both my feelings and the truth. From this moment forward, I'm putting it all out in the open."

She stared up at him, wide-eyed.

"Samantha." Her boss had made his way over to them. "You're both old enough to practice a little more control and discretion."

The tone of her boss' voice pissed Zack off. But he held his tongue for Sam's sake.

"That kiss, in front of numerous witnesses, represents a conflict of interest, don't you think?"

"Actually, Stan, I wasn't really thinking at all."

Zack grinned. This was the Sam he loved. Bold and confident.

"Is that why you want to have a little sit down with me?" Sam asked.

"That's one of the reasons."

"Okay, but there's nothing in any journalism book I've ever read that says it's unethical to fall in love."

Zack loved the way she defended herself. Much differently from the day they'd met.

As Stan's eyebrows shot up and he opened his mouth to respond, her boss' cell phone ringtone sounded. "We'll talk later. First, let me take this call." He stalked a few feet away.

"Quite a character," Zack commented.

"You have no idea."

"So, where do we go from here?"

She shrugged, and peered up at him through long lashes. "How about lunch?"

He smiled. "I have some paperwork, and I'll need to be debriefed."

"Okay, then I'll wait for you at the hotel." She sighed.

"I'm not just talking about today."

Her cheeks brightened. He loved that he could get that kind of reaction out of her.

"I'm open to suggestions," she said in a soft, coy voice.

"How about a vacation? An adventure vacation."

She playfully swatted at him. "Are you for real? You haven't had enough adventure over the last two weeks?"

He touched her lips. They were moist and a bit bruised. Her bottom lip trembled.

That simple move hardened him. Jesus, he wasn't even able to control his own desire out here in the open. He laughed at his own predicament. "I had another kind of adventure in mind. One that includes just you and me in a hotel room overlooking the Gulf of Mexico on St. Pete Beach."

"Sounds like a plan." She grabbed his hand, entwining her fingers in his, and looked up at him with the genuine love and trust he'd been waiting for all his life.

Turn the page to start reading Flatline *by Linda Bond!*

Chapter One

Reporter Rachel Wright's producer had thrown up twice in the car on the mad race over to Tampa Bay Hospital, but it was the blood in Jackie's vomit and the lethargy in her limbs that had her heart whacking against the ribs. An investigative reporter, she thrived on tense situations, but right now every blood vessel in her body had to be constricted.

She slammed her back against the red entrance button on the emergency room, desperate to get help ASAP. Head pounding and arms full, she struggled to hold Jackie up. But it wasn't only the heavy body weighing Rachel's spirit down.

This was the first time she'd been back to the hospital since the night her brother had died.

The ER doors zipped open.

Thank God. Jackie will be fine now. There would be no repeat of the last time.

Rachel took a deep breath and heaved Jackie up. It was like pulling a life-sized rag doll stuffed with rocks through the door.

"Can I get some help here?" She meant to yell but lacked

the air to create any real volume. She maneuvered her friend forward—a puppet heavy on her feet.

The waiting room was almost full, typical for Tampa's largest trauma hospital, but this early on a Sunday morning? Couldn't have been ten a.m.

"Okay. Here." Rachel plopped her friend into the first open chair, between an old man with gray skin hacking something into a dirty rag and a woman rocking back and forth holding her stomach, staring at nothing.

Rachel hated hospitals. *Hated them.* "I'll be right back."

But before she could leave, the woman rocking back and forth lost her smartphone. It slid off her lap onto the tile floor, landing with a ping.

The woman didn't react.

Neither did anyone else.

Rachel knelt down and picked it up. "You lost your phone."

The woman's eyes remained unfocused.

Rachel's gaze flickered between her friend and the poor woman.

Jackie groaned.

Rachel put the phone on the woman's lap and gently placed one of the woman's hands over it. Her skin was clammy. "Hold on to it. I'm going to get help."

As soon as she walked up to the registration desk, the familiar whispers started.

"It's Rachel Wright," a young nurse said.

"Who?" An older woman on the phone cocked her head as if only half listening.

"Rachel Wright. You know, the reporter on the local news. The *investigator.*"

Her stomach turned. Ever since she'd become an investigator, this was how people reacted. Like she was investigating them. Guess everyone felt a little guilty about something. She forced a smile.

Another young woman in bright daffodil-colored scrubs, manning the check-in desk, popped her eyes wide. "Hello, Ms. Wright. I love your stories. Are you here working?"

"Thank you. No. I'm here to register a really sick friend. She went to one of those walk-in clinics yesterday. I don't know what they gave her, but she isn't getting better." Her heel tapped against the floor, but she kept her words slow and even. "She's too ill now to even register herself. She's throwing up what looks like coffee grounds." Rachel directed her next comments to the older nurse at the desk. "Do you have a bucket? Just in case she—"

The older woman put her hand over her phone, nodded at Rachel, and turned to the nurse in yellow scrubs. "Room 5. Get Angelica to take Ms. Wright's friend back right away."

We're bypassing everyone? "Thank you." Funny how people became super-efficient when the investigator walked in. "Can you have someone check on that woman, too?" She pointed to the lady who had dropped her phone. She was still rocking back and forth. "I think she's really out of it."

"Rachel?" Jackie stumbled to the counter, dry heaving violently.

Rachel caught her friend, dread drilling deeper into her bones.

"Sorry," Jackie said. "So sorry."

"Oh, Jackie." Déjà vu hit Rachel. She shuddered. "Don't be sorry. You're sick." She squeezed her eyes shut, trying not to let awful memories make her sick, too.

"Honey, let's get you in this seat before you pass out." A petite nurse, eyes as blue as her scrubs, arrived with a wheelchair. "Sit down, dear." The nurse helped Jackie maneuver into the wheelchair, then she adjusted her feet into the foot holders. "We'll have you feeling better in no time."

Rachel's heart swelled with gratitude. Just the calmness in the nurse's voice relaxed her.

"Let's get you back." The nurse glanced up. "Ms. Wright, I'm Angelica Dawson." The pretty blonde's reassuring smile dropped her anxiety another notch. "Follow me. We're heading to our trauma isolation room."

Until she said that.

"Isolation room?" Rachel stumbled over her own feet. "Why?" She quickly righted herself.

The nurse's stride slowed. "Until we know what's making your friend throw up so violently, we can't take the chance she's contagious."

Rachel exhaled. "Okay." She followed the nurse down the hall, wondering if it was the same isolation room where her brother Jim had died. How many isolation trauma rooms could one hospital have?

Jackie's head collapsed onto the back of the wheelchair. Her eyes fluttered shut. Then her head rolled to one side, bobbing for a second before falling still.

Rachel's breath caught. "I think my friend just passed out." She walked faster.

Nurse Dawson picked up her pace, too. "I'll start an IV right away. Any idea what's wrong with her?"

Rachel shook her head. "She's usually the Energizer Bunny on jet fuel. She has been working long hours in the newsroom due to the flooding we've been having."

"Maybe she caught the flu. A bad strain is going around." The nurse acknowledged another woman in scrubs rushing by. "Not sure if this year's vaccine is stopping it."

"It could also be food poisoning." Rachel's stomach somersaulted. "We ate some nasty fried food yesterday."

"We'll check it out." Nurse Dawson pushed Jackie into an open room.

Rachel stalled. This *was* the room. The wallpaper was the same. She would never forget staring at those doves pasted all over the walls. They'd given her no peace.

"Can you get onto the table, sweetie?"

Jackie opened her eyes and appeared to look right at the nurse, then she blinked and her eyes rolled back, as did her head, and her whole body began to jerk in quick, uncontrolled spasms.

Rachel's heart plummeted. "Oh my God, what's happening?"

"Seizure."

She ran to the nurse's side, grabbing hold of Jackie before she flopped onto the floor like a fish.

"Help me get her on the bed," the nurse huffed the words. "I need to keep her airway open." She called for help.

They lifted Jackie's body, maneuvering her onto the hospital gurney. "Okay, now what?" Rachel had never seen anyone convulse like this.

"Hold her so she doesn't roll off."

Rachel did what the nurse asked her to do.

The nurse tilted Jackie's head back. "Does she have a seizure condition?"

"No."

"Allergies? Other conditions?"

"Not that I know of." *Oh God.* The room started to shrink, corners graying. Rachel couldn't lose another person in this room. She couldn't even swallow. Fear lodged itself like a big fist in her throat.

After her brother died here five years ago, she'd lost both her best buddy and her deep faith. And she'd gained an unexpected daughter in her seven-year-old niece, as well as an obsessive fear and mistrust of doctors.

Rachel shuddered, remembering the emotional agony of that night. The older brother she'd looked up to all her life dying right in front of her. Not even a year after his wife, whom Rachel had adored, had died in a car accident. Another bad night in a sterile hospital. Now their daughter was an orphan, and Rachel was her guardian.

She hadn't stepped foot in a hospital since Jim's death.

"What's going on?"

Her spine straightened. She recognized that voice instantly. His voice had always held that doctor's authority. Deep. Demanding.

Sometimes difficult.

Her pulse picked up, outpacing beeps coming from a nearby monitor. She looked at him.

Doctor Joshua Salvador hadn't changed much.

Tall, muscular, but leaner now, like he'd taken up running. Or still hadn't gotten over the stress of her brother's death and what followed. With those startling blue eyes against his black hair, he had that Patrick Dempsey kind of look, his personality just a shade on the darker side. His big hands were balled up. A big, brooding Dr. McDreamy.

Rachel held her breath, along with her expectations. What would he do when he realized she was here?

He strode across the room with that fierce determination she'd witnessed for years, that confidence that had impressed her.

His feet pounded the floor, his eyes focused on the patient. He left a trail of energy in his wake, heating her skin as he strode by.

She held her breath.

"Dr. Salvador, the patient started seizing about a minute ago." The nurse was still holding Jackie's head. "She's unresponsive. I haven't been able to get all of her vitals."

Joshua strode to the bed. He placed a stethoscope to her chest and listened.

He still hadn't looked at her.

Rachel's heart beat like an intern facing her first confrontational news interview.

How many ER physicians worked at Tampa Bay

Hospital?

Dozens, at least.

And her ex-boyfriend had to be working today?

Rachel placed a hand on her chest. Could Joshua hear her heart pounding? Because she could hear her pulse drumming in her ears. She felt like throwing up, herself. "What's wrong with her?"

"I'm not sure yet." Joshua said, his voice booming.

So he did know she was in the room.

Joshua pressed his fingers into Jackie's wrist. "Nurse Dawson, her skin is a bit jaundiced, pulse is weak." He moved Jackie's sleeve up. "Profound swelling and marked bruising extending over her left upper arm." He continued in a professional, robotic tone. "I need a complete blood count and a metabolic profile."

He still hadn't looked at Rachel.

"Tox screen. Ativan for the seizure."

"She's going to be all right, right, Joshua?" She couldn't keep the doubt out of her voice. She hadn't meant for it to be there. She knew what her doubt would do to him.

Joshua didn't look up, but his body stilled for an instant. It was so quick his nurse probably didn't notice. But she did.

Jackie stopped shaking, but she continued to twitch.

Rachel's knees went weak. This felt like déjà vu. For many reasons.

It had been five years since her brother had died in this very ER with Joshua in the room.

Five years since she'd become a mother to her grieving niece.

Five years since she'd investigated Joshua's ER physicians' group for medical malpractice.

Five years since Todd, the doctor in charge that night, had resigned.

Five years since Joshua had broken up with her over her

series of stories.

Five years since she'd been promoted into the investigative unit, becoming *Rachel Makes It Right.*

Five years since she signed a new contract, which was up in a few months.

Five years since she'd had a decent night's sleep.

The beeps of a machine sped up to an alarming rate.

A baby's cry from another room escalated into a wail.

"Skin is warm to the touch." Joshua pulled his fingers from Jackie's wrist.

He finally looked at Rachel.

The heat of his gaze lit her cheeks on fire. She stumbled backward.

Today felt so different from the day they'd met here in the hospital almost seven years earlier. She'd been with Jackie on that day, too. Jackie had come down with an annoying case of bronchitis. Joshua had been intense. Intensely *flirting* with her. Jackie had noticed and had slipped Joshua Rachel's number.

The man in front of her now had hardened into a different kind of man, and she was partially responsible for his change.

"You're not supposed to be back here," he said.

The frantic activity stopped. For one brief moment, the room calmed, as if the energy had been vacuumed out of it.

Then his words broke the suction. "You're not family. I *know* you're not. You need to leave."

Rachel took a step forward, her breath sputtering. At one time, the three of them had been like family. "I can't leave Jackie. You *know* I—"

His hand shot out, silencing her. "That was not a request. This is my hospital. My trauma room. My order. Get. Out."

Feet wide, she braced herself for a fight. She wasn't leaving until she knew Jackie wasn't going to die.

About the Author

Linda Bond is an Emmy award-winning journalist by day and an author of romantic adventures by night. She's also the mother of five: four athletes and an adopted son from Cuba. She has a passion for world travel, classic movies, and alpha males. Linda currently lives in Florida, where the sun always shines and the day begins with endless possibilities.

You can learn where Linda Bond got part of her inspiration for Alive at Five by clicking on this link right now. The chapters dedicated to riding in a United States Air Force F-16 were inspired by this real life ride. Hear Linda Bond talk more about the making of Alive at Five in this interview. And check out the Alive at Five book trailer on the home page of www.lindabond.com.

Discover more romantic suspense by Linda Bond...

CUBA UNDERCOVER

FLATLINE

Discover more mystery and suspense titles from Entangled...

UNSTOPPABLE

an *Untouchables* novel by Cindy Skaggs

Bad boy Mick Donovan is out to avenge his brother's death, and aligning with Destiny Harper and the FBI Task Force is his ticket. But landing in the mountains amidst a blizzard and a past Dez would rather forget tests what Mick will sacrifice for revenge.

HARD TO PROTECT

a *Black Ops Heroes* novel by Incy Black

Black Ops agent Will Berwick doesn't care what his orders are; he's not taking the enemy—the lovely but arctic Dr. Angel Treherne—to bed. Oh, he'll root out her secrets, but on his own terms. But Angel trusts no one—certainly not Will. What's he hiding? With her life on the line, she needs to know. Preferably without losing her heart.

RISK OF A LIFETIME

a novel by Claudia Shelton

Three years ago, Marcy Bradley let the man she loved go so he could follow his career dream of being an FBI agent. She sent divorce papers. He signed. She never filed them. When a disgruntled client threatens her life, her ex, JB, is all that stands between her and an early grave. With a killer after them, Marcy and JB run for their lives, escaping to a lakeside cabin. Their love is rekindled, and JB realizes they're still married, but will there be time for their passion amidst the explosions and gunshots?

CPSIA information can be obtained
at www.ICGtesting.com
Printed in the USA
LVHW032305210821
695820LV00008B/566